In the battle for a kingdom, every alliance counts…

Princess Valoria only cares about her music and her destiny: to unite the Kingdom of Ebonvale with the House of Song and succeed where her father has failed. As if that weren't challenge enough, she must contend with her marriage to a battle hungry brute of a prince…until she falls for his adopted brother, the orphaned son of a blacksmith. But with a horde of undead gathering to attack Ebonvale, Valoria will have to choose between her personal happiness and the safety of the kingdom. Now the fate of Ebonvale rests in her heart.

I0677330

Books by Aurbie Dionne

Nebula's Music
Messenger In the Mist

Chronicles of Ebonvale
Minstrel's Serenade
Orphan's Blade

Published by Kensington Publishing Corporation

Orphan's Blade

A Chronicles of Ebonvale Novel

Aurbie Dionne

LYRICAL PRESS
Kensington Publishing Corp.
www.kensingtonbooks.com

Lyrical Press books are published by
Kensington Publishing Corp. 119 West 40th Street New York, NY 10018

First Electronic Edition: November 2015
eISBN-13: 978-1-61650-678-0
eISBN-10: 1-61650-678-4

First Print Edition: November 2015
ISBN-13: 978-1-61650-679-7
ISBN-10: 1-61650-679-2

Printed in the United States of America

To Piper, the greatest harpist I've ever played with.

Acknowledgements

I'd like to thank Renee Rocco and Lyrical Press/Kensington for believing in my work. Next comes my agent, Dawn Dowdle, for supporting me through thick and thin. Thank you, Paige, for being such an excellent editor, and to Renee, again, for making my covers so glorious. I'd like to thank my writer friends for cheering me up when things get rough- that's you Cherie Reich and Christine Rains. I want to thank my flute teacher and life mentor, Peggy Vagts, for supporting me in everything I do. Next comes my parents, Andy and Joanne Dionne, and my sister/best friend, Brianne. Finally, thank you to my husband, Chris.

Chapter 1

Shadows

The carriage rumbled on foreign ground as Valoria touched her finger to the window. Could she ever truly call these lands her home? Ebonvale's beauty rested in lush pastures and blooming orchards, but nothing could hide the grotesque mountains of the dead country of Sill. Even now, dark clouds clung to the peaks as if evil brewed. Half of Ebonvale's army had died there defeating the undead.

Ebonvale. Her new home.

"Dreaming about Prince Braxten Thoridian?" Cadence teased from the opposite side of the carriage as she pierced her needle through her delicate embroidery.

Valoria tore her gaze away from the window and glared at her handmaiden. The rocking wheels on the shoddy road had soured her stomach, and talk of her prearranged union churned the milk she'd drunk for breakfast. "No."

"Wait until the prince of Ebonvale sees your silver eyes."

Valoria pursed her lips. Her handmaiden should not speak with such openness to the princess, and the sole heir to the House of Song. Yet, she considered Cadence the only friend she could trust. Why silence the one person bold enough to speak?

"And your hair." Her handmaiden reached across the carriage and ran her fingers along the braid hanging in a loop around Valoria's ear. "Like silky rays of sunset. I only hope he's as dashing as you are beautiful."

Valoria sat back, out of her handmaiden's reach. "I do not give a wyvern's breath if he's dashing."

"What do you care about?" Cadence stabbed an embroidered petal. The red rose in the center of the circle had unusually large thorns. Had she misread the pattern?

"My music." That wasn't entirely true. Her home ranked high in her heart along with pleasing her father. But, her music had always been first.

Valoria glanced at the top of the carriage where she'd strapped her harp with the strongest golden cord in the House of Song. She'd argued with the Chief of Song to bring the instrument aboard, but Echo had insisted she ride as a lady and allow the minstrels' trumpets and drums to protect them. Even now, the repeating fanfares rattled her teeth. Best to lull the enemy to sleep with a few plucked strings than call them down from the hills of Sill to blare in their ears.

Could the undead hear?

"You won't need your music where we're headed." Cadence placed her embroidery on the velvet seat cushion and folded her hands in her lap. "The Royal Guard, with Braxten in charge, can defeat the most horrid enemies. Or so the ballads say."

The mist rolling off the foothills of Sill pressed against the window. Valoria's fingers tingled and she longed to stroke her harp. "We shall see."

She'd never traveled past the forest of Bluewood Pines surrounding the House of Song. Without the mossy trails of glitter motes strung together in the trees by her people's song, the carriage lay exposed. Even worse, without her harp, she had no defense.

Cadence had lost her usual sly smile. "What troubles you, my lady?"

"Shadows." Valoria traced the highest peak on the glass.

Cadence leaned forward and rested a hand on her knee. "There hasn't been an undead attack since King Artemus Rubystone slayed the great Necromancer King three decades ago. Besides, we have the earsplitting trumpets to protect us."

A half smile crossed Valoria's lips. "Earsplitting, indeed."

Cadence spoke true wisdom, like always. Sill should not concern her. Braxten Thoridian was enough to worry about. Meeting him for the first time made her toes curl in her slippers.

Her father had told her of his wish to unite the kingdoms ever since the first time she'd plucked her harp. "You were born to make this journey, to unite the people of Ebonvale with the House of Song, to succeed where I have failed."

Where he'd failed. He'd loved Danika Rubystone, now Queen Thoridian, and might still, which was why he didn't accompany Valoria to the castle. Her father had lost Danika's hand to her own bodyguard and never fully recovered, even after he'd married mother and Valoria was born. Mother had lived in a shadow of love compared to the stunning ruler of Ebonvale.

Now Danika Thoridian would be her mother-in-law. How she could ever forgive the woman who'd stolen her father's heart and thrown it away, Valoria didn't know.

Her father's half-hearted love had killed her mother. Would her own predestined union end the same tragic way? Would she wither and die with a lackluster love?

No. She was made from stronger stuff. Her mother completed her duty by having Valoria, and Valoria would complete her duty by uniting the kingdoms.

She glanced at Cadence's embroidery. That rose had too much sun. How could a woman pluck that stem without gouging her fingers?

The trumpets stuttered, and the fanfare broke into disharmony.

"Are we there already?" Cadence slipped on her boots.

"Not unless our horses can fly." Ebonvale was a day's ride from where her father had seen them off at the edge of the bluewood forest. Yet, the sun hadn't reached its zenith in the sky. Besides, the minstrels wouldn't end the royal processional fanfare in such a haphazard muddle.

Valoria cranked her window open and stuck out her head, not caring a wyvern's scale about what Echo would say. An arrow flew past her nose, hitting the lead rider in the back with a sick, wet thump. His trumpet fell from his fingers, and he slouched forward in the saddle as a red ribbon of blood flowed from his silvery overcoat. Another arrow clanged off the glass of the window beside her and fell to the ground.

Cadence yanked her away from the window. "Lyric's lyre! Get back!"

Shock numbed her silent as they crouched on the carriage floor in between the velvet cushions. Was it the dead army, come back to claim vengeance against King Artemis while he lay in his grave and his heart-stealing daughter ruled? The thought of dead fingers grasping her arms and legs sent shivers all over her. She'd rather die than end up as part of that soulless horde.

If only she had her harp. A low hum reverberated in the pit of her stomach as the minstrels began their Song of Power. They'd used it against the wyvern She-Beast and her brood, casting the entire horde into a comatose state. Her eyes grew heavy, and Cadence shook her. "Cover your ears. Do not harken to it."

Even though the minstrels aimed their song at the enemy, the side effects were powerful enough to knock her out. Valoria fought against the urge to lie down, focusing on the carriage window. Corpses didn't fight with arrows. They lunged in a squirming mass, clacking their rotten teeth.

Cadence poked her head up. "Raiders! Those desperate bastards."

At least if they died, they wouldn't turn into the enemy. Valoria's relief came with a dose of shame. Raiders were just as dangerous. "Are you certain they aren't the undead?"

"They look ragged enough, but they are not rotting."

Valoria rose to the window and Cadence held her down. "No. You are too important."

Was this woman a handmaiden or a bodyguard? "I want to help."

The carriage stopped, and Cadence fell back against the seat. They froze. After hours of bumping around, the stillness numbed Valoria's legs.

Cadence's eyes grew wide as swords clashed beside the carriage window. "Why in Horred's name have we stopped?"

Valoria stood up, gained her bearings, and glanced out the window. Two minstrels lay face down in the long grasses of the meadow. "Either Echo and the others are too busy fighting, or the horses are all dead."

Lackluster love might kill her over time, but she did not plan to die this day. "We have to get out of here. I must get my harp."

Cadence clasped her arm like a vice. "You are not going anywhere."

She ripped her arm out of her grasp. "Yes, I am. And I'm not leaving you. Come on!"

Valoria unhinged the latch and opened the carriage door to the sounds of grunting men and clashing steel. Echo fought two ragged raiders with his short sword. Ratty brown hair covered their heads and faces in a wild tangle. Haphazard scraps from old leather, stained fur, and muddied cotton made up their clothing. The wind changed direction, and the raiders' filth wafted to Valoria. She covered her mouth from the stink of old sweat and mold.

Echo lunged, pulling off the cloth covering one of the wild man's ears. The man fell to his knees, grasping at the side of his head as his ear bled a red streak down his cheek to his neck. The Song of Power hummed around the battlefield like a giant tuning fork hit with a sledgehammer. Raiders poured from the long grasses like field rats, circling the carriage and what was left of the retinue. Each one had cloth stuffed up their ears. In time, their numbers would overrun the minstrels.

At least she'd go down playing her harp one last time.

As Echo turned to the second man, Valoria climbed the side of the carriage. Her harp glowed golden in the sun, exactly where she'd left it. Relief poured through her as she untied the first knot holding the instrument down.

Cadence grabbed her ankle and tugged. "Come back inside before an arrow spears your thick head!"

The second knot had hardened in the sun. Her nails broke against the cord. "Help me untie it."

Cadence sighed in exasperation. "You are the worst ward I've ever had."

As her handmaiden climbed the side of the carriage, a new fanfare broke from the horizon. This music lacked the deft touch of the minstrels' hands. The rough tone and horrid intonation would summon only scowls from the enemy. No one from the House of Song would be caught dead playing with such coarseness.

A line of silver caught her eye as the Royal Guard crested the hill.

"Look!" Cadence joined her on the carriage roof. "The banners have the insignia of the two swords. 'Tis Braxten Thoridian's army."

"And their awful horn blowers." Army or not, Valoria untied the last knot holding down her harp. She swung the instrument from the carriage roof and landed on her feet. Closing her eyes, she strummed a mysterious chord full of dissonance. She did not have the power to bring the raiders to their feet like Echo's haunting tenor voice, but she could elicit the doubt inside their desperate hearts.

She knew the taste of desperation.

The Royal Guard rode into battle at full speed, trampling the outside line of raiders with their horses. As they fought to reach the minstrels, Valoria focused on her music, stringing together chord after chord of unresolved harmonies. Some of the cloths weren't enough to block the sound, and a few raiders fell to their feet before they reached the retinue. But, most of them charged with vengeance, wielding pitchforks, broken glass, and whatever they found on the side of the road.

Another arrow ripped by Valoria's face, and she fell back against the carriage. "Lyric's lyre! 'Tis not working."

"You have to find something that does, or we'll all be joining the gods." Cadence reached in her boot and pulled out a dagger.

Valoria stared at Sill. The dead lands tempted her even though father had warned her of manipulating nature with song. Music could control a person, but it could only entice a force of nature to do its own bidding. Nature had its own way of deciding people's fate.

She breathed deeply. Could she harness the mountain's power long enough to save them all? With everyone's life in jeopardy, risk didn't matter.

A clump of raiders broke from the group, running toward the carriage. Echo's voice surged as he threw himself in front of them. He was no warrior. He would not be able to hold them all off.

Cadence growled beside her. "Let them come. They'll have to get through me first!"

That would take all of three heartbeats. Her handmaiden had a fierce tongue, but her battle skills were limited to needles and embroidery. If only the enemy were thorny roses.

Valoria turned her attention back to Sill and took a deep breath. She sensed a greater presence lurking in those mountains. Now, she had to call it to her. Her voice rang out, sweet and clear as morning's first light.

"Beyond the borders
Of shadowed paths
A bright dove calls."

A vast consciousness stirred with a low rumble as if waking from a long sleep. Valoria sensed a power far greater than hers with an insatiable hunger for anything with blood running through their veins.

"Valoria, what are you doing?"

"Saving us all." Her voice rose.

"Save her brethren
And her enemies
Are ripe to pluck.
Their hearts bleed
With fiery vengeance.
Let their passion
Draw you near."

An icy breeze blew through her, tossing her gown around her legs. A wall of cool mist rode the wind, pouring from the foothills. Valoria held a melancholy high note, allowing the tone to echo over the meadow before tapering away into the minstrel's humming. One by one, the raiders emerged from the mist disoriented, giving the minstrels enough time to pull the cloths from their ears. They fell as the dissonant hum of the minstrels' Song of Power rang in their heads.

Her attention returned to Echo. Four of the five raiders surrounded him. He'd killed one of them, but the others wore him down. He wouldn't last long. A memory of the old man teaching her harmonies on the harp tightened her chest. She would not see him die.

The lead charger of the Royal Guard hacked at raiders all around him. With one swift blow, he sliced through two attackers, then trampled another with his horse's hooves. He lunged at a clump of raiders emerging from the mist in the opposite direction.

But, he wouldn't be going in that direction for long. Valoria strummed her harp. She did not know this particular warrior, but she knew the desires lurking in every soldier's heart.

"Honor bestowed
On a savior.
Justice is served
When one man outnumbered
Has a second chance."

The rider turned around. His armor shone brilliantly in the sun. He wasn't overly large and muscly, but lean and swift, riding with the grace of a dancer, as if his horse were an extension of his legs. With his visor down, Valoria could not see his face, yet his actions took her breath away.

As Echo swung his blade desperately in an arc around him, the soldier came up from behind, spearing one of the raiders. The others turned toward the soldier, their attention diverted. Clutching a gash on his shoulder oozing blood, Echo fell to his knees.

"No." Valoria dropped her harp.

Cadence grabbed her hand. "It's too dangerous. Too many raiders still run free."

"Look." She pointed to where the mist dissipated. "They flee toward the hills."

Cadence's grip tightened. "Still, you should get back in the carriage. There is no place for a lady on a battlefield."

Valoria ripped her hand out of her handmaiden's grip. "Tell that to my new mother-in-law."

She ran toward Echo, darting in between minstrels gathering the wounded and tending to the horses, while the Royal Guard captured prisoners. Her mentor lay on his back in the grass, his gaze skyward, as if he longed to meet Helena and Horred in their sacred temple.

Valoria fell on her knees beside him. The gash ran from his neck to his shoulder, his skin split open by a crude blade. The earth below him blossomed with red. Denying his condition, she tore a piece of cloth from her dress and tied it tightly around the wound. "For a harp teacher, you're quite good with a blade."

"Necessity dictates action, my dear." He studied her face, raising a finger to her cheek. His usually ruddy complexion had paled. His hair seemed grayer and thinner against the long-stemmed grass. "Shouldn't you be in your carriage?"

"Like a prize to be won?" She shook her head. "I missed my harp too much."

"I bet a wyvern's egg you did."

"Come on." She hefted him up. "Your carriage awaits."

"Am I to take your place?"

She laughed, wishing it were so. "I don't think Braxten Thoridian would like that."

As if summoned by a name, the solider turned toward them and dismounted. All four raiders lay at his feet. He pulled his helmet from his head, and brown, curly hair fell around his shoulders. His eyes were a rich, amber brown, his features sharp and rugged. He fell to one knee and bowed before her. "Princess, allow me to help you."

Hope glimmered in Valoria's heart, followed by a swell of desire. This man had led the Royal Guard into battle. His armor had Ebonvale's double sword crest and the deep violet colors of the ruling house. It had to be Braxten Thoridian. "Yes, help me carry him to the carriage. My handmaiden can tend to his wounds."

The soldier took one arm, and Valoria took the other. They lifted Echo and walked carefully to the carriage. Around them, the soldiers patrolled the fields as the last raiders fled.

The soldier glanced at Valoria with melancholy. "My apologies, Princess. It seems for many of your retinue, we came too late."

"Helena looked upon us with grace today. We're fortunate you came." Valoria gave him a thankful nod. His modesty impressed her. He'd just defeated an entire horde with only a brigade, yet it was a sad victory. He spoke as if the fallen were his own.

"Another raid held us up. We had planned to meet you at the forest's edge."

She studied his profile, wondering if he was as kind as he was handsome. "Another raid?"

"These are dire times we live in. After the wyverns destroyed the southern towns, many of Ebonvale's people fled north. We only had room for so many refugees, so the rest had to fend for themselves. Who knew they'd become outlaws."

They hefted Echo into the carriage. He grunted and held his wounded shoulder.

Cadence covered him with a blanket. "I'll keep him safe, my lady." She stole a glance at the soldier, then looked back to Valoria and raised her eyebrows.

Valoria ignored her unspoken question. "Thank you." She placed her hand on Echo's cheek. "Rest now." His eyes flickered as he fell in and out of consciousness.

She exited the carriage, picked up her harp, and took the reins of a fallen minstrel's horse.

The soldier followed her and offered his hand to help her mount. "You are not riding in the carriage, Princess?"

She snorted. "This is where I should have been in the first place: riding with my harp tied to my back."

His eyes held amusement and something more. Was it admiration? "Better to fend off foes?"

She held her breath. Did he know she'd called the mist from the hills to disorient the raiders and buy the minstrels more time? "Better to protect my people."

She adjusted the saddle and kicked the horse into line with the others. Just because they were promised to each other didn't mean she should lose her head like a giddy girl at Summer's Eve fest. Many had died that day, and she had to honor their memory. "Tell your army they'd best let the minstrels play the fanfare."

"'Tis not my army, Princess."

She yanked the reins and her horse swiveled back in his direction. Was this some sort of game? "You are Braxten Thoridian, are you not?"

Ironic amusement passed through his eyes. "You are mistaken. I'm Lieutenant Nathaniel Blueborough, son of the late Alhearn Blueborough, the blacksmith of Shaletown. Queen Danika Thoridian and her husband adopted me. I'm Braxten's brother, if not by blood, then by name."

He mounted his own horse and called over his shoulder. "Around the castle, I'm known as Nip."

Chapter 2

Paintings

Nathaniel rode to the front of the line distracted and intrigued by the princess of the House of Song. Had disappointment flickered in her gaze when he told her he wasn't Brax? How could she not know he was the adopted son? Had she never left the resonant walls of the House of Song?

He resisted the urge to turn back and study her large, silver eyes. She was Brax's intended, and he had to remember his place. Even though he was the elder brother, he had no blood ties to the throne. Since Brax had achieved legendary warrior status, becoming even stronger than his father, Bron Thoridian, Nathaniel had no chance in commanding the army either.

Guilt weighed him down. The king and queen had opened their hearts and adopted him, so he should have been grateful for any place in Ebonvale's castle. Even as a scullion. They could have left him to die as a beggar in the ashes of Shaletown, and he might have turned into a raider himself.

Grasping the reins, he reminded himself of his debt to the House of Thoridian. He'd served them well all his life, and he wasn't about to squander his honor on one lovely girl.

"Battle leave you with ill feelings, my lord?" Timber Rollins kicked his horse up beside him. Flecks of blood and earth painted his timeworn face. An old scar from his left forehead to the bottom of his right cheek shone white and fleshy in the sun.

"Not battle. Fate."

"Ah, a vile beast. Fate can give you the world, then take it away." The old man had been in battles long before Nathaniel could hold a sword. He'd served King Thoridian, and King Rubystone before him. He was one of the few men who'd seen the dead rise at the necromancer's hand and lived to speak of it.

Although Brax passed him off as an old fogey, Nathaniel listened to his council. "My life is the opposite. Fate took everything away, then dealt me a decent hand."

"Decent?"

"Better than the one I had before. I was to become a blacksmith's son, and now I'm second in command of the Royal Guard. So why am I not content?"

The old man placed a hand on his armored shoulder. "Nothing can replace what you lost. No matter how illustrious or grand."

The minstrels' fanfare picked up tempo as they crested a hill. Ebonvale's stone ramparts claimed the horizon. Built around the remnants of Helena and Horred's temple, the stone buildings piled up upon one another until lofty turrets poked from the mass, towering above the highest ramparts. Purple pennants waved in the breeze as soldiers patrolled the battlements.

"She's beautiful, isn't she?" Timber goaded his horse forward.

Nathaniel nodded, taking a moment to reflect upon the first time he'd ever seen the castle as boy. "She's home."

They passed the orchards and the farmlands, reaching the city walls. Nathaniel rode ahead. He recognized the guard at duty, yet he still presented the Royal Seal.

"Tough journey, my lord?" The guard ran his eyes up and down Nathaniel's muddied armor.

"Thank the gods we delivered the princess in one piece. We need medics immediately."

"I'll send word." The guard nodded, allowing the entire retinue through.

Nathaniel led them through the courtyard, ignoring the other nobles' stares. Minstrels weren't to be trusted since one had stolen King Rubystone's wife many years ago. Hopefully, having the House of Song's princess would remedy those prejudices. He held their gazes as he dismounted and the minstrels' fanfares resolved in a beautiful harmony his trumpeters could only dream about playing themselves. Medics rushed to the wounded as the carriage came to a halt.

Nathaniel found the princess glancing nervously at the forming crowd. He walked to her and offered her his hand. "Princess. If you will, I'll announce your arrival."

She took his hand, squeezing hard. Her fingers shook. "Please, by all means."

Nathaniel helped her down, then brought her before the crowd. "Come to us from the House of Song, the only daughter of King Valorian and the late Queen Mayweather, may I announce Princess Valoria."

Whispers filled the air. One person managed a meager clap. With Nathaniel's insisting glare, light applause spread.

"They do not trust me," Valoria whispered, loud enough only he could hear.

"Not yet." Nathaniel turned toward her and gave her the reassuring look he usually gave to the troops before a battle. The way she'd chosen to ride instead of retreating to her carriage told him there was more to her than a simple minstrel's daughter. "But in time, they will."

She surveyed the crowd with a tight-lipped smile, then turned to him. "Please, I must see my people's wounds cared for."

"Of course. Medics usher them to the infirmary as we speak. You can stay there as long as you like. But, keep in mind the king and queen are waiting to receive you."

She pursed her lips as if weighing her personal needs with offending her new family. "I'll stay only long enough to see them tended to." She pulled her harp from her back and handed it to her handmaiden, a brown-haired girl with a fierce look about her.

"Very well." He offered his arm. Better to keep her beside him then have some hired assassin pull her into the crowd. Ebonvale's hatred for the minstrels ran deep, even though they had helped them win the wyvern war. "Come with me."

The crowd parted before them. Her retinue followed as they walked the cobblestone from the main square to the apothecary, a stone building with vibrant stained glass windows. Various bottles, vials, and rolls of bandages lined the walls. Behind the counter, a backroom filled with beds took up the space of an old, attached barn. Patients from previous raider attacks filled half the beds. Hopefully they'd have enough room for Valoria's people and the prisoners they'd captured.

Guilt stung his chest as he saw one of the raiders chained to the bed. He'd have to interrogate him later on, a chore he never liked. But, if he let Brax get to the man, he'd be dead by morning.

Valoria rushed to the bedside of the older man Nathaniel had helped her carry back to the carriage. The intricate embroidery on his overcoat labeled him as someone of high status in the House of Song. Perhaps a music teacher? His kind eyes reminded Nathaniel of Ludo, the baker in Shaletown who used to slip him sweet biscuits when his parents weren't looking.

She touched the medic's arm with insistence. "Will he live?"

"He'll have an ugly scar, but yes, he'll live to see another day." The medic nodded curtly and rushed to the next bed where another minstrel clutched an arrow speared through his shoulder.

Valoria leaned over the old man, and his eyes flickered open. "Did you hear that? A hideous battle scar. Your pupils will listen to you now."

"Anything to get them to practice." He chuckled, then held onto his shoulder as if the movement pained him.

Valoria took his hand in both of hers. "My father will be proud of your bravery."

"And yours." He tapped her hand. "Although you should have listened to me and stayed in the carriage. You're too important to both kingdoms to lose."

"Lose?" She laughed cynically. "I'm not going anywhere."

"Hopefully, you're going to the throne room, my lady. Shouldn't keep the king and queen waiting." The older man glanced at Nathaniel. He nodded, then backed farther away. He shouldn't have been eavesdropping on their conversation. This unhealthy preoccupation with his brother's intended had to stop.

Valoria leaned over and touched the old man's forehead. She whispered something in his ear, then left him to survey the other wounded minstrels.

Nathaniel kept his distance. Instead of following her to each of her people's beds, he approached the chained raider. He was just a boy with red fuzz for a beard and freckles sprinkled across his dirty cheeks. Sprawled across the bed in tattered clothing, he breathed laboriously, as if each intake of air would be his last. A nasty gash stretched across his stomach. Nathaniel's gut tightened. This boy must have been close to his real brother's age the day the wyverns attacked Shaletown.

Pill. His true brother. He hadn't thought of him in years.

The boy spit at Nathaniel, wriggling against his bindings. "You might as well kill me now, because I'm telling you nothing."

Nathaniel leaned down, examining the cut. The medic had staunched the bleeding, but the wound ran deep. With so many of their own people needing care, the battlefield surgeon would treat him last. He probably wouldn't live through the night.

This could have been him, or Pill, if he'd survived the attack. Where had Ebonvale gone wrong?

"Listen closely, I'm not here to weed out your friends, just relocate them. Temple monks purge the southern lands as we speak. Soon the soil will be ripe for planting. All Ebonvale needs are people willing to go back."

The boy winced and held his stomach. "Lies. All of it. That soil won't grow a sprig if you brought your royal horse to fertilize it himself."

A few soldiers standing by the door placed their hands on their hilts and stepped forward. Nathaniel waved them back. "How do you know if you do not try? It cannot be much worse than raiding caravans on the road for scraps."

"Starve here or starve there, the only difference is the scenery."

The prisoner was right about that. The wyverns had scorched most of the south, leaving a dry wasteland. The temple monks had a large undertaking in reclaiming it. But, they'd never succeed without volunteers to cultivate the land.

The boy grabbed his arm, leaving bloody fingerprints on his armor. "What do you know of loss? You have a castle, an army, fancy armor, sprawling orchards."

Nathaniel met the boy's accusing stare. "Shaletown was my home. The wyverns took my entire family away from me. You have to make something of what fate has given you, or else you'll always be a victim."

"I'm not a victim. I'm a fighter." The boy pulled his arm away.

Nathaniel shook his head, wishing he could believe him. When he looked down at that bed, he saw himself.

Someone cleared their throat behind him. Nathaniel turned around, feeling as though he'd woken from a daze.

Valoria crossed her arms and steeled her gaze like a warrior charging into battle. Blood stained her white gown across her breasts and down her arm. "I'm ready."

If only he could bring her a new dress. Nathaniel thought of the shop across the street, then paused. Perhaps she'd done this on purpose to show the effort and the loss the minstrels had poured into this union. Who was he to take that away and pretty her up like some prize to be won?

"Very well." He signaled to the soldiers at the door and offered his arm. She placed her hand on his armor, light as a feather, and he led her back outside where her retinue waited. The minstrels still able to play began their fanfares, and they walked to the throne room.

When they were out of earshot from the others, Valoria turned toward him. "Tell me about your brother."

Nathaniel kept the emotion from his face. What could he tell her and still be truthful without driving her away?

"Brax is a strong and proud man, and a born leader. He has a clear vision of what Ebonvale should be and fights for that ideal every day of his life."

Valoria pursed her lips as if he'd told her nothing she wanted to hear. "Is he kind-hearted?"

Nathaniel resisted the urge to flinch. Kind was not the appropriate word to describe Brax. "He has a strong sense of justice."

"That is not the same thing."

"No." But it would have to do.

They climbed the marble-veined steps to Helena and Horred's ancient temple. Most of the rock had been reconstructed or replaced, but a few of the great steps of the past remained. Nathaniel always felt honored to walk upon them.

They entered the main antechamber and climbed the spiral steps to the main hall above. Paintings of the previous monarchs and their families adorned the walls. Valoria studied each one carefully. Why not give her some information that might help her at court later on?

Nathaniel pointed to the first painting. "This was King Artemis Rubystone, slayer of the great Necromancer King, and ruler of Ebonvale for twenty-five years." He motioned to the painting beside it, this one framed in rubies and gold. "Here is his first wife, Islador of the Northern Isles. She died of a fever only a year after they married, but he never stopped loving her memory."

"So I've heard." Valoria raised an eyebrow.

He wondered if she knew the king's undying love for Islador had driven his second wife into the minstrel's arms. "This is his second wife, Sybil of Jamal. Although you may have heard the stories of her exile, she now lives in the farthest turret on the southern side of the castle and advises her daughter, the queen."

Sybil's delicate, youthful face in the painting was much different than the wrinkled, sun-splotched old woman she'd grown into. Yet, she'd grown wiser as well, at least in Nathaniel's eyes. Although not well liked by Ebonvale's people, she was like a grandmother to him.

"I'm not like others. I do not judge matters which I'm not a part of."

Nathaniel nodded, impressed. This minstrel woman would be a fair ruler someday. He pointed up ahead. "Next are the king and queen."

Danika stood with Bron at her side. Her fierce stare showed the passion underlying her regal composure, while her hand gripping tightly on Bron's arm showed her undying love for her husband. She'd risked the kingdom's safety taking Bron instead of Valoria's father as her husband. She loved the warrior more than anything in the world.

Nathaniel paused, studying the pair. Maybe someday, he'd find such a love.

"Finally, here's the portrait you've been waiting for: Braxten Thoridian, son of Danika and Bron." His brother stood in his silver battle armor, brandishing his thick, jewel-crusted claymore as if preparing to slay a wyvern.

Valoria paused at Brax's painting. The paint revealed the hard lines of his massive jaw, sleek shaved head, and barrel-shaped nose. Some women were drawn to intimidation and strength. But her face gave away no emotion.

Nathaniel leaned toward her, searching her silver eyes. He'd be lying if he told himself he didn't care what she thought.

Chapter 3

Empty Throne

Valoria struggled to keep a straight face as she beheld her future intended. With arms wide as tree trunks, a square nose and beady eyes, he reminded her more of a raging bull than a man. He oozed masculinity and strength, but lacked tenderness in his blunt features. He looked more apt to slice off her arm than bring her flowers.

She glanced away, unable to hold Brax's war-hungry gaze. One painting was missing from the rest. Where was Nathaniel's likeness?

The soldier stood at arm's length, studying the painting of the king and queen. Still, she could feel his gaze burn her cheek when she wasn't looking in his direction. "Why are you not on this wall?"

"I have no place there. I am not of their blood. Come." He gestured toward the throne room. "We should not tarry."

Valoria bit her tongue. Right. When the question focuses on him, he ushers her ahead. How could she tell him she wasn't ready? Would she ever be?

The large oaken doors spread open, inviting them in. Attendants wearing velvet robes in Ebonvale's purple colors bowed as the procession passed and entered the main audience chamber. The pennants of the house of Thoridian dangled from lofty rafters, waving lazily in the breeze from open windows.

On the floor, marble tiles depicted the galaxy above, with swirling cosmic clouds and glinting stars of mica. The artist's work represented Ebonvale's never-ending reach throughout the world, stretching throughout the universe. Valoria tried not to compare their arrogant design with the House of Song's peaceful dome.

At the center of the cosmos stood three thrones made from the pillars of Helena and Horred's temple before the dead army stomped their palace to ruins. Ancient craftsmen had carved climbing ivy and wandering butterflies in the ivory. Some of the images had broken off or crumbled. Yet, by the places where the artwork remained unscathed, she could sense how beautiful the ancient temple must have been.

The doors closed behind her, leaving her to face her new family with no way to escape. If only she had her harp to calm herself with soothing tones.

King Bronford Thoridian sat on the largest throne to the right, wearing his battle armor. His shaved head gleamed pale white like his son's. But this man had kinder eyes. Whether because of the slight wrinkles around them, or by a hint of sympathy, Valoria did not know.

Beside the king sat Danika Thoridian, the woman who'd stolen her father's heart. Even though the queen had aged past her prime, her blonde hair glowed golden in the sun, and her sharp green eyes sparkled like emeralds. A necklace of five violet pearls lay around her neck. She was gorgeous, and Valoria could see why her father had been taken with the former princess.

The queen's foxy features showed compassion where Valoria thought there'd be none. "Helena's sword! Are you harmed, my child?"

"No, my lady." Valoria bowed slowly before them, ensuring all saw her bloodied dress. "But the House of Song has sacrificed much to come."

"As it always has." Sadness weighed down the queen's pretty face.

Valoria straightened, studying her. What other emotions lurked in the furrow of the Queen's perfect brow? Regret? Valoria crossed her arms. "And will continue to do to ensure our people's union." Her chest tightened. Had she said too much?

Danika Thoridian's lips pursed as she stood. "Hopefully, your sacrifice is at an end."

Hadn't it just started? An uncomfortable silence reigned as Valoria struggled to keep that last thought to herself. As if to ease the awkwardness of the moment, the king stood and walked down the steps to take her arm. His fingers were rough with calluses and thick as sausages, but his skin was clean. She'd heard he hadn't been in battle since he'd damaged his left knee running after raiders last year.

His tone was soft and kind. "You've had a rough journey. Please, take my son's seat by our side."

Valoria glanced at the empty chair resting beside the king. Where was Braxten? Should he not find the time to welcome her? Anger ripped through her, followed by a humiliating sense of relief. She'd have to face him some day, why not get it over with?

"Braxten is defending our southern border with the Royal Guard." The king showed her to her intended's throne. She sat upon the white ivory, feeling like a child in a giant's chair. Hard stone pressed against her behind, and the armrests were cold as winter's chill. Hopefully, the man who sat there didn't take after his throne.

Nathaniel approached the king and queen, bowing before them. As he briefed them on the attack, Valoria tried not to watch him too closely. She found her eyes returning to the solid lines of his face every chance she got. He was the only one among the Thoridians who made her feel at home.

But he wasn't a Thoridian, now was he?

The doors to the hall burst open, and Braxten strode through, his armor chinking with each step. The portrait had not done his size justice. He towered over the other men, wide as an ox with bulging arms and legs. A bloody gash crossed his left cheek, and he wiped the blood away as if it was sweat. His wide-set eyes were dark and fierce, his gait purposeful and swift. A brown sack dangled from his fist.

Valoria's throat constricted. Was it a gift for her?

The underside of the sack dripped dark liquid on the marble floor. If it was a wedding gift, than it was a strange one indeed.

Not even glancing in her direction, Brax approached the king and queen and upended the sack. A round head of wet black hair bounced twice, then rested with two glaring eyes staring at Valoria. Its mouth lay open in a silent scream. Horror and disgust rolled through her. She tightened her grip on the throne, fingernails digging into the ivory.

"The leader of the resistance." Brax's voice was deep and velvety, growling with each word. It resonated deep inside Valoria's gut. It was a voice she'd remember, a voice that would haunt her dreams.

The queen covered her mouth. The king waved her back. His face remained stoic as he approached his son. "Have you forgotten what day this is?"

"I thought you'd be proud, father." Brax bowed his head.

"I am always proud of you, son." The king put a hand on his shoulder. "But, now you must forget our battles. Your future wife has come."

The king gestured toward Valoria, and Brax turned in her direction. She tried to keep her face expressionless as his eyes bore into her, pulling her apart bone by bone. He seemed disappointed somehow, as if they'd given him a toy he didn't need. Still, Brax bowed his head to her. "My lady."

She nodded once, acknowledging him, but she could not accept him in her heart.

The warrior stood and turned back to the king. Although he spoke under his voice, Valoria's trained minstrel ears could hear. "I expect a counterattack in the next few days. I must fortify the southern border."

The king sighed. "My son—always thinking of the safety of our kingdom." He put a hand on Braxten's shoulder. "Be back by tonight's dinner feast. You must take your seat next to our future princess."

"As you will, father." Brax nodded, then stormed off as quick as he'd come with his men following him. Awkward silence fell as his footsteps receded down the hall.

Nathaniel took the sack and covered the head. He turned to the nearest of the Royal Guard and whispered under his breath. "Get that foul thing out of here."

Valoria hunched over in her chair as a sick pang hit her stomach. Panic rose inside her. Could she retain her composure, or would she explode from disappointment in front of the entire audience in the main hall? Grinding her teeth, she straightened and held onto the throne with both hands. She did this for her father, and for the House of Song.

Nathaniel addressed the king and queen. "The princess has had a rough journey. Allow me to escort her to her quarters, where she can rest for the evening's festivities."

"Of course." The king smiled at her, and it was not unkind. If only his tenderness had passed to his son.

Valoria stood and accepted Nathaniel's arm. They exited the throne room in silence. Only after the doors closed behind her did she breathe again.

"The king and queen have chosen the finest quarters for you and your handmaidens." Nathaniel gazed straight ahead as if he couldn't bear to look at her. Had her introduction to the king and queen disappointed him? Could he sense her reservation, her fear?

"They are very kind."

"They have awaited your coming for a long time."

"As did the House of Song."

"I'm sure." He glanced in her direction. "I'm not sure your father has told you, but as a young boy I fought at his side."

Valoria perked up. Any mention of her father—her home—raised her spirits. "No, he did not say."

Nathaniel smiled as if remembering a joke. "We barely escaped a battle with kobolds in the red woods. From there, we entered the caves of Darkenbite and met the albinos."

"Sounds like quite an adventure." Why had her father failed to tell her of it? "Who else was on this quest?"

"The king and queen. This happened before they were married, back when Bronford Thoridian was her bodyguard."

Valoria nodded. There was her answer. Her father stayed away from that time in his life as if it were poison. Yet, he could never bring himself to forget.

"It was the greatest adventure of my life." The hall ended in a corridor that parted both ways. Nathaniel gestured toward the right.

At least some good had come of it. "So far."

Nathaniel turned toward her with a question in his eyes.

She smiled for the first time that day. "You have many years left to have more." Even though the story aged him about ten years older than her, for her mother had birthed her two years after the queen had stolen her father's heart.

A smile slipped through his lips before he turned back and showed her to an oaken door. "Your room, my lady."

Nathaniel opened the door to bright sunlight filtering through three large triangular windows. A four-poster canopy bed draped in light blue satin sat at the room's center before a grand fireplace. Threaded rugs from Jamal spread across the marble floor in vibrant azure and vermillion hues. A porcelain tub and wash basin sat beside a mirror as large as the wall. On the other side hung a tapestry of Helena and Horred on their wedding day.

Valoria swallowed hard, trying to remind herself this was not a prison. Or at least, not meant to be. Her trunks had been placed at the foot of the bed, and next to them sat her harp. She knelt beside it, feeling the strings under her fingertips.

"Is it to your liking, Princess?" Nathaniel stood at the doorway, awaiting her approval.

"It is more than enough." She stood, remembering her place. If she was to be queen someday, she couldn't throw herself at the floor whenever she saw her harp. "Thank you, Commander Blueborough."

"Lieutenant. But please"—he took her hand—"call me Nathaniel."

His fingers lingered on hers, and she gave him a questioning look. What did he desire? Her trust? Or was it something more? Would he tempt his own brother's intended?

Nathaniel pulled away. "I'm the second in command of the army. The name does not suit me."

As if that was the reason. Valoria inhaled sharply. "So be it."

He bowed before her. "I must take my leave. I'll see you tonight at the dinner festival."

Yes, he would. But Brax would be there, and she doubted he'd talk to her while she sat next to that warhorse of a man. "See you tonight."

He left, closing the door behind him. Valoria surveyed her room again. The main room led to a smaller antechamber for her handmaidens. Although Cadence's trunk was there, and her embroidery slung across the bed, the room lay empty.

She probably looked after the wounded, which was where Valoria would rather be. But, future queens did not run around without bodyguards, tending to wounded soldiers. Her future was a lonely, secluded one. No matter, Valoria had her harp. She could play soothing arpeggios until dinner. She opened her trunk, choosing a plain red velvet dress and laid the fabric upon the bed. Better not wear the blood-stained monstrosity her betrothal gown had become.

How befitting.

Her intended was a monstrosity in himself. Had he looked at her for more than a few heartbeats, maybe he would have noticed the blood. Then, she might have earned a measure of his respect.

Taking her harp in her hands, she strummed a chord and breathed deeply. Thoughts of the day disappeared as her music echoed through the room. She played an old reverie Echo had taught her as a child. One by one, the chords built upon themselves to reveal a lilting melody. The song never failed to warm her hands and calm her.

Outside, the wind picked up, howling through the towers of the upper battlements. Her triangular windows snapped open, and the curtains flew over her. Valoria stopped playing and swiped the fabric away. She approached the window, dread eating her stomach away.

Beyond the city walls and the blooming orchards lay the dark mountains of Sill. Lightning struck the highest peak as gray storm clouds clustered around the valley separating the foothills from the meadows. A storm brewed.

She moved to shut the window. A voice chanting a strange language rode the wind, holding her still. Valoria leaned over the balcony, the wind whipping her hair from its braids. The stone turned her fingers to ice. For a moment, the voice became clear, and she could have sworn she heard her name.

Chapter 4

Simmering Meat

Valoria's velvet gown weighed her down as she hustled across the corridor. She dared not wear anything more revealing. Any show of skin would only make her more vulnerable, more pitiful in Brax's cold eyes. She was not desperate for his attention.

"It's not my fault you're late." Cadence shouted after her.

"No. But coming back soaked in blood did not help." Valoria struggled to remember the path Nathaniel had taken her down earlier. Was it a right or a left at the large painting of King Thoridian cutting the head off the necromancer?

"I told you not to wait for me." Cadence caught up and tripped on her hem, tumbling forward.

Valoria caught her and hefted her upright. "I'm not attending this alone."

"Very well. But, I'm not following you on your wedding night. Sooner or later you'll have to face him without my company."

Valoria preferred later. After witnessing an arrow pierce a minstrel's back, Echo's bloody shoulder, a man's decapitated head bounce on the floor, and a spine-chilling voice call her name on the wind, she'd had enough unpleasantness to last a fortnight. "All I want to do is get through this dinner."

The stench of roasting meat hit her nose, and she coughed, covering her mouth with her sleeve. Unlike the minstrels' plant-based fare, Ebonvale's people savored their animal flesh. Just one more aspect of castle life she had to accommodate. "This way. I hope they have some roasted turnips or squash."

Cadence smoothed down her dress. "I wouldn't count your wyvern's eggs before they hatch."

They turned the corner into a room lit by flaming chandeliers. Two guards stood at duty, ushering them forward into a room filled with guests drowned in gowns and finery. As she entered, the people bowed before her, lowering their faces toward the floor. The royal family sat at a long table along the back wall below three stained glass windows.

At the center of the table, a roasted hog sat on a silver tray. Brax sat above the snout, gorging on a piece of the hog's leg. He glanced up, and put the leg down, chewing hungrily as he laid his uninterested eyes on her.

Disgust sickened her stomach. Could anyone else be so ill-suited for her? Might as well deliver her to the undead. She could not expect them to wait for her to eat. Yet, she felt like a servant wandering into a ball with no serving platter in her hand.

King Thoridian stood and extended his arm. "Dear Princess Valoria, your presence is a welcome sight. We wondered if you'd gotten lost. I was about to send Lieutenant Blueborough to check on you."

The queen rose as well and gestured to the empty seat next to Brax. Although she'd changed into a burgundy evening gown, she still wore the violet pearls around her neck. "Please join us."

Valoria froze, unable to step toward the lumbering brute with hog juice dripping from his chin.

Cadence poked her finger in Valoria's back. "Get on with it."

"May I escort you to the main table?" Nathaniel appeared beside her like a beacon light in a foul storm. She could not deny him.

"Of course." Valoria took his arm, holding on a little too tightly.

He leaned down and whispered in her ear. "I was beginning to worry."

"My handmaiden needed freshening up."

"So kind of you to wait for her." He smiled warmly.

"Indeed." If only he knew the real reason for her procrastination. Would he think any less of her?

Valoria approached the great table and met Brax's gaze. She bowed her head. "My apologies, my prince. My handmaiden found it difficult to remove the blood stains from her clothes." Guilt panged inside her at her spiteful tone. Her father would not be proud of her throwing words like daggers at her future husband. She glanced at the floor.

"You've endured quite a lot at the filthy hands of the raiders." Brax's voice turned to a growl, as if he couldn't leave his battles from his meal. "I only wish I was able to deal them retribution. Thanks to my brother, you arrived safely."

He nodded to Nathaniel, and Nathaniel gave up her arm and pulled out her chair. "Thank Valoria herself. She fought just as bravely as the rest of us. Next time, the raiders will have to answer to her."

Brax crinkled his thick, black brow in doubt. But, pride surged in Valoria despite his disbelief. She wished she could thank Nathaniel for his vote of confidence. She certainly needed it.

With a small smile, Nathaniel walked away, leaving her with her intended.

"I've set aside a plate for you." Brax pushed a plate of soppy ribs in front of her. "It is the juiciest part."

Valoria covered her mouth, stifling the urge to choke. How could she tell him she only ate vegetables and grains? What would he think of her? "Thank you. But I am not hungry this hour."

Dismay settled across his blunt features.

"I mourn my lost countrymen."

"Ah. Of course." He nodded as if losing men on the battlefield was something he understood deeply. He took the plate away. "I will make sure the raiders pay."

Valoria folded her hands in her lap lest the urge to slap him overcame her. "Wouldn't it be more suitable to deal them a forgiving hand?"

Brax smiled condescendingly. "Dear Valoria, you are naïve to the follies of susceptibility. We must secure this kingdom's future for only those with noble hearts." He spoke as if she were a milkmaid being taught to squeeze the teat of a cow for the first time.

She bit her tongue. Did he mean to cast out half the populace? "Surely every man suffers from vagrancies at some point in his life. And these people have lost everything."

Brax's hand clenched and a vein in his forehead protruded. "That is no reason to murder and pillage, and to attack innocent princesses."

Valoria gritted her teeth. He had a point, but she was far from the idiot adolescent he thought her. "Innocent princesses can fend for themselves."

He spit out a piece of bone and it clanged on the china plate. "If that were true, you wouldn't need Ebonvale, now would you?"

Fury broiled inside her. Talking to him was like talking to a wall. A sweaty wall. She picked up her glass hoping the cold water would smite her temper. "We need each other."

"So our fathers believe." Brax bit off another chunk of meat.

Was that resentment in his voice?

Valoria stiffened in disbelief. All this time she hadn't given a thought to what Brax wanted. She'd always assumed he adopted his parents' wishes. But, it was clear he didn't want her just as much as she didn't want him.

She'd finally found something they had in common.

* * * *

Nathaniel watched the princess stiffen from across the room. What had Brax said now? He hoped his brother hadn't been too blunt. Valoria could fend for herself, but she also had a softer, kinder side. She hid her vulnerability from the world, but not from him. He'd glimpsed it when she'd faced Ebonvale's people for the first time, when she'd leaned over that old, wounded music teacher, and when she'd asked about Brax.

He longed to go to her, but she wasn't his charge.

"Excuse me, lieutenant, an important matter needs your attention." Kent, the medic in training, stood beside him still wearing his bloodied apron.

Nathaniel stood, blocking him from the ladies lest he spoil their dinner. "What does it concern?"

Kent wrenched his hands in a ball in front of his chest. "The prisoner. The boy with the red hair."

Guilt spread through him. He should have interrogated the boy while he had the chance. But Nathaniel couldn't bring himself to torture someone in such great pain. "Horred's temple. Is he dead?"

"Not dead, sir. He's gone."

"Gone?" A wave of relief passed over him. Why he should care so much about a boy—the enemy—he had no idea. "But, he could hardly breathe."

"Or so he led us to believe."

A fork clanged on a glass, and the conversations muted around them as the king stood to speak. Nathaniel ushered Kent to the back of the hall. "Show me the last place you saw him. The gates have been closed for the night, so there's a chance he's still in the city."

"As you wish, lieutenant." At least a little color had returned to the young man's face.

"Do not fret. We will make this right." Before he left, Nathaniel glanced back at Valoria. She met his gaze with a questioning raise of her brow. Her eyes held a flicker of desperation. Could he leave her?

He had to. She was his no more than the claim to the throne. If he were wise, he'd do his duty without any more thoughts of her. Resolve hardening inside him, Nathaniel turned from the dinner and followed Kent into the corridor beyond. He found two soldiers guarding the entryway and dispatched them to gather the others off duty and search the thoroughfares.

"Why did you not bring this to Commander Brax's attention?" Nathaniel whispered as they exited the temple and walked across the city square.

"The Commander seemed busy at the moment with his intended. Besides, I know you will find a way to…soften the blow."

No one wanted to be the target of Brax's fury. But, Nathaniel couldn't keep his superior ill-informed for long. "If we find the prisoner, I may not need to."

A light bell chimed as they entered the apothecary's shop. They walked past the shelves of medicines and hanging, dried herbs to the barn in the back. Most of the patients slept wrapped in white sheets and thick bandages. The older man Valoria had attended to sat propped on a pillow reading a scroll of parchment by candlelight.

Kent led Nathaniel to the back. "We moved all of the seriously wounded patients here." He pointed to an empty bed. The cords used to tie the boy's arms and legs had been cut. "He laid here."

Nathaniel picked up the broken cord. "He must have stolen a scalpel when the medics weren't looking."

Unease stirred in Kent's gaze. "With the bustle from the influx of minstrels, I couldn't watch each patient."

Nathaniel placed a hand on the young man's shoulder. He wasn't much older than the boy who'd run away. A mistake this early in his career would send him back to the farms where he'd come from. "No one will blame you."

"Commander Braxten will, as he should." Kent hung his head, looking at the old planks on the floor. "I am supposed to keep track of all medical equipment."

"Then, I will leave his means of escape in question. It is not important." Nathaniel scanned the rafters above. The barn had no back door, and every floor plank was in place. A single white dove sat by a cranked window. Even in prime shape, that climb would be difficult.

Nathaniel approached the older minstrel. The candlelight reflected a staff with notes on the parchment. What manner of song did he read? Tragic or sweet? Hopeful or sad?

"My apologies for interrupting, sir." Nathaniel bowed. "I regret I did not introduce myself earlier. I'm Lieutenant Nathaniel Blueborough."

The old man glanced above the parchment. "You may call me Echo."

"Echo." An honorable name for a minstrel. Nathaniel wished he could learn more about him and his connection to Valoria. But, they had more urgent matters to speak of. "A prisoner has gone missing. He lay back there in the bed in the far right corner. Have you noticed anything unusual?"

Echo rolled the parchment and brought the candle forward. Admiration shone in his eyes. "I remember you now. You saved my life earlier on the battlefield."

A flash of memory lighted Nathaniel's mind. Raiders swarmed around him, and he cut through the front line, pushing them back. A voice sang in his head, promising him honor. "One man outnumbered deserves a second chance." He spoke the words, but they were not his own.

"Eloquently spoken for a soldier." Echo raised his brow, peering deeper into his soul.

Nathaniel shook his head. "I cannot take credit for my actions. A force pulled me in your direction."

"Indeed." Echo looked away in frustration when Nathaniel had expected surprise. "A force I cannot seem to control however much I try."

The old man gestured toward the empty bed. "The boy was here when the sun set. I woke up a few hours later to the medic's shouts that he'd disappeared."

"Then he couldn't have gone through the front gate." Nathaniel massaged his chin in thought. "He must be in the city." He checked over his shoulder. "The boy couldn't have found many places to hide. Most inns, taverns, and shops are locked after sunset. Patrols march the cobblestone. My guards should have spotted him."

"What of the back gate?" Echo spoke as if he tempted fate.

Nathaniel gave him a chastising stare, as if silencing a child asking to be told a frightful bedtime story. The minstrels hadn't been in Ebonvale for decades, but they should know better. "Contrary to rumor, the back gate hasn't been opened since King Artemis Rubystone's army returned from their triumph at Sill. In the spring, it floods from the mountain pass. The poor lad would have to slosh through the muck of the moors, not to mention the stories of the voices calling from the mountains, and all of those awful bones of the lost travelers and castle runaways..." He closed his eyes, blocking the thoughts from his mind.

Echo lay back, propping his head on the pillow. "Tradition, superstition, and a little bit of muck may not supersede one's desire to be free."

"The gate will be the last place I check." Nathaniel gave the man a steady glance. "Thank you for your help."

"I'll do anything to ensure our kingdoms' unity. These are trying times."

"Indeed. With half the countryside a charred ruin and raiders running amok. At least the wyverns haven't returned. Many thanks to your kind."

Echo raised his finger. "It was the unity of both kingdoms that defeated them."

Nathaniel nodded and turned toward the door. Another reason to support Brax's union with Valoria. "I will never forget."

Chapter 5

Flight

Nathaniel rounded the corner of the apothecary's shop with a lantern in his hand. The silver rays of the quarter moon barely penetrated the shadows. He knelt down and raised the lantern above the cobblestone. A single drop of blood speckled the amber rock. He touched it with his finger. The blood was cold, but not entirely dry.

Seems the boy had some acting skills. He wasn't as near to death as he'd led Nathaniel to believe.

Nathaniel checked the area and found another drop on a storage crate in the alley out back. The bloodied path continued through the empty gin kegs behind the Wild Boar Tavern and stopped at the back door. Unlike most of the village, this tavern stayed open through the dark hours of the night.

A perfect place to hide.

Nathaniel came around the front, not wanting to raise suspicions. Two men stood by the door, chewing black root. They were farmers from the countryside, probably stopping by to drop off their goods and have a drink before the journey back tomorrow. They straightened as he approached, and he waved them back. "At ease."

"A strange place for a lieutenant on duty." The younger of the two men called after him with a teasing tone.

Nathaniel glanced over his shoulder. "We are all on duty every heartbeat of our lives."

The inside of the tavern glowed with golden light from three giant hanging lanterns and a roaring fire in the back. Several men sat at the bar, and most of the tables were taken. Loud conversations provided a din of cheers and shouts.

Barmaids pushed through the crowd with trays of ale, bowls of some sort of thick, brown stew and loaves of bread. No one looked any younger than twenty summers, and nowhere did he see a head of red hair.

Timber sat in the corner by the fire, spooning the thick stew in his mouth and looking off into the distance as if reliving an epic battle from years past. Nathaniel edged his way across the room and sat in the empty chair across from him.

"Seen anything out of the ordinary tonight?"

Timber raised his gray brow in surprise. "I cannot remember the last time I saw you in a tavern, never mind the Wild Boar."

Nathaniel leaned forward and broke off the end of the loaf on the table. "Necessity dictates my actions."

"Well, if you've come to speak to an old man like me, you are truly desperate." He raised his mug and drained the last sip. "No one seeks my council these days."

"Am I no one?" Nathaniel smiled. If King Rubystone had survived the battle at Sill, he'd have sought Timber's council until his dying day. Bronford Thoridian was too proud to ask, and Brax followed in his father's footsteps. Perhaps a good old chase would console Timber. Nathaniel pulled his chair closer and lowered his voice. "I need your help. A certain young raider has gone missing, and the trail leads here."

Timber's gaze changed from dreamy to alert as he scanned the room. "You don't say?"

Nathaniel nodded. A barmaid asked him if he wanted anything and he waved her away.

"You should order a drink to keep up appearances, in the least, sir."

"I do not intend to be here long."

"That table over there has been here for quite a while." Timber pointed to a rowdy bunch of young men by the bar. "And that man over there has a friend who hasn't moved all night. He shields his face with his arm." Like any great warrior, Timber had been keenly aware of his surroundings and who was in them even though he didn't show it.

Nathaniel shook his head. "Too burly." A hooded figure sitting alone in the far corner caught his eye. The man's frame was slight, his shoulders narrow like a boy who hadn't completely grown into his own. He gripped his right arm over his stomach, as if nursing a wound. "But over there…"

Nathaniel nodded in his direction, and Timber took the cue, placing his empty bowl on the table by the fire. Together, they approached the lone figure.

Heads turned as they grew closer. Nathaniel placed his hand on the hilt of his sword. He'd rather not draw it out in front of civilians, but he'd wield it if he had to. The figure turned in their direction, revealing a pale cheek, a red curl, and a fearful blue eye. The boy leapt from his seat and startled a barmaid. Her tray toppled, ale glasses breaking on the floor. The boy pushed a man aside and ran toward the door.

"Make way!" Nathaniel shouted. Everyone cleared his path. He bolted toward the door and followed the boy into the darkness.

* * * *

Servants cleared the third course from the table as the first couples took to the dance floor. Unfortunately, it was venison stew, another plate Valoria couldn't stomach. All she'd had to eat was a roll and a lettuce leaf garnishing the chicken wings of the second course.

"Your minstrels play well." Brax mentioned it as though they'd trained their whole lives to play background music at a feast.

"They do much more than entertain. Are we going to dance?" She'd rather know now and prepare for it, like a soldier going to war.

"Most certainly not." Brax drank another cup of ale so strong, the fumes made Valoria dizzy. He'd eaten every bit of food in front of him and some of hers. At least she was good for something—second helpings. "I do not dance. It is a fruitless activity. I'd rather save my energy for training."

Relief came over her. "How could I not guess?"

He raised an eyebrow as if he wondered if she teased him.

Valoria hid her face behind her glass of wine. "If we do not dance, then what do we do at these events besides eat?"

He stood, and for a moment she thought he would change his mind and offer his hand. "I consult with my generals about our future war plans and I try to earn more allies for the kingdom's cause."

"How diligent."

"We all must be diligent in times like these." Brax regarded her as if she were some silly party princess. "If you'll excuse me, I have matters to attend to."

The king and queen glanced at Brax with surprise and disappointment, but he ignored them and crossed the room, joining a group of soldiers in the back. The queen turned to Valoria with an apologetic face, but she glanced away, not wanting her pity.

She couldn't make Brax love her any more than they could. And she didn't want to.

Frustration brewed inside her. Would she be resigned to watch every night while other couples danced and laughed for all the years of her life? Valoria threw her napkin on the table and stood. She'd rather play with the court musicians. At least then she'd be useful.

The queen called her name, but she pretended not to hear, leaving the table and walking along the side of the room. Where had Nathaniel disappeared to? For a moment, she'd thought he was on her side. But, he could never really be on her side completely. That was Brax's duty.

Two doors opened to a balcony overlooking the courtyard. Valoria breathed the fresh air with relief, closing the door behind her. The glass muted the din of the party, but it could not mute the sore ache in her chest.

She walked to the edge and placed her hands on the cold stone railing. The cobblestone streets of Ebonvale spread out before her. The city was three times the size of her minstrel village. Gabled roofs of inns, taverns, and shops cluttered the horizon in a complicated jumble.

So many people called Ebonvale their home. Was it her duty to protect them? As strong and noble as the Royal Guard was, it had been the minstrel's song that stilled the wyverns so the warriors could get close enough to deliver the fatal blow. When the next threat arose, would it take both sides once again to defeat it? Would only her and Brax's union ensure the safety of these people and her own?

Maybe Brax was right. Maybe Ebonvale didn't need the minstrels after all. A lot of time had passed between the last war with the wyverns, and the fire worms had yet to return. It would be a convenient truth.

The door opened behind her, and the queen stepped onto the balcony. The wind threw up her honey-blond hair. She wore a sumptuous gown, but her body moved like a warrior's. The soft fabric could not conceal the sinewy muscles in her arms, or the fierceness in her eyes. She was gorgeous, and for a moment Valoria understood why her father could not take his heart back. But, her mother had had a soft kindness the queen lacked. In Valoria's esteem, gentleness counted more than beauty.

"Forgive me, am I intruding?"

Valoria bowed her head. "No, your majesty. I needed fresh air."

"As do I." Queen Thoridian joined her, standing on the balcony's edge and gazing at the city below with certainty and pride. "These dinners can be tiresome."

Valoria glanced away, afraid the queen would see the repulsion on her face. "I am thankful for your kindness."

"It is I who should thank you." The sincerity in her tone made Valoria snap her gaze back on her.

Queen Thoridian pursed her lips. In the moonlight, her pearls shone like underwater treasures. Valoria had heard a tale sung about the Sapphire Isles, where a king had tricked a mermaid and stolen the five pearls of wisdom. Were they the same?

The queen turned toward her. "You know of the history between your father and me?"

Anxiety crept up Valoria's spine. At her home, this subject was taboo. "He does not speak often of it, but I am aware of your broken betrothal."

Queen Thoridian nodded, and a sad reluctance settled in her sharp features. "I highly regard him. He is a great and noble man and he treated me well—better than I deserved. But, I did not love him. You see, I am very much like my mother before me even though it pains me to admit it." She shrugged as if she could do nothing about it. "My heart rules my mind. I loved Bron—I still do—more than anything in the world. There is no shame in that. But because of my choice, the future of both kingdoms falls to you, and to Brax."

Great pressure fell on Valoria's shoulders. She struggled to breathe. Her chin trembled as she struggled to hold her tears back. Uniting the kingdoms by marrying Brax seemed so impossible. "I do not think he cares for me."

"Brax is a noble man, but it takes time to win his regard. Once you do, he'll love you more deeply than anyone else could. If you have any of the virtues of your father—some of which I've already seen in you—then, in time, he will."

The queen moved toward her and took Valoria's hands in her own. Her meadow-green eyes pleaded. "It is unfair of me—of anyone—to ask you to choose against your heart. But, who knows what threats lurk on the horizon, and how much of an alliance our kingdoms truly have? Do me this one favor. Be patient. Give Brax time."

Words would not come. Valoria stood frozen with the queen squeezing the blood from her hands. She asked so much of her. But, Danika Thoridian wouldn't have come out and spoken so honestly if she didn't think the cause was worthy. Valoria's own father had asked the same of her since she could talk. Could she disregard all of their hopes after one dinner party?

Valoria nodded slowly. "I'll try."

The queen laughed desperately. "Thank Helena and Horred." She smoothed back Valoria's hair. "You are such a darling child. Your father must be proud."

"I want to make him proud." Valoria smiled, thinking of his long face, his graying hair, and his silver eyes. "He's spoken of me coming here every day of my life."

"I'm sure he has." She glanced away as if the thought of Valoria's father talking about Ebonvale every day seemed unsettling. "Come, let me find your handmaiden. I will bore you no longer with this dinner feast. You deserve some rest."

A little stunned, Valoria allowed the queen to lead her back into the room. She kept to her word, and summoned Cadence from the servants' dining room downstairs. Cadence met them at the door with a smile on her face.

"I trust the dinner was successful." Cadence took Valoria's arm as the queen paced back to her table, velvet gown trailing behind her.

"As successful as it could be with a man who 'does not dance' because 'tis 'a fruitless activity.'" Valoria smiled ironically.

"Hush!" Cadence glanced around in case someone overheard. "Leave your spitfire tongue to your room."

Having Cadence call her a spitfire was quite the compliment to end the night. Valoria pulled Cadence forward. "Shall we embark before my tongue gets the better of me?"

Cadence gave her a stern look. "We shall."

Valoria moved past one of the servants she'd seen waiting on Nathaniel's table. "Wait." She broke free of Cadence's arm and approached him. "Excuse me."

"Yes, my lady." He looked like a mouse caught in a wyvern's claws.

Valoria smiled to ease his anxiety. "Do you know where Lieutenant Blueborough ran off to?"

He blinked in surprise and then bowed his head. "No, my lady. He left suddenly. I hadn't even brought him his second course."

Cadence gave her a hard stare. Valoria waved her hand. "No matter. I had a trivial question about something in my room."

The servant cleared his throat. "Can I help you, my lady?"

"No, no, no." Valoria stepped back as if he'd catch her in a trap. "'Tis not important."

She pulled Cadence away and they retreated down the corridor. He hadn't even finished his second course. Something must have gone terribly wrong. She wished she knew what it was. He'd been so kind to her, and she longed to repay the favor.

Once they were alone, Cadence shook her head. "You shouldn't be asking about the lieutenant, my lady."

Valoria laughed, but it came out brittle and forced. "It was just a matter with my room. That's all."

Cadence furrowed her skinny brow. "I saw the way he looked at you back at the battle, when he was helping Echo into the carriage."

Valoria stopped in the middle of the hallway by a painting of King Thoridian atop a white charger. "Why? How did he look?"

Cadence clucked her tongue in disapproval. "Like you were the Goddess Helena herself, stepped from the Holy Temple in the sky."

Chapter 6

Raven's Eye

Nathaniel launched after the red-haired raider. The quarter moon provided limited light as the boy disappeared down an alley by the butcher's shop and the candlestick maker. When Nathaniel reached the alley, it was empty. He ran alongside the stone buildings, adrenaline pumping in his veins.

Did he truly wish to find the boy?

Who knew what measures Brax would take to get the information he needed? But, Nathaniel couldn't have gangs of raiders attacking every caravan departing from the castle. And poor Kent would be punished if the boy wasn't found. He hadn't done anything wrong. But this boy certainly had.

Glass shattered, drawing Nathaniel to the dimly lit part of town in the north by the back gate. Nathaniel watched his footing as he ran over the broken cobblestone. A shadow disappeared into a building with a crumbling foundation. Nathaniel picked his way over the remnants of the roof sprawled over the floor. Footsteps creaked on the broken stairway. The boy climbed over a hole in the staircase and pulled himself to the upper floor.

"Wait." Nathaniel called after him. This part of town was dangerous, not only for the broken glass and deteriorating wood, but thieves hid in the shadows. Besides, there was only one way out, through the back gate and into the moorland with swamps so deep, entire carriages could sink to the bottom and never be found again.

But what could he promise the boy to come back to? He might be better off taking his chances in the moors.

Nathaniel leapt up the stairs and stepped on rotten wood. His foot fell through, and he tumbled forward. An upturned nail sliced his palm.

"Horred's grave!" He clutched his injured hand against his chest and regained his footing, following the boy to the back room. Pigeons took off from the posts of a sodden bed. Tattered curtains flowed from broken windows. Nathaniel pulled open the closet door, and a bat flew toward his head. He ducked, and pulled out a thick blanket covered in moss. It hung over a chair with only three legs.

No one.

Rats scurried away as he checked under the bed. He turned toward the broken window. A thick clanking resounded from the wall, slow at first, then picking up speed. Chains strained and pulled, and a deep creaking rumbled in his gut.

The gate was opening.

Dread settled in Nathaniel's stomach. He scrambled down the rotten stairs and ran into the street.

Timber caught up, huffing. Fear and surprise lit his wrinkled face. "Helena's sword, what does he think he's doing?"

"Getting away." Nathaniel tied his handkerchief around his palm and raced ahead. Timber followed, running faster than he should for his age. "Leave this to me."

"I will not allow you to go alone." Timber called from behind him.

The gate rose inch by inch as they lurched uphill toward it. Countryside black as soot and endless as the sky stretched out beyond the walls. The dank smell of rot and mold wafted in on a breeze so cool, it settled into his bones.

Nathaniel ran under the gate and stopped abruptly at the edge of the murky water. The spring floods had risen higher than ever before, covering most of the ramp leading to the gate.

The raider had disappeared without even a ripple in the water.

"Would you look at that?" Timber came up behind him. "I cannot even make out the road."

"Must have been a snowy winter up there." Nathaniel gestured toward the darkened peaks. He kicked a rock into the water, and the muck swallowed it with a clump. "He couldn't have gone far."

"That's the problem. You don't have to." Timber crouched and scanned the surface of the water. Reeds and tall marsh grasses blew in the cold wind. "He wouldn't be the first one lost in the depths."

The wind changed direction. Was the howling from a man? He tried not to imagine rowing out there with only a lantern for a light. "We'll need a boat to continue the search."

Timber placed a heavy hand on Nathaniel's shoulder. "Wait until morning."

"I'll have to inform Brax."

"Either way, he's going to know."

Nathaniel nodded, promising himself to cover for Kent when he reported back to Brax. Timber spoke with the wisdom and patience of his age. The boy wouldn't get far. That was if he survived at all.

Only the gods knew why Nathaniel longed to save him, even if it meant crossing the moors.

Just as he turned back to the gate, movement from the dark peaks drew him back. A black mass spread from the highest mountain, thinning into dark specks as it widened over the valley below. A chorus of caws filled the air.

"Crows." Nathaniel squinted at the sky. "Thousands of them."

The birds flew in strange patterns, coalescing into spiral shapes and breaking at the top, like tornadoes unleashing darkness upon the land.

Timber pulled his bow from his back along with an arrow. He aimed as the birds flew over their heads.

"What are you doing?"

"Making sure." He fired, and the arrow pierced a bird, felling it over the gate. They ran back to the city.

The beast lay in the middle of the shambled cobblestone road with the arrow through its heart.

Nathaniel bent over it, as a current of sorrow drifted through his chest. He knew what it felt to be aloft, soaring triumphant and free and to be hit with an arrow through the heart, ending the dream that life once was. "Why did you fell it?"

"Don't touch it!" Timber crouched beside him and used the tip of his bow to move the wing. He cocked its head to the side. A milky, cataract-covered eye glanced up at them. Bald spots covered its body where the feathers had been plucked, or had fallen out. The blood that oozed from the arrowhead was a black, gelatinous goo.

Nathaniel had never seen anything like this in his lifetime, but he'd heard enough stories. "An undead bird?"

Timber nodded, then watched the sky with suspicion.

None of the crows had settled in the city. They'd come and gone so quickly they wouldn't have noticed if they hadn't been standing at the back gate.

Timber glanced over his shoulder at the open gate and the moors that lay beyond. "Spies."

Chapter 7

Dismissal

"I do not understand why they'll deny the future princess of Ebonvale entrance to her own council chambers." Valoria collapsed into a velvet seat, staring down the guards on duty as they stood with their spears crossed over the doorway. The one on the right glanced down with a small amount of guilt pulling at the corners of his mouth, but the one on the left stared straight ahead as if the future queen of Ebonvale were not even present.

"Calm down. I'm sure there's an explanation." Cadence sat beside her and took her hand. "Perhaps they are planning the wedding and wish to keep it a surprise."

"I highly doubt it." If they were planning the wedding, Brax wouldn't even bother to be there at all. "Everyone who's important is in there. Everyone except for me." She'd gone down to breakfast hoping to make headway with her new family only to find the room empty. A servant had tipped her off to where they all were.

"My father would never think to leave me out of meetings." Father had included her in all aspects of running the House of Song and the outlying village. A sickening wave of melancholy overcame her. She missed his quiet, noble poise more than anything. She could use a measure of it herself.

"Perhaps they do not wish to bother you right before the wedding." Cadence tapped the back of her hand encouragingly.

"Bother me? They've managed to do enough of that already."

"Shhhh." Cadence glanced at the guards. "You never know who's listening."

"Let them listen. They can teach these warriors proper manners."

Cadence threw her hands in her lap. "Honestly, I'm not sure what Echo wants me to do. 'Tis like leading a blind goat across a cliff side."

Valoria narrowed her gaze. "What did he put you up to?"

Her handmaiden pouted, guilt saddening her eyes. "He wanted to make sure you...followed through."

"Followed through? Who does he think I am? The Queen of Ebonvale?"

"For Helena's sake, pipe down."

Guilt panged in her gut. She shouldn't have spoken ill of her future mother-in-law. Hadn't she told Nathaniel she didn't judge others? Valoria behaved better than this. Circumstances had unraveled her just like the edges of that dusty tapestry of some forgotten king on the far wall.

The guards moved away from the door, and the large slabs of oak opened with a creak. The king and queen burst through, followed by a retinue of advisors. A woman so old, she could have been a ghost drifted past. Her long, white hair trailed to her ankles. Bone thin with wrinkled withered skin, she clung to a young man's arm as if she'd fall to pieces without his strength.

Was that Sybil, the mother of the queen who'd run away with the minstrel so many years ago? It was hard to believe one waif of an old woman was the source for unending minstrel hatred.

Valoria was here to end that prejudice, to unite the kingdoms, to undo the seed that old woman had sown. If only it hadn't grown so monumentally large.

Nathaniel emerged next. His uniform was rumpled, and a bloodied bandage wrapped around his right hand. He looked as though he'd been up all night.

Despite Cadence pulling on her arm, Valoria broke free and approached him.

He regarded her with welcome surprise. "Valoria. I did not know you were here."

All of her frustration melted away. She touched his hand. "You're hurt. What happened?"

Nathaniel glanced back into the room uneasily. "I am certain Brax will inform you."

She clutched his arm, refusing to release him. The wool of his uniform felt coarse under her fingers, a barrier she could not cross. "Tell me now."

Nathaniel sighed as though he knew he was in the wrong but could not deny her. He pulled her aside by the tapestry. "One of the raiders escaped. I cut my hand while chasing after him."

"Is this why they had a meeting without me?"

"No." He glanced again at the room. Indecision crossed his amber-brown eyes.

She pulled him closer. "Please."

Nathaniel leaned down to her, so close their foreheads almost touched, and whispered, "Spies from the north have crossed into our territory. It seems the next threat to Ebonvale is closer than we thought."

"The north?" Disbelief shocked her, followed by a dark dread, which settled in her bones. Had she awoken the threat when she called on the northern lands for help?

Nathaniel pulled away abruptly as Brax entered the corridor.

"Valoria, I must speak with you." Brax's voice was blunt and businesslike, as if he called on a servant.

Valoria glanced back for Nathaniel. He'd disappeared in the crowd. The old woman stared at her with large, knowing eyes that bored into her soul and upturned all her secrets. Valoria turned back to Brax and cut through the crowd. Anything to escape the old woman's eyes.

She reached him and followed him into the council chamber. Ebonvale's purple pennants hung from lofty rafters. An oily, vermillion scale as large as a carriage hung on a slab of wood on the wall. It must have been taken from one of the wyverns in the final battle at Scalehaven that she'd read about. Old swords lined the walls, probably the weapons of past rulers. This was a place where battle plans were laid down, a place of finality, a room of fate.

Unease crawled over her shoulders. All this time she'd wanted to be in this room, and now the urge to leave crept up her legs.

Brax gestured toward a high back chair with red jewels in the frame and a velvet cushion. "Have a seat."

Valoria shook her head. "I prefer to stand. Why did you not include me in this meeting?"

He blinked in surprise, as if the thought hadn't even occurred to him. "Ebonvale's matters are not your concern."

Anger flared inside her. "Aren't they? If I am to be the future queen?" It was the first time she'd directly mentioned their union to him. She felt absurd stating the obvious fact they'd both been denying. But, sooner or later they had to come to terms with their union and all that it implied.

Brax ran a hand over his face. "One step at a time. First, I must ask you to withdraw the minstrels who are able to travel. They must return to the House of Song."

"Whatever for?"

"There is a new threat to this castle. The minstrels will be safer within their own kingdom, protected by their…" He waved his hand as if he couldn't possibly understand it. "Songs."

Was his skull as thick as it looked? "They should stay here to lend their aid. You will need them."

"They have completed their mission. They've brought you here unscathed. At present, they are distracting my forces and causing dissent in the city when we need unity to present a strong front. Do not fret, I will send a retinue of men to protect them on their journey back."

"They are here to preside at the wedding." Valoria stood as if she had iron in her back. She couldn't order the minstrels home now after they'd traveled all this way and survived such a brutal attack. Besides, she wasn't ready to be left alone with these warriors. The minstrels gave her a semblance of community. If Brax thought he could take that away with a single order, then he didn't know the princess of the House of Song.

"The wedding must be postponed." Not one sliver of emotion crossed Brax's thick nose, thin lips, and wide chin. He could have been remarking on the weather.

Relief flowed through her, and she pushed it back, ashamed of her own weakness. Father's words from her childhood came back to haunt her… *watch what you wish for.* "Surely the king and queen disagree."

Brax shook his head. "They have given me full authority on the matter." He walked toward her and placed a finger under her chin, bringing her face to meet his. "Do not pretend you are not pleased."

She pulled away and eyed him defensively. "I am not pleased. I am…" She struggled to find the most diplomatic word. "Surprised."

He turned toward the window, and whatever openness he'd shared closed like a steel door in her face. "The king and queen are on their way to speak to your retinue. The minstrels who are able will leave tomorrow at first light."

Chapter 8

My Fair Lady

"What'll it be, sir?" The man at the bar polished a tin cup and glanced at Nathaniel with a crooked smile. He had a golden front tooth, but his overcoat had seen better days. Nathaniel lamented the fact this man would get no tip from his purse.

"I'm not here for a drink." Nathaniel ignored the heads that turned in his direction. "I wish to speak with a certain barmaid."

"A barmaid?" The man chuckled. The top button was missing from his coat and the threads dangled loose. "Well, aren't you a ladies' man."

Nathaniel's patience wore thin. He placed his hand on the hilt of his sword. "This is for an investigation conducted by the Royal Guard."

"Of course, sir." The man's smile disappeared as he placed the tin mug and the wet rag on the countertop. "Which maid?"

"The one with the red curls tending tables last night." He scanned the room, but didn't see her. Fortunately, Timber stood outside the back entrance, in case she made a run for it.

The bartender nodded. "That's Masie. I hope she hasn't done anything wrong."

"No. I need to ask her a few questions, that's all."

He nodded and disappeared in the back.

Nathaniel tapped his fingers on the counter, ignoring the stares from the other patrons.

An old man sitting at the bar sipping the leftover stew from last night turned toward him. "Is it true the minstrels are leaving?"

Nathaniel nodded, keenly aware the conversations had quieted across the room. "The king and queen think it best with the recent raider attacks." The less the populace knew, the better. He couldn't have panic spreading like the plague of the undead.

The old man lifted his mug. "Good riddance. Those snobby finger-pluckers told my boy his butcher shop was an 'extravagant show of brutalism.'" He intoned the minstrels' words in the highest, haughtiest voice he could manage.

A chorus of shouts erupted across the tavern with people agreeing and telling their own stories.

"They told me I needed a bath." A woman in the back stood.

"Yeah, well, I caught one of them sniffing my mother's stew like it was dung," called out a young man at a back table.

"Excuse me." Nathaniel held up both hands until everyone quieted around him. At least the Royal Guard still had some authority. "Your future queen is a minstrel. From now on, any insult against them is an insult to the Royal Family and will be considered treason."

Silence fell. Nathaniel settled into a seat at the bar as he reined in his irritation. Why did the insults affect him? He wasn't a minstrel. He wasn't even going to marry one. But they did. They pushed the dagger straight through to his heart.

The back door opened, and the bartender came out with Masie. Her apron dripped with dishwater. She stared at Nathaniel as though he would arrest her right there. He wished he could smile to alleviate her fears, but he wasn't certain of her innocence.

"Come with me." Nathaniel led her outside to a bench in front of the bakery. The sweet smell of baking bread permeated the air and the midday sun cast golden rays on the blue flowers in the window boxes. If only these were peaceful times.

Masie wrung her hands in her lap. Nathaniel couldn't tell if her worried expression was guilt, or just fear.

"One of my soldiers witnessed you serving the young man who ran away last night."

Masie nodded. "He sat at my table, sir."

"Of course." He tried a small smile. "Did you recognize him from anywhere?"

"No, sir." She glanced down. Freckles speckled the bridge of her nose and her cheeks. It could have been just a coincidence she resembled the raider. But, he'd heard of some families who'd split, half their sons residing at the castle, and the other half chancing life on the outlying farms.

"You don't know him?"

"No." She bit her lip.

"I see." Was that the same expression the boy had used when he'd refused to answer Nathaniel's questions? "What is your family name?"

"Smith."

Nathaniel sighed. There were a hundred Smiths all over town. "Did this boy say anything to you when you served him? Anything at all?"

"He ordered water, sir."

"Water?"

"Yes."

"You did not think it odd?"

"'Tis my job to serve the patrons without question, sir."

True, yet from the looks of it, this establishment survived on tips, and no barmaid would serve anyone for very long with no gold in sight.

"Can I go back in, sir? I have to finish the dishes before the dinner rush."

Dinner was half a day away. How many dishes could a single tavern have? Nathaniel touched his forehead, massaging his temples. "Yes, of course. Thank you for being helpful. You may go."

After the sighting of the undead bird, Brax had ordered the back gate shut for good. Nathaniel's search for the raider had come to a dead end.

* * * *

As Valoria entered the apothecary's shop, a minstrel pushed by her on a crutch. Her countrymen had slings across their chests and others hobbled with canes. One man, a servant to her father, had a bandage wrapped around his right eye.

She grabbed a medic by the arm. "Excuse me. These men are deemed able to leave?"

"Commander Thoridian has given the minstrels two carriages to transport the wounded, my lady."

"How kind of him."

The medic smiled, as if unaware of her mockery. "He is kind, indeed."

Kind enough to kick them out. Valoria found Echo propped on a pillow, reading a song of protection against enemies. If anything, she was glad to see him leave. At least near the House of Song he'd be safe. The undead would have to storm all of Ebonvale before reaching the bluewood forest. "Where you're traveling, you will not need such tunes."

Echo raised a gray eyebrow. "I'm not traveling anywhere."

"Am I mistaken? Or have you lost your mind cooped up in this warrior's excuse for a healing dome?"

Echo chuckled and rolled the parchment on his lap. "The medics have deemed me unfit to travel."

"Helena's sword! Are your injuries fatal?"

"Not even close." Echo tapped on a different scroll near his arm. Valoria unrolled the parchment and read the notes. "This is an enchantment of façade. Have you been serenading the medics?"

He smiled wryly. "They love my voice."

"Horred's grave." She collapsed on the side of the bed. "What if the undead attack? You are not in the condition to defend yourself."

"I have a hunch I'll be more use to you here than in the House of Song."

"You'll be no use if you are dead."

He picked up a scroll. "I have my songs to protect me. Come." He gestured for her to lean closer. "There are more serious matters to discuss."

Valoria's stomach churned as she moved closer. "What could be more serious than your health?"

A medic came by, bringing Echo a mug of water and asking if he needed anything. Echo waved him away.

Valoria pursed her lips. "I can see why you want to stay."

"Never mind that now." Echo's gaze grew hard as stone as he placed the mug on the table to his right. "Braxten Thoridian is a proud, arrogant young man. He believes he can squelch this threat without the minstrels' aid."

"You do not need to tell me what I already know."

"Watch him with a wary eye. As the sole minstrel at the castle's back gate, you must make sure the undead do not break through."

"He's sent most of the minstrels home. What can I do all alone?"

Echo smiled fondly. "I heard your song during the battle with the raiders. It was you who turned the tide in our favor. Not Ebonvale's Royal Guard."

Valoria crossed her fingers together and glanced away. Fear resided deep inside her. Echo had no inkling of what she might have summoned that day and it did no good to speak of it now. "They fought nobly and bravely and we must not take that away from them."

"It is you who fought nobly and bravely. You have become more than what I could have ever hoped for. 'Tis time I admit your abilities have surpassed my own."

Valoria's cheeks burned. Echo was the greatest minstrel in the House of Song. He had no rivals that even came close. "Come now, no one can trick a medic like you do."

He wiggled a finger at her. "I do not jest. I have full faith you will save us, and I do not mean by marrying Braxten Thoridian."

She teased him with a mischievous smile. "Does that mean I'm off the hook?"

"Sadly not. 'Tis a cruel fate, but not as cruel as the alternative." He patted her hand. "I'd marry him myself if it would take the burden off your shoulders."

Valoria laughed. "I do not think Brax will like you any better than he likes me."

"Let us hope he likes you a lot."

"Or at least a little." Valoria sighed.

"Give him time. He may possess qualities we have yet to see manifest. And the same goes for you. He hasn't heard you play."

"Oh, please. No warrior here appreciates music the way we do."

Echo smiled secretively. "You may be surprised."

"Even if he does grow to like me even a little, Braxten Thoridian will no sooner allow me on the battlefield than in the council chamber room."

Echo took her hand and squeezed. "So be it. But that doesn't change the fact that you must find a way."

Resolution hardened inside Valoria as she left her old music teacher in the apothecary's shop. He would not leave her to the wolves alone. He would stay beside her, even if it meant tricking the medics with his music to do so. As long as he lived, she'd always have someone on her side.

Speaking of those on her side, Valoria spotted Nathaniel approaching the temple steps from downtown. What business had he in the city?

Nathaniel recognized her and increased his pace. He caught up just as she took the first step.

"Valoria, you should not be out alone. Where is your handmaiden?"

"Taking a nap." She glanced at him with irritation. "And you are not my mother."

"That is certain." Nathaniel smiled slyly. "But it is not safe in this city for any minstrel to walk alone."

"Because of all the hatred?"

He glanced away, as if deciding whether or not to tell the truth. When he looked back at her, his face was solemn, resigned. "Yes."

"All due to Sybil running away with the minstrel years ago?"

"I am afraid so." Nathaniel told her the truth of the matter—like Cadence. She was growing to love that about him.

"This morning, after the meeting, there was an old woman walking behind the queen. Was that Sybil?" She shivered, thinking of how the old woman's fierce gaze had bored into her—seeing the raw nakedness of her heart unfold.

Valoria tripped, and Nathaniel took her arm. "Yes, it was. I am sorry no one introduced you. The commotion from the spies has upset our traditions."

"That's understandable. Although being left out of the meeting was not."

"I have no excuse for that." Nathaniel glanced at their feet as they stepped on one of the ancient, ivory steps from Helena and Horred's temple.

"The excuse is not yours to give." Her reply came out harsher than she intended, and Valoria looked away, watching a noble couple descend the steps on the other side, arm in arm, like her and Nathaniel. The only difference was that couple looked like they were married to each other.

"My apologies on the postponement of the wedding." Nathaniel sounded sincere, but he seemed preoccupied watching the pigeons eat breadcrumbs sprinkled by a boy on the top step.

"No matter." If only he knew how much she dreaded the wedding. "The king and queen must focus on protecting Ebonvale. That is what is important now."

"Spoken like a true ruler." Nathaniel regarded her with pride. "You will be a magnificent queen."

Valoria laughed and glanced down at her slippers as embarrassment heated her cheeks. "I cannot speak of any magnificence. I only want to be fair."

"You will be more than fair. That I know."

Chapter 9

History's Lesson

Whips lashed, and the horses jumped into motion. The two carriages of wounded minstrels rolled down the cobblestone following ten men of the Royal Guard in their silver armor. The minstrels who could ride brought their trumpets to their lips. A fanfare echoed over the cobblestone and reverberated through the stone buildings. They played a song of farewell, wishing Valoria good fortune.

They might as well save their breath.

Valoria waved, portraying a resilient smile while deep inside, she mourned for the countrymen they'd lost, the growing threats on the horizon, and the horrid atmosphere of her new home. She could not show her sorrow to the minstrels. She had to give them a union to believe in, and a future to hope for.

A small crowd of villagers stood on either side of the procession. Woman held children in their arms and on their shoulders, and men brought their drinks from the local tavern into the street. A young boy carried a basket of painted wooden flutes, selling them at too high a price in Valoria's eyes. The crowds' feeble waves made Valoria wonder if they were here to support the minstrels or bid them good riddance.

At least Echo had stayed.

"I am thankful for your compliance on this matter." Brax spoke beside her as he held up his hand to the final soldier. He wore his armor, like every other day of his life. Was he ever rid of it, or did he sleep with a helmet on?

Valoria stiffened. "You did not give me a choice."

"There is always a choice." Brax smiled, but it came across as self-satisfied. "You chose wisely."

He meant she'd chosen not to complain. Frustration prickled her composure. Valoria crossed her arms over her chest. This could not set a precedent for the future. Brax must know she meant for this to be an equal partnership. She was not another servant to be ordered around.

"Which means I'll get my wish on our next disagreement."

Brax's horrified expression curled the sides of her lips. Without staying to hear his reply, she turned and climbed the temple steps. Cadence joined her, lifting the trail of her long, burgundy dress.

"Well, said, my princess."

Valoria glanced over her shoulder and spoke under her breath. "I thought you were supposed to push me into his arms."

"Following through is one matter, but becoming a mute, trophy wife is another."

"Good to know you are still on my side."

"We are all on the same side." Cadence reminded her of the reason why she was here. Not to draw lines but to remove them.

They passed by Nathaniel, standing at the back of the congregation of nobles next to an older solider. He bowed his head and Valoria nodded in return. An unspoken understanding passed between them. What of, she wasn't sure. But, it was enough for Cadence to give her another warning glare.

"That one over there I do not trust at all."

Valoria painted on a face of innocence. "You mean Lieutenant Blueborough?"

"You know very well who I speak of."

Valoria bit her lip. It was as if his name had been burned into her heart and there was no way to remove it. Every time she uttered it, her ears turned red.

You will be more than fair. Valoria had turned those words over and over, trying to find what manner of creature lurked underneath. Had he faith in her leadership abilities? Or did his compliment extend to more of her attributes?

She shouldn't have given the phrase another thought, but there it was, recited through her mind like a nursery rhyme.

They reached the top of the steps and the train of her dress fell from Cadence's hands. She huffed and picked it back up. "You wonder why there are so many."

"They built the castle around Helena and Horred's sacred temple. They couldn't very well tear them down."

"I'm aware of the history. But they could have at least leveled a few."

Statues of the great gods stood watch on either side of the doors. Helena's face had been carved as stoic and certain, as if she never doubted one decision in her life. Horred stood burly and tall, much like Brax with a broad forehead and a strong jaw. But, his expression was more open, as if he'd listen to even the poorest beggar on the street.

"To them the temple is sacred, just like our House of Song." Why Valoria felt like she had to stand up for these warriors, she had no idea. They were full of grandeur and display, when the House of Song valued peacefulness and clarity.

"Every time I climb those steps I feel like ghosts hang over my shoulders." Cadence shuddered. "All I can think of is how the undead stormed Helena and Horred's temple and how they stayed behind to hold them off as the people burned the city around them."

"They gave their lives so others could go on with their teachings, so they could rebuild." Valoria poked Cadence in the arm. "You told me you weren't afraid of Sill. That Braxten Thoridian's army could defeat the most horrid foes."

Cadence's face had turned pale. She swallowed hard. "That was before a bird that should not have been flying at all fell atop our heads."

"Helena and Horred did not have the great wall." Valoria put her hand on Cadence's shoulders. Even though she took a position of strength, she'd said it to calm her own nerves as well. Maybe she'd learned a thing or two from Helena's countenance.

Cadence squeezed her arm. "With all the minstrels gone, except for you, me, and Echo, let us hope that is enough."

* * * *

"The family is not complete without you by their side." Timber murmured to Nathaniel as they stood three steps behind the king and queen.

Nathaniel had caught himself staring as he watched Valoria and her handmaiden leave. It took him a moment to form a reply. "I do not doubt their love for me. But, I have my place and Brax has his."

"You are the elder son."

"Not by blood or by name." He gave Timber a look that told him to let it be. The king and queen had given him so much—a home, a family, a title, and a place in their army. To ask for anything more would be ungrateful. And he hadn't wanted more. Until he'd laid eyes on Valoria.

Ashamed, he pretended to pay attention to the last of the procession. Something Echo had said the other day clung to his thoughts. The old music teacher hadn't been surprised when Nathaniel mentioned the *force* that drew him to save the minstrel. Echo had known exactly who convinced Nathaniel to save him.

That same voice sang in Nathaniel's dreams each night. *Justice is served...when one man...outnumbered...has a second chance.* He'd ignored it until a few moments ago, when Valoria had snapped at Brax in a commanding tone he'd not heard from her mouth before, the same voice from the battlefield.

She'd enchanted him. She'd called on him to protect her former music teacher. That, in itself wasn't a crime. He would have done the same if she'd asked him outright. But, her secret led to another question—had she enchanted him with additional charms? Was this unhealthy preoccupation with her a product of her own doing?

Disbelief clouded his thoughts. Why would she? She was set to marry Brax. Having Nathaniel dote on her would solve nothing. In fact, it would only cause trouble, and she wasn't a troublemaker. Guilt trickled through him for even considering it. So, if she hadn't enchanted him, than his feelings for her were all of his own doing. He couldn't decide which truth was worse.

"Are you well, sir?" Timber pulled him out of his trance.

Everyone had retreated up the temple steps, leaving them behind as a light rain began to fall. The townsfolk had mostly gone except for a young boy still trying to sell wooden flutes from his basket. In Ebonvale, he'd have more luck selling swords.

Nathaniel clapped Timber on the shoulder. "To tell you the truth, old friend, I'm not sure."

"These are trying times."

"Indeed. But, you've been through worse before and lived to tell of it." Nathaniel glanced at the scar running down Timber's face.

"Barely, sir. I cannot say the same for the late king."

"I know you miss him." Nathaniel smiled with compassion, even though he'd only heard tales of Danika's father. The late king had died at the last battle of Sill before he'd ever been born.

They walked into the foyer. Some of the nobles stayed and mingled, chatting over glasses of wine. Valoria was nowhere to be seen. After watching her countrymen leave, he couldn't blame her.

Brax approached him with a solemn nod. Timber bowed, leaving him to speak with his brother alone.

A servant offered them a platter of cheese. Nathaniel declined, but Brax took a large wedge. He was never one to turn down food. "We have not spoken much as of late."

Nathaniel smiled to show no harm had been done. "You have been busy with your future bride."

"As if." Brax bit into the cheese. "There are too many threats to think of marriage at a time like this."

"You could leave them to your father. He is still king." Nathaniel gestured to where the king and queen stood surrounded by a ring of nobles and advisors.

Brax shook his head. "He wants to see me rule. Ever since he damaged his knee, he has taken a back seat. I must not disappoint him."

"You will never disappoint him." The king's love for Brax ran so deep, it had overshadowed everything else in his life, except for the queen. After Brax was born, there was no room for an orphan son from a burnt village. They had an appropriate heir.

Brax studied Nathaniel with his beady eyes. "You have always been my greatest supporter when you've had so much reason to despise me."

"You are my younger brother, and it is my duty to do so." Nathaniel took a glass from a servant's tray and raised it to Brax. "Besides, I have no desire to be king."

"That is fortunate." Brax scanned the room as if sizing up every noble there and finding them wanting. "We have enough problems as it is."

Chapter 10

In the Deep

Cold, putrid air wafted over the battlements. Nathaniel pulled his cloak around his shoulders, scanning the dark moors for any sign of movement in the moon's silver light. The surface lay untouched, stagnant and dead like the land beyond.

If only he knew what the enemy had planned. Sill had stirred, for certain. But was it shifting in its sleep or had it fully awoken?

Shuffling came from the eastern ledge. A dark shape hunched to the side took slow steps forward. Nathaniel's heart stopped.

Was it an undead? How did it get up on the battlements?

The shape approached with slow determination with a distinctive stumble favoring the right side.

Nathaniel's hand fell to the hilt of his sword. "Who goes there?"

"Only an old man." The figure stepped into the torch's light.

Nathaniel breathed in relief and surprise. "My king, what are you doing up this late hour?"

Bronford Thoridian's battle armor gleamed as if it had never been used. A slight dent in the breastplate and a scratch on the right arm told otherwise. His thick, jeweled claymore hung on his belt. "Sleep has eluded me. I wanted to take the morning watch."

"That is not necessary. We have enough men."

Bron leaned on the stone wall. "I have done nothing for too long. The queen keeps me locked away as if I were a cripple, unable to defend myself."

Nathaniel breathed to speak, but the king raised a hand to silence him. "It is only out of love. She fears I will meet a horrible end."

Nathaniel smiled. "So will we all someday."

"But not today." The king smiled fondly and touched Nathaniel's shoulder. "It seems like forever since we've talked."

Nathaniel shrugged, although he had to admit he was pleased to spend this time together. "I try to stay out of the drama."

Bron laughed. "I remember a little boy named Nip with a wooden sword who very much enjoyed drama."

Nathaniel placed his hand on his brow. "I have since grown out of that horrid phase."

The king smiled. "You have come so far and done well for yourself."

"That is because *someone* gave that little boy a chance."

Bron waved his compliment away. "I gave you what I could. I wish I could have given you more."

Nathaniel paused. The king had never spoken of such things. "I do not know what you mean."

"All these years tradition has tied my hands. In the eyes of the law, you have no place in noble society. The queen and I have had to act accordingly to ensure the people have a clear heir, to ensure Brax's reign."

"I understand. You do not have to—"

The king raised his hand to interrupt. "Let me speak." He shifted his weight on the stone wall. The suit of armor must have been heavy for his damaged knee. Yet, a warrior would not yield to his own weakness.

"I cannot give you my inheritance, but you will always have my love."

Nathaniel's heart warmed. All of the times the king had favored Brax over him melted away. "Thank you, my king. That is all I ever wanted." A wave of melancholy hit him. Bronford Thoridian would never replace his real father, but they'd shared so many moments alike to that of a father and a son.

The king reached out and placed his hand on Nathaniel's shoulder. "I am proud of the man you've become. Brax may be more fit to lead a battle, but you have more wisdom to rule a kingdom."

"It is not my place to judge."

"Yes, but as a father to you both, *I* must judge if I am to ensure the kingdom survives."

Nathaniel froze, feeling as though he trespassed on sacred ground. What was the king leading to? He couldn't want Nathaniel to take Brax's place, could he? Nathaniel would never agree to such an upheaval. Even if he did, the people would never accept him as their king.

"Brax is hotheaded at times, but he has a noble heart, and I love him deeply—just as much as I love you. Promise me, when I am gone, you will look after him and steer him on the right course when he falters."

Nathaniel gave him a stern glance. "You are strong and healthy with many years—"

The king took his hand and squeezed. Desperation filled his eyes. "Just promise me."

"I promise." The words came out easy. He'd only ever intended for that himself.

"Good. Now I'll be able to sleep at night." The king winked. "Now leave and allow me to take your place, just this once."

Nathaniel nodded. As he moved past the king, a low moan chilled his bones to the core. He ran to the other side of the wall and glanced down into the moors. The torchlight flickered over brownish muck and oily black waters. A pale hand broke the surface, grasping blindly at the wall beside the ramp. Dirty fingers groped as another hand, then another broke free.

"Sound the alarm!" Nathaniel called to the watchmen on the other side of the wall. "The water has concealed their attack."

The sound of metal sliding rang behind him. Nathaniel turned to see the king unsheathing his sword. Hungry eagerness lit his eyes, and his face was rigid, and brave. "Then we will fight."

Nathaniel had never been a religious man, but he drew the sign of Helena's sword across his chest. "May the gods save us all."

* * * *

Valoria tossed in her bed. A simmering agitation filled the crisp night air, and every nerve in her body stood at attention. She kicked against the sheets until she lay on bare satin with goose bumps prickling her skin. A putrid stink wafted from outside, and she covered her mouth with her hand. Had the servants emptied all the chamber pots under her window?

A man shouted from the northern part of the city.

She bolted upright, gasping in air. "Cadence, did you hear that?"

The door to her handmaiden's room lay open by a crack, but no answer came.

"Cadence?" Valoria hissed as she jumped out of bed. She ran to the balcony, but could see nothing in the darkness.

"What is it, my lady?" Cadence stumbled in wrapped in her blanket like a caterpillar in a cocoon. Her braid had moved to the top right side of her head, reminding Valoria of a unicorn.

"I thought I heard something."

Cadence tugged her arm. "It must have been a nightmare. Let me get you back to bed. You need your rest."

"It couldn't have been a nightmare because I haven't slept a wink." Valoria's stomach churned. She hadn't lived in the castle for long, but she sensed something wasn't right. "Do you not smell that foul stench?"

Cadence rubbed her eyes, already bored. "My nose is stuffed. 'Tis all the old tapestries."

Clanging chimes made Valoria's body rigid. A church bell rang as if it were broad daylight.

Cadence's eyes widened. "Has the bell boy gone mad?"

"No, not mad." Panic bolted through Valoria's veins as she heard additional shouts, all coming from the wall. "That's an alarm." Valoria launched back into her room and dug out her riding suit.

Cadence followed her, then stood like a scarecrow and stared with her mouth wide open. "What are you doing? Are *you* mad?"

Valoria slipped on her underskirt and riding coat. "I'm lending my assistance."

"Oh no, you're not. Echo will have my head if I let you go out there." Cadence placed herself in front of the door.

Valoria strapped her harp to her back. "He'll have your head if you stand in my way. Echo was the one who told me I have to go."

"What?" Cadence didn't budge, but she'd lost some of her earlier resolve. "I cannot believe that nonsense."

"It's not nonsense." Valoria stared her down. "Echo believes I can help."

Cadence put a hand on her side. "Just you, all by yourself with your harp?"

Valoria nodded. "I know I can. Just this once, will you believe in me? Will you let me go?" If Cadence didn't, Valoria would have to knock her upside the head and leave her unconscious. Besides, if her own handmaiden couldn't believe in her, then maybe Echo *had* lost his mind in that apothecary shop.

Cadence nodded. "All right. But don't do anything foolish."

"I will stay safe." Valoria kissed her cheek. "Besides, you do not play a harp from the front line."

* * * *

Nathaniel hefted a bucket of hot oil over the wall. As it fell, archers raised their bows with flaming arrows. The oil splattered on the pale heads of the undead, then burst to flame.

The undead writhed, climbing upon each other blindly until the flames ate their skin away and nothing held their bones together. Nathaniel uttered a prayer as their bodies fell into the muck. Could the undead join Helena and Horred in their holy temple in the sky?

"Over here, sir! Look!"

His soldiers called from the battlements above the gate. Some of the undead had walked from the mud with flames engulfing their bodies. Instead of blindly throwing themselves against the stone walls, they fell at the thick oak of the gate.

"Water!" Nathaniel called from the wall. "Bring it to the back gate."

He glanced over his shoulder. The king stood with a battalion of soldiers behind the gate with their swords drawn. If the undead breached the wall, how many of those young men would lose their lives and join the ranks of the other side?

"Now!" Nathaniel threw himself down the steps and grabbed a bucket carried by a servant. He ran back up the stairs three at a time, reached the wall, and dumped it over. The small splash disappeared in the flaming ball that had become the back gate.

"We need more water!" He ran down with the empty bucket.

Beside him, the gate crumbled into ash. The first few undead stumbled through engulfed in flames. Behind them, a line of bodies hobbled forward like a force of nature beyond anyone's control.

Nathaniel stared in horror. Not since the time of Helena and Horred had undead crossed the border into Ebonvale. They were worse than the foulest tales he'd ever heard. No story could have prepared him for the unnatural jolting of their limbs, or the lolling of their white eyes. If they'd been people once before, they had no resemblance to them now.

He threw the bucket at the horde and unsheathed his sword. A crude trumpet call sounded behind him. The battalion shouted war cries as they ran forward.

A body who used to be a man lunged at him, teeth clacking. Nathaniel stabbed the man's chest with a sickly thump that would have felled anyone living. The body pushed himself into his sword, and the rotten smell almost knocked Nathaniel to the ground as the teeth came inches from his face.

"Chop off the heads!" King Thoridian shouted from beside him. "End the evil at its source."

Nathaniel kicked the corpse back and yanked out his sword. He whirled around and swung at the neck. The head and body fell in two pieces, and three more undead took his place.

A woman wearing a stained cooking apron stumbled forward along with two women wearing velvet dresses caked in mud. Nathaniel paused, peering underneath the oily strand of hair that covered their faces.

Nathaniel stepped back. It could not be. He would not strike a woman whether dead or alive. The undead woman raised a hammer. She stumbled one step forward, then blinked into black smoke.

Before he could make sense of it, the undead woman blinked back into existence inches from him. Her hammer hit his arm, and he stumbled back in pain. The two women in velvet blinked beside him. One of them lifted his arm and raised his wrist to her black teeth. She clamped down on the leather, and he felt pressure on his skin.

One heartbeat later, her head was gone. King Thoridian sliced into the undead with the apron and kicked the other velvet woman back. "Your wrist! Has the skin been broken?"

Nathaniel blinked in surprise. He pulled back the leather and ran his finger over his veins. "No."

"Thank Helena." The king swung his blade around them, staving off more undead as they crept in. "Whether 'tis woman, child, or man. You must fight."

Nathaniel shook his head to clear the haze of shock and raised his sword.

Chapter 11

Soul Song

Villagers ran south through the cobblestone streets, carrying infants, travel bags, small dogs, and valuables. Fear drew their faces long and pale. Some had tears running down their cheeks. Others openly sobbed, calling out to Helena and Horred to save them.

Valoria eddied around them in shock and denial. Had they already lost?

"Follow me up Chandler's Lane. We'll break through at Bluebird Square." Brax shouted to a brigade of soldiers.

Valoria ducked behind an old man with cages of birds heaped over his back and allowed the brigade to pass as they headed north. She fought her way through the chaos like a fish swimming upstream and followed the soldiers. Grunts and shouts echoed off the crumbling buildings as she drew closer. Below the clamor of swords was a chorus of long and low moans chilling the marrow of her bones.

The undead.

They were in the city.

A raging fire lit the streets up ahead. A line of soldiers kept the dead from pouring into the city, but the soldiers fell back with each step even as more joined them. They wouldn't last forever.

"You, over there! Get back to the city." One of the soldiers had stopped running and pointed to her.

Valoria ducked into an alley hoping the soldier had more pressing matters then chasing a runaway girl. A stairway led to the upper stories of an old tenement building. She climbed the steps, hoping to gain a view of the battle because she couldn't help anyone by charging in the front line with her harp. The minstrel's duty lay behind all the glory, which was why they were always overlooked when the battle was won. To this day, those narrow-minded warriors believed they'd defeated the wyverns by themselves.

She wasn't in it for glory or to prove a point. If the undead overtook Ebonvale, it wouldn't be too long before they spilled into the countryside, and then crawled through the bluewoods to the House of Song. No, Echo was right. She had to end the plague here before it spread.

Unfortunately, thick-headed Brax had sent most of the minstrels home. Valoria hardened her heart. She could do this alone. She had to.

Torn sheets fluttered in the wind, hanging on nails from the railings. In the darkness, the sheets looked like ghosts, but nothing was more frightful than the creatures below. Valoria tore the sheets over her head and ducked into a doorway.

Fresh apples lay in a basket on a table in the center. An overcoat hung on a chair by the door. Dirty teacups sat in a bucket.

Someone lived here in the ruins of the northern city. Valoria didn't have time to investigate. She barreled through the back room to a small balcony on the other side. The battle raged below her. Soldiers cut down the undead like farmers scything their crops. More and more came through the hole that had been the back gate. The mass pushed forward with sheer numbers of writhing limbs and scraggly haired heads. So many dead. So many more to come.

Valoria swung her harp in front of her. Her voice cracked as she began a song to ward off enemies. The first three verses had no effect. Her fingers shook as they plucked the strings, failing her. Below, the undead pushed in a relentless tide. The soldiers had retreated from two houses down to the one before hers. If she couldn't think of something, undead would climb that back stairway.

A group of soldiers had broken from the front line. Undead eddied around them, closing off their escape. One by one, the soldiers fell as the circle grew smaller and smaller. In the front stood a warrior with a slight body, a quick, sinewy strength and two breasts in her chest plate.

The queen.

Beside her, a broad shouldered man slashed over and over to keep the line.

No. Valoria ran to the edge of the balcony. Whether she wanted to marry him or not, Brax could not die. He was the sole heir to the throne.

A single soldier broke from the line and threw himself at the horde toward the ring of soldiers left behind. He moved slowly, whacking three undead with each stroke, but he favored one side, making each circle lopsided and opening himself to attack.

King Thoridian.

If she didn't act quickly, everyone that mattered in Ebonvale would be dead. Ebonvale would suffer the same fate as it had so many hundreds of years ago with Helena and Horred. Her world's very existence hung by threads.

She had to use everything in her power to save them, even if it meant taking the risks Echo had taught not to take. Valoria strummed a dissonant chord, breaking a fingernail. She closed her eyes and moaned, channeling the dark energy emanating from the horde.

Pain traveled from her limbs to her head. Overwhelming emptiness ached in her chest.

She pictured the time when mother had asked her to stay inside and work on their embroidery. The cottage had been dark and cold, and her mother had been sullen that morning. She'd run outside into the sunshine to play with father. The next day, mother had fallen ill, and after that, she'd never had another chance to choose her mother again.

Valoria remembered the day her father had asked her to travel to Ebonvale to marry Brax. She'd thrown her vase across the room—the one he'd given her on her twelfth birthday, the one her mother had painted before her death. It had shattered to pieces on the floor. Gone forever, like her mother's touch, her mother's voice.

Or the time when she'd found a baby deer injured by a hunter's trap in the forest. She'd sat with the animal's head in her lap and sung a healing chant. Its gaze turned from fearful to blank as the life leaked away. She couldn't save it.

Such vast emptiness surrounded her. She hung over a great abyss of darkness. It ate away at her soul, devouring any hope or life. But, she couldn't stay at the precipice forever. Her world needed her. She was not dead, only feeding off those who were. Valoria touched the surface of the void and came back with a dark power she could not control.

The sound that rose up from her throat was something she'd never heard before: sorrowful, painful, resigned, remote. It grew louder and resonated from within her, riding on currents of power as they wracked her body.

Through the darkness, a face emerged. Black, blotched skin stretched taut over edgy bones. Cheekbones too high to be human framed endless eyes of black.

The necromancer.

"Valoria." He beckoned with a lifeless voice. "You belong with me."

"No." Valoria opened her eyes. The dead had stopped their attack, moaning in unison the same chant she'd summoned from the dark depths of her soul. King Thoridian had made it to the ring of soldiers. He stumbled, falling on his knees as the queen and Brax took each arm.

The soldiers cut through the dead around them, and one by one they silenced their moans until the song of death lessened and ceased all together.

Valoria fell to her knees. Hot, sticky blood covered her fingers, and her harp strings dripped with red.

* * * *

Nathaniel climbed over the bodies of undead. Some of them were almost bare skeletons held together with threads of thin flesh, while others could have been normal men and women in slumber. Thank Helena and Horred. The gods had saved them. But, Nathaniel was too distracted to pay them much heed. King Thoridian had fallen to his knees just as the undead gave up and sang to the gods in the sky. The old man shouldn't have been on the front line, and if the king hadn't volunteered to stand watch, the queen could have held him back.

Nathaniel should have looked after him. He'd been distracted by preserving the gate. The last he'd seen of him, the king had saved his life.

He reached the circle where the queen and Brax stood. King Thoridian knelt on the ground, his head hanging low.

"Someone get a medic right away!" Nathaniel called around him. "That's an order!"

"It's too late." Brax spoke in a daze, his eyes bleary as he approached him. Black blood splattered his armor. "He's been bitten."

The queen collapsed in front of the king and held his head in both hands. "My dear, my one true love."

"No." Nathaniel couldn't believe it. He was the one who should have been bitten. The king had saved him. But he hadn't saved himself.

"It cannot be."

Brax clapped Nathaniel on the shoulder. "'Tis my fault. We'd broken apart from the group and the undead were overwhelming us. My father threw himself into the horde. He kept them at bay. He saved us."

Nathaniel moved to go to him, but Brax held him back. "Let them have their moment."

Brax was right. Nathaniel had had his time with the king on the battlements. At the time, he'd had no idea it would be his last conversation. At least it was a good one. "What about you?"

"I'll stay and make sure he journeys to the temple in the sky and not to the necromancer's horde." Although Brax's face was stiff, his eyes were red. Nathaniel was no stranger to loss. But, he hadn't been forced to deliver the fatal blow to any of his own family.

He squeezed Brax's shoulder and stood with him in silence as the king and queen said their piece.

"I cannot let them take you away." The queen's voice broke on her words.

Bronford Thoridian faced his end with no fear. "Fate has caught up with me, my dear. We both know this was my destiny."

The queen shook her head. "I shouldn't have let you out of my sight."

"You kept me safe for too many years." He drew the sign of the sword across his chest. "I look forward to sharing the sky with Helena and Horred."

She smoothed the hair on his head. "You saved us all, just like they did."

A small smile crept into his face. "'Tis the best way to leave."

"I do not regret one heartbeat of the time we shared."

"Nor do I."

Brax moved toward the queen and gently pulled her up.

She fought against him. "I will not leave him."

The king smiled. "Go, and remember me the way I am now. Allow me the same honor I paid to your father."

Nathaniel didn't know much about what had happened to King Artemus Rubystone at that fateful battle of Sill, but Bronford Thoridian's comment must have struck a noble chord in her heart. The queen kissed his forehead, then turned away.

Nathaniel took her arm and led her through the solders piling the undead in wagons, giving Brax his last moment with his father. The queen squeezed his arm. Tears ran down her cheeks and pain contorted her face. Every step seemed like it took all her courage. "I was with you when you lost your world, so it only seems fit you are with me when I lose mine."

"You haven't lost everything." Nathaniel placed his hand on hers. "You still have Brax and me."

"Aye." She nodded, biting her upper lip. Her entire body shook. Nathaniel had never seen her so close to falling apart.

The queen stumbled and fell forward onto her hands and knees. "I cannot go on."

He crouched beside her. "You must. This kingdom needs you just as much as I did when I was a little boy."

She glanced at him as if seeing him for the first time. "And such an adorable little boy you were. I remember wanting to take you home as my own the first time I saw you in the ash."

"And here I am, needing you still."

Around them, soldiers began to clap and shout. Nathaniel stood, scanning the area. At first, he thought they cheered their victory, but all heads glanced at a single balcony above them. Valoria stood on the railing with the wind in her long, auburn hair, holding her harp.

Shock and worry hit him hard in the gut. What if one of the undead had attacked her? He pulled on the nearest soldier's arm. "What is the princess doing here?"

"Saving us." The soldier raised his arm to her in salute.

Nathaniel had had an inkling of her power back on the battlefield, but he hadn't heard any kind of minstrel song. "What do you mean?"

"You saw the undead stop. You heard them moan."

It was as if someone had collected all of their puppet strings and hung them up. "They gave up, crying out to Helena and Horred in the sacred temple."

The soldier laughed, then grew solemn. "No, they did not sing to the gods. They sang to her."

Chapter 12

Bound

Valoria awoke to blindingly bright sunlight. Her entire body ached and her head felt like a bruised plum. She shielded her eyes. "Lyric's lyre. What's happened?"

"There you are." Cadence pressed a wet cloth to her forehead. "Just get some rest."

Images flooded her mind. Undead swarming, bloody fingers, and a black hole sucking her heart away. "Am I dead?"

"You most certainly are not." Cadence gave her a stern look. "Soldiers carried you in this morning. They said you passed out after you saved the entire kingdom from ruin at the hands of the undead."

"I did?"

Cadence pursed her lips. "I'd think you'd remember that."

"I remember more than I care to." The horrible, black-holed eyes of the necromancer stared back at her, and she gripped the sheets with the palms of her hands as her whole body turned icy cold and goose bumps pricked her skin. Sure, she'd saved the kingdom, but she'd also let him in.

"There, there. It's all over now." Cadence took her hand.

"'Tis not over." A part of her had been eaten away by that horrible thing that wasn't even a man. Even now, she felt him inside her mind, squirming like a black worm to find the center of who she was. She blocked the images and tried to focus on the bright sunlight pouring in. It felt a world away.

"How many dead?"

Cadence patted her hand. "You mustn't worry about that now, my lady."

Valoria batted Cadence's hand away. She bolted up into a sitting position. "How many?"

Cadence glanced down. "There are still many missing."

"Do not treat me like a child."

Cadence wiped at her eyes. "Maybe a hundred, mostly soldiers."

Valoria thought back to the battle before she'd tapped into the black energy. Soldiers had been stranded, and someone had gone to save them. "The king?"

Cadence shook her head. "Dead."

Sorrow took her breath away. She hadn't known the king well, but he'd only shown her kindness. The queen must have been reeling.

Valoria's chest tightened. "And Brax?"

Cadence smiled. "Very much still alive."

At least someone was still in place to run the kingdom. Valoria hadn't entirely failed.

"What about Lieutenant Blueborough?" She didn't care if Cadence chastised her. She had to know.

"I haven't heard about him. I'm sorry, my lady. I didn't think to ask." Cadence must have thought she'd had enough trauma without her handmaiden nagging her because she didn't press it any further.

A knock came from the door.

Cadence stood. "Perhaps that's Brax now, come to check on the woman who saved his kingdom."

Valoria settled back into bed. Was she ready to face him? Could she find the right words to acknowledge the grief he must feel? She'd have to try. They were to be married one of these days, and she couldn't hide from him forever. Since the battle, everything had changed, even if her feelings for him did not. The warriors and minstrels needed each other. There was no way either of them could fight such an evil force on their own. Her union with Brax was more important now than ever. She could not allow her personal feelings to bring down two kingdoms. She had to grow up and accept her responsibilities. "I'm ready."

Cadence patted her hand, then jogged across the room and opened the door. "Lieutenant? I didn't think to find you here."

Valoria perked up. It had to be Nathaniel.

"I'm sorry to intrude. Will Valoria see me?"

Relief filled her with joy at the sound of his voice. Nathaniel was alive.

Cadence paused. "She's still very weak."

"Allow him in." Valoria called in the most authoritative voice she could muster. "This instant."

"Very well." Cadence gave her a wary look, then opened the door further.

Nathaniel rushed in, his handsome face full of worry. He bowed his head. "My lady."

Valoria tapped the chair where Cadence had sat. "Please, sit down." She glanced at Cadence. "Leave us."

"My lady? Are you certain that's appropriate?"

"For Lyric's sake, he is checking on my health on behalf of his brother."

Cadence bowed her head. When she glanced up again, she gave Nathaniel a suspicious look. "I'll be a shout away."

After Cadence disappeared into her room, Nathaniel took the seat beside Valoria.

Valoria touched his hand. "I am most sorry to hear of the king."

Nathaniel blinked as if staunching tears. "He died in battle saving those he loved. For a warrior, there is no better way to go."

They sat in silence. Valoria could think of nothing appropriate to say after such loss. She realized she was still holding his hand but she didn't let go. "I'm sorry I couldn't save him."

Nathaniel turned to her with eagerness flashing in his face. "Did you really save the rest of us?"

Valoria held her breath. She'd said too much already. "I did what I had to."

Nathaniel wouldn't allow her to look away. He locked his gaze with hers. His tone was questioning. "I did not hear a minstrel's song."

"I did not sing one."

He shook his head. "I do not understand."

Valoria sighed. It was too late to hide the truth. Besides, he'd only ever been truthful with her, and she couldn't bring herself to speak a lie between them. "I tapped into the dark necromancer's magic, but in doing so I exposed myself."

Shock and horror passed his face. "Horred's grave. Are you all right?"

She shrugged. "Only time will tell. We're told not to expand our powers beyond simple songs. I've broken the minstrel's code of conduct." She squeezed his hand. The thought of him renouncing her made her sick. "You must know I had no other choice."

"I understand." A strange suspicion crossed his face. "Had you ever used this type of power before?"

Valoria's skin chilled. It was time she told someone, time she owned up to the consequences of her actions. "Only once in the battle where we met. I called down the mist from the hills to blind the raiders so the minstrels would have a fighting chance. It was then I sensed the evil in the mountains and asked it to do my bidding." She wiped her hand over her face. "In doing so, I woke Sill. I am to blame for the attack. All the dead are on my conscience." For that she would never forgive herself.

Nathaniel held her hand to his chest. "No. To believe that is folly. Sill has been festering for years. The swamp has slowly spread from the valley to the city walls. You did not awaken Sill, my dear. You saved us all from a fate in the making these many years."

Valoria gasped in relief as tears rolled down her cheeks. His words had lifted a burden from her shoulders. "You are certain?"

"I am. But..." He paused as if considering whether or not to speak of what was on his mind.

Valoria nodded eagerly. "Go on."

"Have you used this power on me?"

What a ridiculous thought. She laughed, relieved. "Not the evil power. Just a song to encourage you to lend aid to Echo, my music teacher. I hope you do not mind."

"No." He sighed. "Not at all. But, there is nothing else you've cast?"

Valoria crinkled her brow, thinking of every song she'd sung these past few days. "I've been singing to calm my nerves, to give the minstrels strength in their journey home, and for the people of Ebonvale to have open minds, but I cannot think of any such song directed at you. Why?"

"You would tell me, would you not?"

He was acting very strange. "Nathaniel, I just told you my darkest secret since arriving here at the castle. If there was anything else, you would know. I'm not sure why, but I trust you more than any other warrior here."

Nathaniel turned away, and Valoria wondered if she'd said too much. She hadn't mentioned Brax. But, she'd spoken the truth. She trusted Brax as much as she trusted a bull not to kick her.

"I must take my leave." Nathaniel stood, avoiding eye contact. He bowed. "I wish you well in your recovery."

A heartbeat later, he'd disappeared out the door. Valoria covered her chest with her hand as embarrassment set in. She was the biggest fool in all of Ebonvale. She'd practically told him she preferred him to Brax at a time when her union to Brax was the most crucial move she could make. For a noble man to hear of such betrayal must have been poison to his ears. She'd driven him away.

Would he report to Brax?

Valoria tried to calm herself. Surely not. It wasn't like she'd said anything too criminal, and Nathaniel was no gossip. But, she couldn't be seen with the lieutenant any longer. She'd gone too far, and she had to take a few steps back to remedy the situation. If only doing so didn't break her heart to pieces.

Cadence opened the door and peeked in. "Oh, I didn't know you were alone. Where'd he run off to so suddenly?"

Valoria wiped her eyes and stifled a sob. "I have no idea."

Cadence locked the door and shook her head. "Coming to visit you is most forward, indeed. Especially for a man who is *not* your intended."

Valoria swallowed a lump in her throat. "Do not worry. I do not think he'll be coming back."

Cadence admired her with wide eyes. "You sent him away? I am so proud of you. Braxten Thoridian should be the only man in this room. It's his grief keeping him away, my lady. I'm sure of it. Just you wait and see. When he's better, he'll come calling and you'll be glad the lieutenant is not in the way."

If only the world were as simple as Cadence saw it to be. Did her handmaiden feel the hatred against the minstrels? Did she not miss her home? "Have you had any trouble adjusting?"

"No, my lady. I like it here." Cadence folded a blanket and stashed it in the chest at the foot of the bed.

"Do you ever miss the House of Song?"

"I never fit in there." Cadence walked over to the windowsill and dusted it a little too immaculately. "I struggled with every instrument there was before I decided to be a handmaiden. To tell you the truth, I feel more at home with these warriors."

"Oh, I did not know." Valoria hadn't asked much about Cadence's past, and now she wished she had.

"Of course you didn't. My parents were not proud of my lack of talent, so they tried to hide it any way they could. I am certain they did not mention it for my appointment to be your handmaid." She squinted out the window. "Looks as though a storm is coming."

"From where?" Valoria stiffened. Energy charged the air. She rose from the bed and peered over Cadence's shoulder to the dark mountains of Sill. Gray clouds churned and lightning struck. Seconds later, a deep grumble rumbled in her stomach.

Valoria closed her eyes. She stood on a mountain ridge as rain pelted the air and lightning struck the ground below. In the muck of the valley below, bodies writhed. Men and women stood on the cliff's edge as undead pushed them into the dark waters. They screamed as they fell, and then disappeared into the mud. Seconds later, they emerged moving in jolts, their skin blotched purple and black as they were reborn.

Glass shattered and Valoria opened her eyes. The shards of a vase lay scattered on the floor as Cadence shouted her name.

"My lady, you disappeared. You blinked away, and then came back in a puff of black smoke."

Horror and disbelief rattled Valoria until her hands shook. "I saw through the necromancer's eyes."

"What did you see?"

"Get my evening dress. I must see Echo."

Cadence took her arm and pulled her back to the bed. "You must rest. You've been through a lot."

"There is no time for rest." Valoria snapped, and then she shook her head apologetically as she searched for a clean dress. "The necromancer is planning another attack."

* * * *

Nathaniel walked in the Wild Boar like a traveler after a long trip on an unforgiving road. The tavern was quiet this early in the day. A barmaid swept the floor in the back, while a young man tended to the fire. An older couple sipped stew by the fire, and an old man slept on the other side of the bar.

"Here to interrogate another of our barmaids?" The bartender gave him a defensive stare. He wore the same overcoat with the missing button, but today he had a clean black scarf around his neck.

"No, I'm here for a drink." Nathaniel took a seat. "That's if you'll serve me."

"We'll serve anyone with the gold to pay." The man came over and his face softened. "What'll it be?"

"Hot cider." Nathaniel took a seat. After his conversation with Valoria, he had to give himself some distance from the castle. She hadn't cast any spell on him. His irrational feelings for her were his own doing.

His last words to the king were a promise to take care of Brax and Ebonvale. Any further conversation with Valoria would only break his word.

If only it wasn't so hard to leave.

"Here you go." The bartender slid a mug of cider over. "Although it looks as though you could use something a little stronger."

"I do not drink on duty."

The man nodded as if he understood and touched the scarf. "We all mourn the loss of our king."

As if Nathaniel needed any reminder of that horrible night. "He fought bravely and will go down in history along King Artemis Rubystone, and Helena and Horred."

"Aye." The bartender filled his own mug and lifted it. "To Bronford Thoridian."

Nathaniel raised his mug.

The bartender added, "May Braxten Thoridian's rule be one of peace."

He drank to that, even though he didn't think they'd seen the last of the undead.

The bartender wiped his chin. "Ever catch that lad who ran away the other night?"

"No." Although Nathaniel wondered if the young man's corpse was among those undead piled up by what remained of the back gate. He'd looked for him that morning, but could not find one familiar face in the horde.

Thank the gods for that.

The bartender wiped a rag over the countertop. "What will they do about the gate?"

"A mason is already at work closing the hole with giant stones."

"Stones, eh?" He knocked his fist on the counter. "Much better than wood."

"We hope. I cannot help but feel we are ignoring the real problem. How does one rid himself of an ever-spreading swamp?"

"You pack up and find another place to live, in my opinion."

"Move the castle? Abandon the steps of the holy temple?" Nathaniel shook his head. "Somehow I think if we do move, the swamp will continue to spread. It will catch up to us one way or another."

The bartender pursed his lips. "As does all evil."

"Only if you let it." Nathaniel placed a gold coin on the counter and stood.

But, the bartender wasn't finished with his commentary. He threw his rag into a bucket on the floor. "Heard the minstrel princess turned the tide of battle last night."

"'Tis true." Nathaniel glanced away, fearing his fondness for her played clear on his face. "Thank you for the cider."

The bartender nodded, pocketing the gold. "Maybe we misjudged them after all."

"I'm as guilty of that as the rest of us." Without looking back, Nathaniel pushed open the oak door.

Chapter 13

Blue Fire

Valoria counted the doors past the fourteenth painting of Braxten Thoridian wielding his mighty sword. She'd followed the servant's directions, yet it seemed as though they'd put her old music teacher in the darkest, narrowest corridor of the entire castle.

Might as well put him with the horses in the stalls.

She knocked on the door and waited, trying not to gawk at Braxten Thoridian's muscly arms. You'd think he would have smiled for at least one of the fourteen paintings, but every face he made was arduous, as if he looked upon the world and found it lacking.

Echo called from inside in his lyrical voice. "Come in, come in."

Valoria opened the door. The room was small but cozy with a single window looking out over the chicken coops, a small cot, washbasin, and dresser.

"Valoria, I thought you were another medic. They've been coming every hour with more potions and herbal tinctures. I told them I was healing well, but I think my songs had a little too much effect. Have a seat." He gestured to a stool in the corner. "'Tis the best I can do considering."

"You'd think in this entire castle they could find a bigger room."

Echo waved her concern away. "They weren't expecting me to stay. Now what's this I hear of you commanding the army of the undead?"

Valoria choked. Echo was never one to follow the chicken around the hen coop. "You told me I had to do everything I could. I had no other choice."

Echo's face slackened. "Then, the rumors are true? You used dark magic to beat the necromancer at his own game?"

"I did. And it's not the first time, either. Back in the meadow, when the raiders attacked, I drew the mist from the mountains of Sill."

"I thought you might have." Echo ran his hand through his graying hair. "Oh, Valoria, my dear. I did not want this for you."

"I had to. Soldiers were dying. Braxten and the queen were in trouble. There was no other way."

"I see." Echo collapsed onto his cot and rubbed his head.

Valoria felt like she'd stolen biscuits from the baker. Shame weighed heavily on her chest. She could not bear Echo's disappointment in her. "I'm sorry. I thought it was the only way."

"It may have been." Echo wiped his face. "'Tis my fault. I knew you were powerful, that you'd surpassed my teachings, but I did not know how strong you'd grown, that you were capable of controlling nature, of tapping into evil." Echo glanced down at his hands as if he were the one who'd called upon the dark forces.

"Why is it so bad to use dark power if it is for good?"

"'Tis a slippery slope." Echo reached out and took her hand. "Many minstrels have tried. The few who were successful were consumed by it in the end."

The black eye sockets of the necromancer flashed through her mind. If she'd forced herself to look closer, she would have noticed the shape of his robes. "You mean the necromancers were once minstrels?"

Echo nodded sadly. "Aye."

"Why does no one speak of this?"

Echo raised his eyebrows, and the wrinkles in his forehead made him look so much older and more helpless than ever before. "The people of Ebonvale already despise us. What would they think if they knew the truth?"

Valoria sat in stunned silence. He was right.

Panic slowly edged its way in. "What am I supposed to do? The undead will attack again. I've seen it through the necromancer's eyes. But, I cannot keep fighting him with his own magic. Every time I do, I lose a little of myself."

"Calm down." Echo reached out and took her hand. "We will think of something. How much time do you think we have?"

Even though Valoria shuddered to revisit her memories, she thought back to that horrible moment when she lived in the necromancer's head. His thoughts had been so clear. He needed time to rebuild the army, along with the strength of the next full moon. "A fortnight, maybe more."

Echo nodded and pursed his lips. "We'll need to gather an army unlike any other. Minstrels, warriors, and maybe even raiders if we can get them to join our cause."

"But, we cannot see the undead coming in the swamp. We have to take the battle away from Ebonvale's walls."

"The swamp." Echo drummed his fingertips over his knees. "I've heard it's been spreading for as long as people can remember."

"Lieutenant—someone mentioned that to me, yes." Valoria glanced away.

"There is an old song I learned as a boy…something about fighting fire with fire…"

"But there is no fire in a swamp." Valoria frowned. Had Echo finally lost his mind?

Echo ignored her, still singing the song to himself. "And water with the mermaids' breath. That's it!" He slapped his knee. "Blue fire."

Valoria studied him with concern. All this talk of her using dark magic had overtaxed his senses. "Maybe you need to rest."

Echo batted her away. "I'm fine, as I've already stated to the medics. But you, my girl, are to pack your things."

"Whatever for?" Were they going back to the House of Song? As much as it would fill her heart with joy, Valoria knew that wasn't the right path. Retreating home would solve nothing.

Echo looked her up and down as if she'd just won her first music competition. "You're journeying on a quest."

* * * *

"I advise you not to bother him. He's been stabbing that scarecrow all morning." A young soldier approached Valoria as she walked across the muddied training field behind the weapons hall.

"He will have to listen to me." Valoria pushed by him, walking in her traveling boots hidden underneath her black, mourning gown. "He owes me a favor."

Brax shouted as he whirled around and sliced the arm off a man made from hay hanging from a training pole. The arm flew through the air and landed by Valoria's feet. Hay spilled around her boots. She had to re-convince herself she was making the right decision to ask for his aid.

Today, Brax wore a simple leather tunic stretched across his broad chest. Sweat slickened his tan face and arms. A flash of surprise, and then a hint of annoyance crossed his blunt features as he recognized her. "Women are not allowed on the training grounds."

"Tell that to the queen." Valoria stepped toward him.

He still held his sword in the air as if he'd slash her down. "Women warriors are the only exception."

"I must speak with you." Valoria held his gaze with the fiercest expression she could muster. "About the secret to saving your kingdom."

He lowered his sword. For the first time, she saw the hurt in his eyes. He grieved for his father the only way he knew how, by training with his sword. "Is it true your song stilled the undead?"

She nodded. "But, I fear it will not work next time. We need a means to end the spread of swamp, to burn the dead waters away and unite the people of this land to fight together."

He looked her up and down as if he'd appraised her unjustly before. Did admiration spark in his eyes or had she imagined it? "And you have this answer."

Valoria used the most commanding voice she had. "I do. But, I will need a warrior's help and you owe me a favor."

Brax wiped his brow as he considered it. It was a far cry from dismissing her at the dinner.

"I see. And what does this favor entail?"

"A journey to an island off the eastern coast, and something valuable enough to trade."

He shook his head. "I cannot leave my duties here. Not at a time like this."

"The next attack will come in a fortnight. I know this because I saw through the eyes of the necromancer when I stole his song. Their army will be vaster, and they will not stop until we are all dead. We must regain the ground between the walls of Ebonvale and the valley of Sill. We must burn away the swamps."

Winning the battle had done more than save Ebonvale, it had given her credence in his eyes. At least enough for him to consider her thoughts. "And you know how?"

Valoria nodded. "Blue fire."

Brax narrowed his dark, beady eyes. "I have not heard of such a thing."

Valoria wanted to tell him there were a lot of things he probably hadn't heard of, but she needed his help, and she wouldn't win him over with snide remarks. "It is made by the mermaids of the Sapphire Isles."

He snorted. "'Tis a myth."

Valoria stepped so close, she could have touched his chest with her finger if she'd cared to poke him. "'Tis the truth. Only the eldest minstrels know of it. The mermaid's potion is strong enough to burn away the swamp and give you the battleground you need."

He studied her as if seeing her for the first time. This close to him, she noticed green flecks in his dark eyes, a trait of his mother's. Not all of him came from the stout-hearted late king.

"I will go whether you come with me or not. But the question is, do you wish to place the quest for the one thing that will win this battle in the hands of another?"

Brax crossed his arms over his chest. A small smile curled the corners of his mouth. "You are cleverer than I thought."

Valoria narrowed her eyes. She'd see if he was cleverer than she thought as well. "So you will come with me?"

"On one condition. We must take the one person I know who can negotiate an honest trade, someone who has history with the fishermen who navigate those waters. Someone I trust with my life."

Did such a man exist? He sounded like Horred himself. "Who is this man of whom you speak?"

Brax's face softened, and for the first time, he looked noble and kind, almost handsome. "My brother."

Chapter 14

Brothers in Arms

Nathaniel pressed his palm against the solid granite chunk as three mules heaved it into place underneath the arch where the gate had once stood. Would it be enough to hold the undead back?

Flames licked the sky behind him, warming his back as soldiers seared the corpses. The air stunk of rot and burnt flesh. As a boy, he'd never thought anything would smell worse than a dead wyvern, but he'd been wrong.

As dangerous as the wyverns were, they never pierced your soul the way seeing an undead woman or man did. The wyverns fought for their right to survive, whereas the undead took all life away. If Nathaniel had to choose a greater foe, he would have chosen the one he faced now.

Better now as an adult when he could do something about it.

"Nothing will move that stone. Not even I." Brax surprised him from behind as he came up to tap his sword on the chunk of granite.

"I thought you were training." Nathaniel clapped him on the shoulder. Losing the king last night had only strengthened the bond between them. Nathaniel knew what it was like to lose a father. Now he'd lost one twice. But, this time his adopted brother lived to share the burden.

"I was, but a princess convinced me otherwise." Brax lifted his eyebrows as if a pig had taken off in flight.

"You mean Valo—I mean Princess Valoria?" Only hours ago, she'd seemed more inclined to go to him than Brax. What had changed?

Brax gestured toward an area where the workers wouldn't overhear their conversation. "She has come to me with a way to win the next battle with the undead."

Nathaniel followed him. "The next battle?"

"Did you not suspect they'd return?"

He sighed. "I did. I only hoped they wouldn't."

Brax nodded. "So did we all. But the princess claims she has seen through the enemy's eyes. She knows what he is planning."

A current of jealousy spiraled through Nathaniel, and he stifled it. Why hadn't she mentioned this to him? Because he'd left in a hurry? Had he not given her a chance?

"And what is her plan?"

"She knows of a potion which will burn the swamp away. It would give us a level playing field and bring the battle away from Ebonvale's walls."

"What is this potion?"

"Blue fire. She says it comes from the mermaids in the Sapphire Isles."

As ridiculous as it sounded, the idea held a kernel of truth. "Ah yes, as a kid I heard of such a tale. But, I thought it was only a story told by imaginative sailors and fisherman to while away the hours on their boats."

"So did I." Brax shook his head as if the world were stooping to foolishness.

"You trust her enough to leave our kingdom and search for this blue fire?" Didn't the princess and Brax have trouble getting along?

"To tell you the truth, I wouldn't have when I first met her. I thought her a spoiled, naïve princess who embroidered pillows and plucked trivial melodies on her harp. But after seeing what happened last night, I realize I've underestimated her. She controlled the undead as if they were her own. If she says she knows what the necromancer has planned, I believe her. If her idea to burn the swamp has any credence, than I would be a fool not to follow it. What I want to know is will you travel with us?"

Shock took his breath away. To accompany Brax would place himself in front of the one person he wished to avoid. "Go with you and the princess? To the Sapphire Isles?"

Brax put a hand on his shoulder. "I need someone with knowledge of the fishermen's ways and experience in trading. You grew up in Shaletown, did you not?"

"Aye."

"And you negotiated the metal trade with the albinos as a young boy?"

"I did." Nathaniel had trading in his blood. His father had made deals as far as the continent stretched to get the precious metals he needed for his blacksmith work.

"Then, why do you hesitate?"

How could he speak the truth? He chose his words carefully. "This journey is the perfect chance for you to acquaint yourself with the princess. I would stand in the way."

"Nonsense. I cannot put my personal concerns in front of the kingdom's." Brax did not look concerned in the least. In fact, was he avoiding a lone journey with her? Would Nathaniel have to mediate between the two of them the entire way?

Brax smiled. "We both know you are the best man for the task."

The best man for the task, maybe. The most appropriate travel companion? No. "Who will stay to make sure the queen recovers from her grief?"

"My mother is a strong woman. Give her some time and she'll have this kingdom back on its feet. She needs the distraction."

"I do not think she will ever completely recover." She'd lost the love of her life, the man she'd bent the law to marry.

Sorrow tinged Brax's face. "Perhaps not. But, you forget, she led Ebonvale for years by herself after her father died. She can handle it now."

"Even if she could, she won't ever agree to both of us going."

Brax polished the hilt of his sword with a handkerchief as a self-satisfied grin stretched across his face. "She already has."

* * * *

"I cannot believe you are leaving." Cadence watched helplessly as Valoria stuffed her traveling bag. "And not taking a single dinner dress, no less."

"This isn't a quest for looking pretty." Valoria wished she had more practical clothes. How was she ever supposed to pass for a farmer's daughter in her silk evening gowns? She glanced at Cadence's simple skirt and apron.

"My lady, you look as though you would swallow me whole."

Valoria smiled. "Fancy doing a trade?"

"A trade?"

"My clothes for yours. You can have whatever suits your fancy."

A spark of excitement flashed in the handmaiden's features before her good sense won her over. "I cannot possibly walk around the kingdom wearing your gowns."

"It will be a necessity, if you are to impersonate me." Valoria found a small travel knife and tossed it in her bag.

Cadence scoffed. "Impersonate you? Why?"

"I do not want to spread panic, or have raiders looking for me to hold me for ransom. Never mind what they'd do if they thought the castle was vulnerable."

"But, that would be treason."

"Not if the queen is aware."

"Is she, my lady?"

Valoria nodded. "Hand me your plainest working clothes."

Cadence scrunched up her nose as if Valoria had told her to drink from the chamber pot. "If that's what you wish." She rummaged in her room and returned with a simple, brown tunic, dark brown leggings, and knee high boots.

Cadence held the garments up as if they were made of poison. "These are for scrubbing the floor."

"Wonderful." Valoria unzipped her dress and pulled the tunic over her head. "Do you have a few extra ones?"

"Of course." While Valoria dressed, Cadence brought three more from her room and placed them in the top of Valoria's bag. "You'll be able to scrub the floor for days on end."

"Or at least look like I have." Valoria smoothed the front of the work clothes and studied herself in the mirror. The tunic brought out her arms in an athletic way, while the leggings gave her the freedom to run and spar with a sword. Dressed as a servant, she'd never felt more invigorated and free in her life.

"You can hide your figure, but you cannot hide your porcelain skin and silver eyes." Cadence smiled. "You still look like a princess to me, my lady."

"Farmers can have pretty daughters." Valoria handed her a burgundy evening dress with black, velvet trim—a hideous concoction she'd had to wear at the last concert at the House of Song. "Your turn."

She helped Cadence slip into the evening gown and zipped up the back.

"My, this is heavy and hot." Cadence teetered over.

Valoria picked her up and positioned her in the front of the mirror. "Walking in twenty pounds of finery is an art. You'll learn."

"I'll have to if I do not want to fall on my face." Cadence ran her hands over the smooth fabric and smiled. The velvet trim gave her a regal look, commanding authority. The red brought out the highlights in Cadence's brown hair and the dark chestnut of her round eyes. She could have passed for a princess any day. "I'm beginning to enjoy this."

"Good. Have fun. You look marvelous."

"I do not, however, look like you."

Valoria waved her concern away. "All you have to do is stand on balconies and wave. From there, the people will see you as the princess." She held up a finger. "No one must know the prince and I are gone if Ebonvale is to remain safe from raider attack. When I'm traveling, I'm to be known as Val, daughter to a local farmer."

A laugh escaped Cadence's mouth. "And who will Brax be, your fool?"

Valoria gave her a look of warning. "No, he will be my brother."

Cadence stifled a smile. "And the lieutenant?"

"My brother as well."

"My, you have a lot of brothers."

Valoria strapped her bag to her back. "In Ebonvale, the farmers have a lot of children to run the farm."

"And who will see to it they do not compromise your honor?"

"I will." Valoria gave her a stern look. "Not that Brax is interested." She thought she'd leave Mr. Blueborough out of the picture.

"He is, you'll see." Cadence fluffed the fabric around her ankles. "Are you sure you do not want me to come with you?"

"You must be my eyes and ears here. Besides, a large party is more likely to draw attention and I do not want the raiders knowing they have nobles roaming through their lands."

"So leave the lieutenant here and take me instead." Cadence grabbed her arm and pleaded with her. "I like pretty dresses, but my duty lies with you."

"I wish I could." Valoria squeezed Cadence's shoulder. She was so loyal and brave. So what if she couldn't play an instrument or sing a tune. Valoria would have chosen her over a talented minstrel any day.

"But Lieutenant Blueborough knows how to trade with these people, and neither I nor Brax have much knowledge of any place south of Ebonvale's borders." Having Nathaniel come along only complicated the journey, no matter how much her heart wanted him to.

"I understand." Cadence released her grip and narrowed her eyes. "Watch your back. Do not trust him. I fear he's out to steal your heart."

He might already have a piece of it. Valoria pushed the worry away. "My heart does not matter in this situation."

The velvet rustled as Cadence walked her to the door. In the gown, she looked wiser and mightier than her years. "It matters if you cannot silence it."

Chapter 15

Country Girl

Fireflies sparked in the training field as the covered wagon pulled up to the back door of the servants' quarters. Brax pulled on the reins, halting the horses as Nathaniel pulled a hood over his head and jumped off.

He knocked three times in rhythm.

An answering knock came from the other side.

He knocked again, this time with four knocks, and the door opened. Valoria peered from a hooded, dark cloak, as one lock of her auburn hair slipped free. She wore a simple servants' tunic, leggings, and slender boots that brought out her shapely legs. Dressed as an equal, she looked even more elegant and lovely.

He bowed. "Princess—"

"Call me Val. And do not bow." She touched his chin, bringing his head up. A mischievous smile flashed in her face before she wiped it away. "Not if I'm your *sister*."

"You are right…sister." The word fell off his tongue awkwardly. Sister was not how he thought of her. Even though he should. She would be his sister one day. That harsh reality twisted his stomach.

"Did you acquire the necessary items of trade?"

Nathaniel nodded. "The queen was more than willing to part with them."

Surprise lit her features. "Truly?"

This was not the time to speak of the queen's loyalties. Nathaniel only nodded. "Come with me."

He offered his hand and Valoria slipped her hand over his. He felt her cool, soft skin as he lifted her into the back of the wagon. All too soon, she released her grasp and disappeared inside.

If only he could go with her. Nathaniel shook his head to rid his mind of his wild thoughts and joined Brax in the front.

Brax turned to him. "Cargo acquired?"

Nathaniel nodded, still trying to rein in the force pulling him toward her.

"How did she appear? Fearful?"

He shook his head and smiled. "Fearless."

Brax whipped the horses and they set off at a canter. "If this was not her idea, I would not allow a woman, a minstrel no less, to come."

Was he having second thoughts? Anger hardened like a fist inside him. Brax's doubt in Valoria was grossly misplaced. "That minstrel saved our kingdom singlehandedly with her harp."

Brax glanced over with a tired, defeated look. "I need no reminder."

Was she that difficult for him to grow fond of? Helena's sword, it wasn't like she looked like a toad. Nathaniel shifted in his seat. Without giving away his immense admiration, he thought another vote of confidence was needed. "She will prove herself a useful ally, you will see."

Brax sighed as if resigned. "She already has."

They rode through the sleeping city with soft hoof clomps and rickety creaks. Tavern signs blew in the midnight breeze. A black cat scurried across the cobblestone, disappearing into an alley. Black smoke from chimneys wafted through the moon's light.

So many people with enough faith to stay. Nathaniel hoped their loyalty would be rewarded. Ebonvale had been lost once before. He vowed to Helena and Horred to keep it safe.

They reached the main gate, and Brax needed only a single nod for the gatekeeper to raise the chains. The gate opened and closed behind them, and Nathaniel bid farewell to the city he'd grown to call home. They headed south, to the home he'd lost.

Melancholy tainted his thoughts. He wasn't eager to return.

Light harp strings plucked from the back of the wagon as they took the main road through Ebonvale's orchards and farmlands. Now and then Valoria's sweet voice would rise and a phrase would waft to their ears: *veil of shadow*, *silent footsteps*, and *we are but trivial travelers*.

"You'd think she'd sleep with such a journey ahead." Brax glanced over his shoulder.

"She protects us with her enchantments." Amusement curled Nathaniel's lips.

Brax gave him a doubtful look. "Two warriors in their prime, protected by a minstrel girl and her harp?"

Nathaniel smiled in a self-deprecating way. Taking the minstrels in meant accepting their ways. "Stranger situations abound."

* * * *

Morning broke in a blush of red and orange light. A dove began its song with a three melancholy notes. As the mist cleared, the last few farms of Oakendell rose up on either side.

"There." Brax pointed to an old barn with three cows grazing around it. A small cottage stood on a hillside of white flowers. "That was my father's farm."

"Are you certain?" It looked more like a house for an old woman.

Brax nodded. "He took me for a ride one day when I was a boy. I met his brother, Hule, who'd inherited the farm. There'd been some tension between the two of them for years, because my father had made it to the Royal Guard and Hule had been forced to return to the farm. But, he welcomed us without any ill feelings and invited us in for a piece of apple pie. My father wanted me to meet my cousins, but he also wanted me to see that every man is important. Every man, no matter his station in life, has the potential to be great."

Sorrow stung Nathaniel's gut, knocking the air out of him. "The king told me that as well." He smiled sadly, remembering the day Bronford Thoridian promised him a spot in the army. "He was teaching me how to fight with a sword. I was only a boy with a piece of wood shaped like a claymore. I tried to attack him, and he defeated me in one stroke. I was so angry at the world back then. I told him I'd never avenge my family, that they all died and I couldn't save them."

Compassion softened Brax's face. "You were a boy. There was nothing you could do."

"That did not stop me from feeling guilty." Nathaniel touched the wood of the seat, bluewood, just like his wooden sword. Where had it gone? He would have loved to hold it one more time. Or place it on the king's grave when he returned. "He said I could become a warrior and 'save lots of people.'"

"Lots of people, eh?" Brax smiled.

Nathaniel thought back, remembering the smell of the orchard and the way the sun hit Bron's face. "He said, 'All you need is courage and someone to believe in you.' 'Who would believe in me?' I asked. You have to understand that everyone I ever mattered to was dead. The king said he would believe in me, and then he promised me the spot in the Royal Guard." Tears stung Nathaniel's eyes. He missed the king as much as he missed his own family.

Brax patted his arm. "He was a good man and he loved you like his own son."

Immense grief passed through him like a tidal wave. Nathaniel turned to Brax. "You remind me of him so much that I feel as though he sits beside me."

"It is an honor too vast for me." Brax shook his head. "He was a greater king than I'll ever strive to be."

Helena's sword, Nathaniel had never seen Brax with that much self-reflection and vulnerability. Even though he understood Brax's struggle, he could not argue with his faults. Brax didn't have the late king's kindness, or his sense of self-sacrifice. But, Brax had the capacity to learn, especially if he accepted his flaws. "The future is not set in stone."

They sat in silence until they reached the edge of the meadows. Up ahead, dust clouds shifted over the barren earth where the wyverns had burned every living plant and seed. Raiders didn't chance crossing into Ebonvale's guarded lands, but this vast southern wasteland was ripe with corruption.

"Better rest now." Brax pulled to the side of the road and directed the horses behind a copse of white birch. "We'll need our strength for what's ahead."

Nathaniel nodded. "I'll get some food from our supplies."

He rounded the wagon and lifted the leather to peer inside.

Valoria sat against the bench on the floor with her legs stretched out in front of her and her harp on her stomach. She plucked a note while her eyes fluttered, close to sleep.

"You're still awake?" Nathaniel climbed in.

She perked up immediately. "Why do you think we've traveled without any delay?" Her fingers were red. She must have played all night.

Nathaniel knew better than to argue. "Must have been your excellent playing."

"I'd like to think it had a part to play and my voice isn't hoarse for nothing." Valoria stood and brushed hay off her tunic. "Thank you for standing up for me." She had a few strands in her hair, and he resisted the urge to pull them out.

Nathaniel picked up a bag of supplies to keep his hands busy. "I do not know what you are referring to."

"You spoke up when Brax doubted taking me with you."

How could she have heard in the back? He studied her with suspicion. How much of their conversation had she picked up? "Minstrels have excellent ears."

She placed her harp on the bench. "You would do well not to forget it."

"I'll keep that in mind." He hefted the bag over his shoulder and lifted the leather covering. Valoria slipped underneath his arm, her hair brushing his chest as she jumped down.

They joined Brax on a rock outcropping beside the wagon. Nathaniel handed him a heel of bread and a wedge of cheese with an apologetic smile. "It's not what you're used to." He'd been on the road a lot as a boy, but the prince had never traveled far from the castle.

"I'll manage." Brax bit a chunk off the cheese and swallowed it down with a draft from his sheepskin. He nodded to Valoria but said nothing.

Valoria sat three rocks apart from him. She took her own bread and cheese from the bag. "Such a lovely night." She broke off a piece of cheese. "Sometimes I'd go out with my father and we'd watch for falling stars."

Nathaniel waited for Brax to respond, but he shoved bread in his mouth as if he were a starved beggar in the streets. Would he leave Valoria's comment unanswered? Nathaniel took up the thread of conversation. "My father took me stargazing as well—my real father, I mean." He gave Brax a meaningful glance, not wanting to speak of the king in such a familiar manner with a guest, even if she would be in their family soon.

"How about you, my prince? Ever gaze at the stars?" Valoria leaned over. She'd stopped eating, studying Brax as if he were a riddle she could not solve.

Brax took a swig from his sheepskin. "I do not have time for such frivolities."

She glanced down as if he'd slapped her. "I see."

Brax's slight to Valoria made Nathaniel's chest pang. He squeezed his hand into a fist, then released his fingers. "What were you singing of?"

"Songs to protect us, ward off danger, and make us seem uninteresting to passersby." Valoria ripped off a piece of bread and tasted it with a sullen face.

Was she sullen because of Brax's disinterest in conversation, or because she didn't like the bread? Nathaniel felt compelled to cheer her spirits. "Powerful songs, indeed."

Brax stood. "I must see to the horses."

"You do not want dessert?" Valoria stood as well, offering a small parcel. "I brought fig cakes from the best baker in the House of Song."

Nathaniel gave Brax an emphatic look. He never turned down food.

"I have no taste for figs." Without looking back, the prince disappeared on the other side of the carriage where he'd tied the horses.

Valoria stuffed the parcel in her backpack. Her shoulders sagged as if she were defeated.

Nathaniel didn't know which move was worse: to console her by trying a fig and strengthen the already compelling bond between them, or to leave her be. With all of his comments so far, it was better not to tempt fate.

"For your benefit, I've never seen him eat a fig."

She smiled and then covered her mouth as if she shouldn't make fun. "I had hoped it would be easier to speak to one another without the formality of the castle."

'Twas always easy for Nathaniel to speak with her. He longed to put his arm around her and comfort her. The fault was not hers. Brax did not share a love of the stars, or desserts. Or beautiful princesses, from the looks of it.

The late king's face flashed in his memory. *Promise me, when I am gone, you will look after him and steer him on the right course when he falters.*

Nathaniel clenched his hands into fists, breathing hard as he reined in his feelings. If he wasn't careful, someday they'd grow too large to control, and he could never let that happen. Not if he wanted to keep his promise. "Brax is a man of few words. Give him time."

Chapter 16

Barren Ground

"Hey, there! Help an old man on the side of the road?"

"We cannot leave him."

"What if he recognizes one of us? What if it's a trap?"

"There's no chance a farmer's ever been to the castle, never mind seen me up close."

Valoria awoke to voices. She jerked upright as panic strangled her throat. How long had she been asleep? She reached for her harp and grasped thin air. Lyric's broken string! Staying up all night to ensure their safety must have caught up with her. And now they'd paid the price.

Someone on the road had noticed them.

Relief coursed through her as she found her harp in the hay by her feet. Clutching the instrument to her stomach, she waited, listening.

The wagon slowed and stopped. Had both men lost their minds? What if they were recognized this close to the castle?

"Can we be of aid, sir?" That was Nathaniel's voice.

Valoria peeked out the leather in the back. The sun was on the verge of setting across a land of bare, blackened trees. She must have slept all day. At least they weren't near Ebonvale's borders any longer. The risk of being recognized wasn't as great as she thought.

"Raiders stole my bags and my horse. I need transportation to the nearest village." The voice had the grittiness of an old man's.

"Where are you from, sir?" Nathaniel's voice grew softer as if he'd jumped from the wagon to approach the old man.

"New Shaletown. I was on my way to help my son. He's moved up north to work on a farm. Doesn't like the barren ground." The old man sounded sincere, however far-fetched the story was. Yet, Valoria picked up a slight rise in his voice at odd intervals. Anxiety crept up her spine. Knowing Nathaniel, he wouldn't deny someone in need.

"We're traveling south." Brax barked.

For once, Valoria appreciated his shortness.

"I'll go anywhere. Just don't leave me here." The man pleaded. "I have a bad leg, and I won't be able to walk far."

"Come with us." Nathaniel's voice softened. "Either we'll pass another party going north, or we can take you back to Shaletown. I mean, New Shaletown, and you can find another horse."

"Mar's the name. Old man Mar."

A grunt followed, like someone hefting another person into the front of the wagon.

"I'm Blue. This here's my brother, Axel. Our sister, Val, is in the back."

Valoria bit her lip to keep from smiling. Nathaniel had chosen Blue like his last name, Blueborough. Axel had some of the letters of Brax, and Val was what her mother had called her. Very fitting, but an odd bunch of names put together. Hopefully, Mar had an odd enough name not to question theirs.

Brax shouted to the horses with his rumbling bass voice, and the wagon began to move.

"You moving down south?" Old man Mar picked up his voice to speak over the din of the horses' hooves and creaking wheels.

"We are." Nathaniel sounded young and hopeful, just like someone trying to make a new life. "Work on the farm has dried up."

"Ain't that the truth." The old man coughed. "'Tis a hard world we live in now, nothing like the peacefulness of my youth, back when wyverns were just a fireside tale." Fabric rustled and the bench creaked as if he shifted in his seat, maybe glancing backward at the wagon. "Brought everything down with you?"

The question was odd in an abrupt sort of way. Why did he need to know what they carried in the back? Valoria pursed her lips. Perhaps she was being overly cautious. He was an old man, not a warrior with a sword.

"Everything we own, which isn't much." Nathaniel's answer was clever. Valoria's mother had told her never to admit having anything of value to a stranger, even if he was an old man.

"Some provisions for the road?" For an old man, Mar was inquisitive.

"If you're hungry, I have a heel of bread in my pocket." Nathaniel answered.

"Thank you much, Blue. Your brother doesn't talk much, does he? Look at those arms—thick as tree trunks. Has he had warrior training?"

Valoria tilted her head. An underlying anxiousness and eagerness had crept into Mar's tone, and it wasn't from being robbed. This man was hungry, but not for a heel of bread.

She picked up her harp, took a deep breath, and strummed a unique chord.

"Honesty is key
In a world where truth is veiled.
Loosen your tongue
So I can see
The fact from the tale."

"Val loves her music." Nathaniel laughed nervously. He may have thought Valoria would give them away, but they'd done enough of that themselves. She continued stroking the chords, building the dissonance until it could not be ignored.

"I am tired of this ceaseless banter." Brax growled. "Small talk makes my feet itch in my boots."

"Must you always be so impertinent?" Nathaniel chastised. "Sometimes I think you have no polite words in your thick head."

Valoria smiled and kept strumming. If only her sense of morality would allow her this opportunity every day.

"And you have no simplicity. You prattle on and on, tying your words into tapestries of riddles. You might as well be a minstrel." Frustration lined Brax's voice.

Valoria plucked an angry note, almost breaking her spell. Wincing, she returned to her chords of truth.

"How do you ever expect to marry one if you cannot stand their 'tapestries of riddles'?" Nathaniel shot back.

"My marriage is none of your concern. I cannot even concern myself with it at present, nor do I wish to." Brax's voice rose with each word.

Nor does he wish to? Valoria's chest panged.

"Go on, go on. All I have to do is keep you two distracted for another two miles." Old man Mar interrupted just when the conversation was turning interesting.

"And why is that?" Nathaniel changed his tone to one of intrigue.

"For the ambush."

"Whoa!" Brax must have pulled on the reins, because the wagon veered to the right and halted abruptly.

Valoria stopped playing and steadied herself against the forward pull of momentum. Quickly, she picked up her chords where she'd fallen off.

"And who is going to ambush us?" Brax growled. Fabric rustled and boards creaked as the old man cried out. Valoria bet Brax had the man's throat in his hands.

"My band." The old man's voice turned fearful.

"Who is their leader?"

"Gibson." He cried. "Gibson the great. He's going to bring prosperity back to these lands."

"Prosperity?" Nathaniel sounded dumbfounded. "More like murder and crime."

Valoria put her harp down and pushed her head through the leather. Hot, dry air stung her face. A flurry of wind threw ash and soot in her eyes. She'd heard stories about the ravaged country in the south, but to stand in the middle of it sucked her lungs dry. Now she understood why so many people turned to raiding. Who could find hope in so much death?

As expected, Brax held the man by his throat. The old man's face turned red, and spittle drooled down his chin.

"Do not interfere, *sister*," Brax scolded her. "We have matters under control."

"Do you?" She strummed three distinct notes, each one higher in pitch.

Nathaniel winced, and Brax brought his hand to his forehead. The old man's eyes rolled into his head and his body slackened. Brax removed his hand, and shock lit his face as he laid old man Mar down on the bench.

"Did you kill him?" Nathaniel gawked.

"Of course not." Valoria placed her hands on her hips. "I suppose you think he spoke the truth of his own accord."

Brax blinked in astonishment and eyed her defensively. "You cast a spell on us. Back when we were talking, and again just now."

"I had to. You accepted a spy as a friend."

"Not I." Brax crossed his thick arms across his chest. "I would have left the scoundrel on the side of the road. Nathaniel gave in to his cause."

Nathaniel frowned, studying the old man. "He looked so helpless, how could I leave him?"

Valoria touched Nathaniel's arm. "If we had left him on the side of the road, we'd have no knowledge of this impending ambush. You were right to help him."

"But, what will we do with him now?" Nathaniel scanned the area. "We can't bring him back to Ebonvale to stand trial."

Brax unsheathed his sword. "We cannot let him live. He knows too much."

"Hold on." Nathaniel commanded as he raised his hand.

Valoria pushed by Brax and positioned herself in front of Mar. "He will not remember this when he wakes."

"Are you certain?" Brax's dark, cold eyes bore into her.

Valoria nodded. "Leave him on the side of the road where we found him."

Brax's jaw tensed and a vein in his forehead pulsed. "And let a traitor, a raider, go free?"

Valoria refused to allow him to bark orders as if she were a servant. "We can't drag him with us the entire journey."

"We should leave him like Valoria says." Nathaniel placed a hand on Brax's shoulder. "If he went missing, the raiders would suspect the Royal Guard at work."

Surprisingly, Brax calmed. "You are wise, brother." He sheathed his sword and took the man's feet. "Help me move him."

Of course, when she suggested they leave Mar it was preposterous, but after his wise brother suggested it, Brax relented. Valoria breathed to calm her temper as Nathaniel and Brax carried the man to the side of the road. Ash wafted as they dropped him on the ground. His hands were calloused, like those of a farmer. They were not the hands of a petty thief. Had he been a farmer before the wyverns came?

Pity softened her anger. One day she'd right the wrongs afflicting these people, but first she had to staunch the flow of evil up north. Both men were speaking quietly, and Valoria jumped from the wagon bench and joined them on the side of the road. They quieted as she approached.

If they would not speak, she might as well take the lead. "And what of the ambush?"

Nathaniel pointed southwest. "The hills we think they are hiding behind lie just a few miles south before the dried lake. My father and I used to sit upon them in the spring when we delivered our goods from Shaletown to the north."

Nathaniel turned east. "There is a path through the dead forest. It will take four days longer, but we can avoid the entire area."

Four days? Valoria calculated the risk. "That would not give us much time to find creatures no one's seen in over a century and convince them to trade their most valued good. We *must* return to Ebonvale before the next necromancer attack."

Brax wiped sweat from his broad forehead and sized Valoria up with mild admiration. "I agree with the princess. I'm more inclined to stay and fight."

Valoria stared in disbelief. Brax? Take her side?

"We do not know how many people they have in their party." Nathaniel's voice was calm and patient, like the voice of reason. "If they capture us or steal our wagon and horses, we may not return to Ebonvale for quite some time. And we have the princess with us."

Brax ran his hand over his shaved head and frowned. "There's that."

Valoria narrowed her eyes. She expected as much from Brax, but from Nathaniel? "If I wasn't here, you'd both be killed in an ambush." Honestly, how many times did she have to save them to prove her worth?

Valoria shook her head, trying to think beyond all of the macho chauvinism. She turned to Nathaniel. "You say you know which hills?"

He nodded. "They are the only hills in the next several miles."

"How close can we get before they know we're here?" Valoria's fingers itched for her harp.

Nathaniel glanced at Brax. "I'm not sure. The wagon is fairly loud."

Brax shook his head. "Not very close."

Valoria nodded definitively. "Then, someone needs to stay here with the wagon while I'll go ahead on foot."

Nathaniel's jaw dropped. "My lady…"

Brax crossed his arms across his chest and grinned as if she were a little girl trying to lift a horse. "Do you plan to take on the entire raider party?"

"No." Valoria jumped onto the wagon. She strapped her backpack and her harp on her back. It was fortunate she'd slept all day, because this would take all of her energy to prove successful.

She leapt down and took off. Let them argue, she would waste no more time. "I'll send a sign when it's safe."

"My lady?" Nathaniel called after her.

"Princess," Brax spoke in a commanding tone.

Brax would have to learn she was not a dog to be ordered to his side. Valoria ignored them even after they jogged after her.

She kept her pace as Nathaniel caught up with worry all over his face. Brax looked as though he'd pick her up and sling her across his back. He reached toward her, but he must have thought better of it because he snapped his hand away. Even in anger, he could not bring himself to touch her. His voice was stern. "Hold on. We cannot have you walking around alone."

Valoria stared straight ahead in rebellion. She'd take no more orders from that brute. "Come with me if you like. But, someone has to stay with the wagon."

Nathaniel touched her arm gently. "What are you planning to do? You can't take them all on by yourself."

"I will not have to." Valoria's lips curled as she thought of it. "I'm planning to put them all to sleep."

Chapter 17

Lullaby

"Release yourself from this damaged world
To a place of quite solitude
Pleasant memories unfurl
To placate your hungers and fears…

"Starshine fades to darkness
As the world dips away
Momentarily your mind wanders astray."

"Let yourself drift.
To the cherished places in your heart."

Valoria sang the refrain again, then let the note taper away to silence. Normally, the crickets' chirps and frog peeps would take up the empty space. But in this dead land, nothing sang back to her.

She placed her harp on her lap and kicked Nathaniel.

He blinked, shaking his head. "For a moment there, you had me, too."

"Like I said before, try not to harken to it. It was not meant for you, so its power is somewhat lost, but you will still feel some of the effects."

He rubbed his head. "I'm in such a fog."

Valoria stood. "That's the point. Now shall I go see if they're asleep?"

"No. Helena's sword. Give me a moment." Nathaniel waved her back. "Stay here. I'll go."

He climbed the hill. When he approached the top, he crouched down until he lay on his stomach and peered over the ridge. He turned to her and raised his hand. Too bad she couldn't see his face. She wagered he was smiling.

Valoria turned to the north and mimicked a bird call by whistling three tones. She waited a few heartbeats. Then, an answering call came from the darkness. At least Brax responded to that. If only she could get him to talk to her.

"He's coming." Nathaniel whispered over her shoulder.

Valoria whirled around, startled. "My, you move quickly."

Nathaniel smiled. This close, she could see every edge of his face. "Warriors in Ebonvale are trained to be quick as the wind and silent as stone."

"Brax is silent, all right." She didn't know about quick as the wind.

Nathaniel face sobered into a professional mask. "Brax has never had to learn manners. Not like I." He laughed. "As a boy, I had very ill manners. But after the king and queen took me in as their ward, I lived in a place where everyone constantly questioned my existence. I learned very quickly how to please and play the game."

"Seems it worked to your advantage."

"In a few ways." He sounded melancholy.

"Not all?"

"There are some things I can never change, not even with good manners."

"Good manners go very far in my book."

Creaks sounded from up the road. Valoria pulled away before she said too much. "Brax is on his way."

"Wait." Nathaniel held her back.

Valoria's heart skidded as she turned back and met his gaze. What did he mean to say?

"Can you not cast a spell on Brax? Make him appreciate the... opportunities provided to him?"

Shock slapped her face. "Do you mean make him love me?"

Nathaniel nodded, his face turning sad and somewhat guilty. "I know 'tis not what you'd want..."

"It's not that." She stopped him before the conversation spun out of control. "Minstrels have a code of honor. There are songs we can sing and songs we should not, or only in certain circumstances." She gestured toward the sleeping raiders beyond the hill.

"Unifying both kingdoms is not a sacred cause, worthy of such a song?"

She shook her head. "Even if I could by our code, it would not work. You see, we uncover what is already in people's hearts. We draw it out, lure it to the surface. If it's not there to begin with, then there's no way to manufacture it from smoke." Her eyes burned on the verge of tears.

"I understand." Nathaniel placed a hand on her shoulder.

The creaks of the wagon grew louder, and anxiety crept up Valoria's spine. She should not be having this conversation with him and they should not be dallying when so much lay at stake.

"We must go." She propelled herself forward, eager to escape a conversation that would lead nowhere.

Valoria reached the wagon, threw her backpack in, and climbed aboard with her harp still strapped to her back. If she had her choice, she would never part with it, not even during fancy dinners.

Brax pulled his hood away from his face. "You are certain they do not stir?"

"They might as well be dead." Valoria sat next to him.

"You are certain?" Doubt crept into Brax's voice.

"They sleep like babies in the womb." Nathaniel caught up and climbed in.

Valoria had to scoot closer to Brax to make room. With Brax to her right and Nathaniel to her left, she kept her arms close. As much as she wished to avoid the awkwardness, she'd be a fool to go back inside. If someone had not heard her song, they'd need her.

Brax gave her a wary glance, shifting an inch away from her.

Anger burned in her face. Lyric's lyre! She wasn't about to kiss him or take his hand at a time like this. What kind of nonsensical hussy did he think her to be? She pulled the harp over her head and began to pluck soft notes in the remnants of the melody. Even though the song was strong enough to put the raiders out for an entire day, if not more, she didn't like taking risks.

They entered the ravine between the hills. Nathaniel drew his sword. Each creak of the wagon wheels sounded like the wail of a banshee. Valoria strummed harder, and began to hum the refrain. She nodded for Brax to spur the horses.

Every heartbeat took an eternity as they crept forward. Black clumps of ash and dried leaves blew across their path like ghosts. Nathaniel scanned the hills.

Would he be able to detect a raider if they cocked an arrow? Valoria's heart sped. She breathed deeply to calm herself. She must have faith in her powers. Half the reason why the song had worked was because she believed in it. She'd practiced every day of her life, took lesson upon lesson. Echo himself had said she'd surpassed his teachings. Yet, that sliver of doubt blossomed and grew in her heart if she let it.

Valoria strummed again, plucking the strings until they threatened to break. Her belief could not waver now.

They passed the shadow of the hills and rode into the moon's silver light. Valoria breathed with relief as Nathaniel sheathed his sword.

"You've done it!" His whisper was on the loud side, and Valoria shushed him. Pride rose inside her. Let Brax demean her abilities now.

Something whizzed by her face and hit the backboard of the bench. Valoria turned and her skin chilled. The end of an arrow flapped back and forth, purple feathers falling on her lap.

"Duck!" Brax's large hand came over her head, pushing it down.

"One shooter. To the right." Nathaniel jumped from the carriage. "Look for others, I'm going after him."

"No!" Valoria moved to run after him, but Brax held her still.

"If he gets away, he'll wake the others."

She turned to Brax with defiance rising inside her like a wyvern's fiery breath. "I'm going to help."

"You are better use here." Brax scanned the area around the carriage and drew his claymore.

Valoria launched forward again, but Brax moved swifter than she'd expected. He grabbed her arm, pulling her to him.

Indignation burned in her face. She shot him an accusatory glare as if he meant to force himself on her, and he released her right away. His face softened, desperation leaking in. He knew he couldn't keep her beside him. "Trust in his skill. He trusted in yours."

Valoria stilled. The brute was right.

Another arrow flew over their heads.

Brax pulled them both down. "Helena's sword, there's two of them."

"At least." Valoria was keenly aware of his arm around her. He'd sheltered her and brought her to cover, yet he did not release her.

"Is there a way you can lure them into the light?" Brax whispered.

Valoria struggled to think over the shock of Brax asking her for help. "There's a song of identity, but that's more for a face-to-face confrontation."

The horses reared up, and Brax gripped the reins to hold them back. "Anything you can think of to give me at least a direction to go on."

"All I can do is make him miss."

Brax nodded and removed his arm from her shoulders. "Very well."

Valoria took a deep breath and sang the song of misfire. Arrows whizzed over the wagon. She had no idea what Brax had in mind, but at least the arrows would not find their mark.

Brax stood as if he wore a suit of armor. Valoria's voice rose as disbelief and shock riled her heart. He believed in her. So much so, he was willing to stand against arrow fire without a shield.

Should he?

As Brax walked forward, Valoria sang with all her heart. His life hung on her shoulders. One mispronunciation or sour note would give the archer the time he needed to aim true. Even though she did not favor him above all others, a strong urge to keep him safe rose up inside her. With the king dead and the queen grieving, Ebonvale needed him. She needed him. Not for comfort or love, but as a strong ally against the greatest threat the land had faced since Helena and Horred's time. Her fate and the fates of all she cared about were tied to his.

Arrows flew by Brax in all directions. He walked in steady, long strides without flinching. It seemed as if he repelled the arrows with bravery alone. Head held high, Brax climbed the nearby hill and disappeared into the darkness.

Valoria barely stopped for breath as she sang the refrain. She'd never felt so alone, sitting under the wagon bench with both men gone and the sound of her voice to keep her company. Again and again she sucked in air and looped the end with the beginning, singing an unending song until her throat dried and her fingers ached.

"It is done." Brax's voice woke her from her stupor.

Valoria crept out. Brax stood in the silvery moonlight, sheathing his sword. A thin ribbon of blood dribbled down his arm. One of the arrows had grazed his skin.

Horror ripped through her. Valoria jumped down and scrambled toward him. Brax stepped back as she approached, but she paid his reticence no heed. She rose on her tiptoes and pressed her hand against the wound. "You've been hit. 'Tis all my fault."

"My princess." His words were solemn.

Valoria stilled. He'd never called her *his* princess before.

"'Tis your fault we are still alive." He took her hand from his wound and held it to his chest. His fingers were hard and course, his skin fiery hot. "For too long, I've discounted your abilities. First, at the battle at the north gate, and second back there in the valley. I can no longer deny the truth."

The truth? Valoria blinked in astonishment. Which truth was that?

He bowed his head down to hers and his voice grew soft, almost vulnerable. "I was wrong to think we did not need each other."

Need each other? In which way? Valoria had so many questions, but they all stuck on her numb tongue. This vulnerable side of Brax hit her heart with full force. She'd tamed a lion and found a soft underbelly.

"Ahem." Nathaniel stepped from the other side of the wagon dragging a thin, scraggly young man by the arms. He'd tied the boy's hands together with his handkerchief. "I've caught the archer."

Valoria stepped back from Brax in revulsion. While Nathaniel had spared life, Brax had taken it away. No matter the softness he'd just shown her, he would never be rid of his hard-edged sense of justice.

"And what do you expect us to do with him?" Brax's hand hovered over his hilt.

"We're going to question him and take him to Shaletown." Nathaniel hoisted the boy toward the wagon.

Brax stood in the way. "He's a liability. You forget too easily how he and his friend tried to kill us."

The boy narrowed his eyes and spat on the ground.

Nathaniel sighed. "The boy and I have an understanding. Besides that, we have a hostage, someone to barter with if it comes down to it." Nathaniel eyed Brax. "I do not suppose you thought of that before you hacked the other man down with your claymore."

Brax's gaze turned cold. "He would have shot us in cold blood, and this one will slice our throats if he gets the chance." His fingers tightened on the hilt.

Valoria could not bear to see more bloodshed. She touched Brax's arm. "He will not. I'll watch him. Leave the interrogation to me."

Brax studied her as if sizing up her determination. His gaze dropped to the place where her hand rested on his arm. He made no move to remove it, which gave her some relief. "Very well. Blue and I will sit up front, and you may do your work in the back."

Valoria's mind went blank until she remembered Nathaniel's alias. "Blue. That's right."

Brax ignored her slip and turned to Nathaniel. "Take him to the back and tie him to the bench."

Nathaniel nodded and pulled the boy inside.

Valoria moved to join them. Brax reached out and stilled her gently with a hand on her shoulder. "Not so fast."

Giving orders again? Would Brax never learn she moved of her own accord? Valoria whirled around with a haughty attitude and raised her brow in question. "Yes?"

"That's the second favor. Now you owe me one." His lips curled ever so slightly before he turned solemn once again.

Dazed by disbelief, Valoria shook her head as she entered the back of the wagon. There was no doubt about it. The prince had flirted.

Chapter 18

Treasures of the Heart

"You have two choices: speak freely from your own mind, or babble on about every embarrassing detail of your life." Valoria held her harp in front of the boy's face.

He looked only a year or two younger than she was, reminding her of the stableboy at the House of Song. He had the same wide, blue eyes and curly black hair.

"I know your kind." The boy snorted. "Weasels you are, oily slick tricksters who enchant innocents with songs that bend their minds."

Valoria sighed. Did everyone in Ebonvale despise her? "We only show you what is truly in your heart. Now do you want to tell me freely, or should I pull it from your mouth?"

He sniffed. His nose was crusted with dirt. "There's not much to tell, really."

Valoria sat across from him. She placed her harp on her lap and drew out the knife she'd stuck in her boot, just in case. Nathaniel had tied the bindings so tightly, the boy's fingers had turned white, but Brax's words still haunted her.

He'd slice our throats in his sleep if he could.

She hoped it didn't come to that. "Why don't you start from the beginning?"

"You mean what I ate for breakfast? Nothing. Same for midday meal and dinner."

Guilt panged in her gut. She popped the top of her sheepskin and offered him water. "No. I mean where were you born? What brought you to where you are today?"

He took a long sip. The water dribbled from the corners of his mouth, leaving streaks on his dirt-caked face. "I was born into this world of ash, in a barn with crumbling black walls."

"Is that where you live now?" She offered him a piece of smoked beef. He opened his mouth. She dropped the piece in and he chewed while talking. "No. My mother had a lot of food stored underground, where the wyverns couldn't get at it. But the stores ran out. We had to move around, looking for food where we could get it. We tried living in the city on the streets, but she couldn't find work."

"What does she do now?"

He glanced at the floor. "She's dead. Died of flu last year."

"I'm sorry." Sorrow thick as a heavy blanket covered her heart. "Why haven't you tried working for the monks revitalizing the land?"

He snorted. "That'll take years before they see any kind of food they can eat, not to mention make a profit. That's if the land comes back at all. Gibson gives us food and shelter now."

Valoria perked up. That was the same name the old man had uttered. "Gibson?"

He closed his mouth like a clamp and glanced away.

Valoria dangled another piece of smoked meat.

He gave her a snarly frown. "Why do you want to know so much?"

She shrugged. She couldn't tell him she was to be the ruler of this hunger-plagued land. "Because I don't know much about the south. This is my first time traveling here."

"You should have stayed wherever you're from." He glanced at her servant's garb as if it were a gown. "There's nothing to be had here. It's just a pack of wolves growling over scraps."

Valoria stiffened. "I didn't have a choice in the matter. Now, are you going to tell me about this Gibson man, or should I start strumming?"

He pursed his lips as if thinking of how much to tell her. "He runs things. Tells us who to attack. He offers us protection, and he takes care of his own."

"Sounds like a reasonable man."

"That's if you aren't on the other end of his attacks. It's either join him or become his prey."

A chill crept across her shoulders. "So, you didn't have a choice?"

He glanced hungrily at the bag of beef. "I did. I chose to live."

* * * *

The horizon glowed golden amber as the sun peeked from the edge of the dead lands. As eager as Nathaniel was to leave the barren grounds, he did not relish the thought of returning to New Shaletown. He hadn't gone back since he'd left it in ruins as a boy.

Nathaniel glanced at Brax, trying to convince himself the ugly souring of his stomach was not jealousy. "You and the princess seem to be getting along better."

Brax shrugged. "It makes no difference. The end result is the same."

"It makes a lot of difference." Nathaniel whipped the reins a little too hard and the horses picked up their pace. "If you want the union to develop smoothly, you must make an effort."

"An effort?" He sounded like it was poison.

Nathaniel exhaled in frustration. "Talk with her. Develop a rapport. Discover what she finds dear and give her those treasures."

The leather moved behind them, and Valoria peeked her head through. "The prisoner is sleeping. I have some information you may find of use."

Nathaniel shifted uncomfortably, thinking of her keen minstrel ears. Had she heard any of their conversation?

"Join us." Brax moved over on the bench to make room for her. "We are about to find a place to rest."

"Then you will need to hear this." Valoria climbed over the back and plopped down in between them. "Gibson is definitely their leader. He's a mercenary who's promised the raiders food and protection if they follow him and death to those that don't."

"He will learn the hand of justice." Brax growled.

Nathaniel stifled the urge to subdue Brax like a master reined in his pit bull. He wished the world were as black and white as Brax saw it. But, it was not his place to lecture the prince.

Valoria pointed ahead. "We should rest in that burnt barn. There are two more ambush points along this road, so we'll need to veer off course slightly to avoid them."

Nathaniel regarded her with surprise and awe. "How did you get all of this information?"

She crossed her arms. "I promised him what he wants most."

Brax's eyes widened in disgust as if she'd promised him something illicit. "And what was that?"

"Safety and food. Oh, and leniency once we reach New Shaletown." She spoke as if it were as easy as giving him a piece of copper.

Brax's jaw tightened. "That is unreasonable. You have no right to impose your own will on the law of the land."

Valoria's face reddened and her eyes widened in fury. "I have every right to do everything in my power to ensure our quest succeeds."

Brax leaned over Nathaniel's lap, pushing his face a breath away from hers. "And that means letting a raider off the hook?"

To Nathaniel's surprise, she didn't back down. She stared right back at Brax, pushing her face even closer to his. Her determination and passion made her all the more beautiful. "His name is Ardent, by the way. He's an orphaned boy who's had to scrounge for food all his life. And we're not letting him off the hook. We're giving him the means to reform, to start a new life."

Brax turned away as if the argument was finished and he'd won. "He will have to answer for his misdeeds."

"That he will." Valoria sighed.

Nathaniel studied her. Would she let this drop? He didn't think so, and he was beginning to know her quite well.

Sure enough, Valoria spoke with her next breath. "But that doesn't mean you have to kill him or imprison him for life. Think about what's best for the land. We need workers to plant it."

Brax's fist clenched. "What's best for the land is to purge it of scoundrels."

"Enough." Nathaniel raised both his hands. If he didn't stop this, they'd continue for days on end. Both parties were as stubborn as mules. Although Valoria looked as different from a mule as one could get. "We'll talk about this once we reach New Shaletown. Right now we all need our rest."

They both fell silent, like scolded children. Brax sat back with a tired, bored look on his face. Valoria crossed her arms over her chest and breathed deeply.

Nathaniel listened to the creak of the wheels as they simmered down beside him. He'd never thought a rickety wagon would be music to his ears. "I'll check on our prisoner, *if* I can trust both of you not to kill each other while I'm gone."

"You have my word." Valoria glanced away haughtily. "Although for someone like Brax, restraint may prove impossible."

"Helena's sword." Brax stood. "I refuse to be spoken to this way." He pointed a finger to Valoria. "You should give your…brother more respect. *I'll* check on the prisoner."

As Brax disappeared into the back of the wagon, Nathaniel pulled on the reins, guiding the horses into the charred doorway of the barn. With the stalls burned to the ground, there was enough room to hide the entire wagon. Unfortunately, the walls stank of soot. Sunlight leaked from a hole in the roof.

Valoria held her head high as if her argument with Brax didn't bother her. But, tears glistened in the corners of her eyes. Pain etched in the hard line of her delicate jaw.

Nathaniel longed to console her, but any gesture would only lead the way down the wrong path.

"He means well." He jumped from the bench and gave the horses water. They'd ridden for too long without rest.

"So do I." Valoria jumped down and petted the lead horse. Her aura of confidence had cracked to reveal her vulnerability. Even a minstrel princess able to charm an army had doubts. "Can you see my way? Or am I a complete fool?"

The façade Nathaniel had built to hold her at arm's length melted. "I always see your way."

Brax emerged from the back of the wagon, dragging the boy behind him. "I'll take the first watch and keep an eye on the prisoner."

"Good." Valoria pushed by him. "If anyone needs me, I'll be asleep." She disappeared into the wagon.

Brax pulled Ardent to a beam that had fallen from the ceiling. He tied the boy's hands to a nail. "There. You shan't run away now. We'll see if your suggestions are what they seem. But, if you plan to trick us, you won't be alive to see the profits. I can guarantee."

"I told her the truth." Ardent seemed softer now, as if Valoria had brought reason to his thoughts. "She would have known otherwise."

"We shall see." Brax gestured for Nathaniel to join him on the other side of the barn.

When they walked out of earshot, Brax shook his head. "I'm not sure which one is more difficult, the raider or the princess."

Metal clanged against metal. Golden amber light glowed from the forge at the center of the room. A figure stood before it, raising a hammer. He pounded it into a piece of silver, and red sparks flew. The figure wore a long, brown leather apron and tall black boots.

Father.

A sweeping wave of melancholy hit Nathaniel. He was back in Shaletown in his home. Everything was in its place. Horseshoes hung from nails on the wall. A pile of old, chipped swords lay in a heap by the fire. Jars of hand-forged nails sat on the worktable.

Why did he feel out of place?

The miller and his son ran by the windows outside, pointing at the sky. Then came Ludo, moving quicker than he'd ever seen him move before. He still wore his white baker's apron and flour wafted after him.

Nathaniel approached the window with a growing sense of dread. He knew what they were running from. He'd been here once before.

"Quickly, my son. Put this on." His father held a gleaming silver-pink breastplate built for a warrior twice his size.

Nathaniel shook his head in disbelief. Usually his father wouldn't let him touch a finished product. He feared he'd scratch the shiny surface or smear the silver with his dirty hands. "It's too big. It won't fit."

"It's not meant to." He lifted the armor over Nathaniel's head.

When Nathaniel saw his father's face again, he looked sad. "Crouch behind it and don't move." His father smoothed the hair over his head. "I only wish I'd been fast enough to make enough for ma and Pill."

Outside, people screamed as someone rang a cowbell. A long, winding serpent curled in the air like a green ribbon. Then, two great, leathery wings unfurled like the masts of ships. The fireworm opened its narrow jaws. Fire lit the sky in a red streak.

His father pushed him behind the anvil, and Nathaniel ducked.

The son of a blacksmith was no stranger to heat. But, the gust of dry, searing air that surrounded him scorched his skin like no burn he'd ever suffered from before. His eyes ached so painfully, he couldn't open them. He felt sticky wetness coming from his face. His nose was bleeding.

He called for his father, but no one answered. The world lay silent, like the dead of night. Except, he'd always heard crickets chirping out his window, and he didn't even hear that now.

Nathaniel wiped his eyes and stood. The breastplate fell to the ground at his feet.

The world was soot and ash. Only one side of the barn still stood behind him, black and charred like bread left in the oven for too long. His father, his house, his family, everything was gone.

"Blue."

Nathaniel clutched his arm against his chest. "No."

A gentle hand touched his shoulder. "Blue, wake up."

He opened his eyes. He lay in the black ash, with charred wood above his head. A gorgeous face hovered over him with eyes silver as gleaming fish in the stream.

"My la—"

She pressed a finger to his lips. "Shhhh. You're not well."

Helena's sword! He'd almost given her identity to the raider.

Nathaniel sat up, trying to shed the haunting feeling clinging to him from his dream. Brax prepared the horses while Ardent lifted a bowl of soup to his lips. His hands were still tied, but enough slack was given to feed himself. "How long have I been asleep?"

"Most of the day."

"In Horred's name, why didn't you wake me?"

"I've only just woken up myself." Valoria offered him a bowl of soup. "Axel made dinner."

"He cooked?" Nathaniel took the bowl and his fingers brushed against hers. His skin tingled where she'd touched.

Valoria smiled. "'Tis not tavern fare, but 'tis edible."

Nathaniel brought the wooden spoon to his lips with hesitation. He sipped a light chicken broth. Large chunks of meat sat at the bottom of his bowl and a few leaves and herbs floated at the top. It was crude, but reminded him so much of Brax—simple, meaty, and to the point with no nonsense. He had to give Brax some credit.

"What were you dreaming of?" She dragged her spoon around, but her bowl was empty.

Nathaniel breathed heavily as the image of his father's face resurfaced in his memory. "The past."

Valoria raised an eyebrow as if intrigued. "What about the past?"

He didn't want to delve into his tragic story, so he spoke in general terms. "How fate can take away everything you hold dear in a matter of seconds."

Valoria nodded. "I know what you speak of. I lost my mother when I was a child."

Nathaniel's voice grew soft, so only she could hear him. "My apologies. I had heard something about the ruler of the House of Song joining Lyric in—what do you say—the rhythm of the world."

"That's correct." She studied him. "Not many warriors know of the minstrels' religious beliefs. But, you are not a warrior by birth are you?"

"No." Nathaniel sipped another spoonful. Every turn of conversation led him back to his dream. "I'm not."

Valoria placed her soup bowl in a bucket of water and washed it with her hands. "My mother died long before her time."

"If you do not mind me asking, what did she die of? No one ever said."

Valoria's face turned solemn with a hint of anger, or was it bitterness? "A starved heart."

"A starved heart? How does one die of such a thing?"

She glanced back at Brax as if she'd already stayed too long. "When there is not enough love."

Before Nathaniel could reply, Valoria stood and walked over to where Brax packed the wagon.

Nathaniel placed the bowl in the water and washed it with both hands. His eyes never left the princess as unease stirred in his gut. Was she anything like her mother?

Chapter 19

Ifs

"Break from the path here." Ardent pointed to a ridge up ahead. "Best to be on higher ground. They tend to wait in the valley."

Valoria nodded at Nathaniel. "Go ahead."

Nathaniel raised both eyebrows. "Are you certain he's telling the truth?"

Valoria had already tested Ardent with a slumbering *awaken thee liar* lullaby, but she didn't want to give up all of the secrets of her trade. She strummed her harp. "Want me to sing the song of truth?"

Nathaniel shifted uneasily. "If you think it's necessary."

His unease piqued her attention. What secret was he hiding? Perhaps it was better she not know. It would go against the minstrel code to lure it out. "'Tis not necessary."

Nathaniel breathed with relief. He spurred the horses up the incline. Whatever secrets he held dear, she wouldn't know. It surprised her how much she wanted to.

Ardent threw a rock on the side of the road. A puff of soot and ash came up when it hit. "Go ahead. Try your song on me. You already know enough to imprison me until Helena and Horred walk again on this earth."

"You will not spend your life in prison." Valoria threw her own rock, stirring up another cloud of ash. "You're to make something of yourself." She couldn't save everyone. At least not yet, but she could make a difference in one life. That's if he'd let her.

"Tell that to the lumbering ox snoring back there." Ardent raised his chin, gesturing toward the back of the wagon where Brax slept.

Valoria's lips curled despite her attempt to hold a serious expression.

Beside her, Nathaniel gave Ardent a chastising glare. "Excuse me, that is no way to address the…man who spared your life."

Valoria breathed in relief. Nathaniel had almost said *the prince*. She was sure of it. If they were ever to pull off this disguise, then they had to act the part better than they were. None of them would be cast in a Temple Day play, that's for certain. She turned to Ardent. "*You* speak with Axel. Tell him you only want to have food and shelter, that you'd do honest work. Unless you wish to spend your days working for Gibson."

Ardent picked at his dirty fingernail. "I don't know any other life."

"You will." Valoria patted his arm, then snapped her hand back just in case he was still the wild animal Nathaniel had captured. "If you want it badly enough."

They reached the zenith of the ridge by midday and stopped to give the horses water. Brax came out to eat with them. After a short rest, Brax took the reins while Nathaniel and Ardent moved to the back of the wagon. Despite her longing to discover Nathaniel's secrets, Valoria chose to stay with Brax. She had to convince him of a great many things. So many it overwhelmed her. So she started with the easiest matter on her list.

"As you can see, Ardent has stayed true to his word."

"So far," Brax grumbled. Was he annoyed she'd decided to stay with him instead of following Nathaniel and Ardent?

Valoria shifted on the bench to study his profile. With his blunt nose and large forehead, he looked like an impassable mountain. Stubble darkened his jaw, but his head was slick as if he'd shaved it that morning. Interesting priorities. If only she could read him better. "What will you do with him once we reach New Shaletown, if he keeps his word?"

"I do not live my life building plans around *ifs*." He spoke as if she had suggested he knit dollies in his spare time.

"I see." Valoria resisted the urge to grin. "I like *ifs*. They bring with them numerous possibilities."

Brax glanced at her as if she were mad. "Possibilities are fantasies that waste time."

Her whimsical streak rose up, and there was nothing she could do to contain it. "Come now, you've never fantasized about anything in your life?"

"No." He stared straight ahead. "Unless you count reaching goals through hard work."

Valoria sighed. Could he be any more tedious? "That's a start."

* * * *

After two more days, the ash and soot gave way to green growth. Barren lands became meadows, and the trees turned from scraggly, bare limbs to small leaves and white buds. The smell of fresh rain and the sea wafted on the breeze. They passed a few small barns, cottages, and a wayside tavern.

Valoria's nerves tingled. She swung her legs and kicked her boots on the back of the bench. They were close.

Beside her, Nathaniel squinted at the horizon. Dread had crept in his gaze. What did he expect to see?

They crested a hill, and the pinkish and grey roofs of shale filled the valley below. Every building stood in perfect lines along clean streets of cobblestone. Valoria admired the perfection until she remembered it had been rebuilt only fifteen years back. The shiny new city rested on a graveyard.

Nathaniel breathed deeply beside her as if gazing upon it gave him unbearable pain.

"What troubles you?" Valoria longed to trace the line from his ear down his chin and run her hands through the curls in his hair. She wove her fingers together and held her hands firmly in her lap.

He gestured toward the western part of the city. "There. That was where my father's shop was. And beside it, the cottage where I was born."

Reality chastened her, stilling her swinging legs. She'd remembered him telling her he was from Shaletown, but to see the ruin firsthand brought a fresh pain to her chest. "Were you here when they attacked?"

"Aye." Nathaniel swallowed hard.

His dream, the way he spoke of loss, it all made sense. How horrible it must have been to be orphaned as a child. Thank Lyric the king and queen took him in. But, to grow up with such a debt knowing you could never be the rightful heir must have been heartbreaking. How could she have spoken of losing one person as if it were the same as losing an entire village? If only she'd known more about him. Compassion overwhelmed her. "I'm so sorry."

"'Tis fate." He urged the horses forward.

An entire brigade of soldiers stood at watch atop the gate to the city, examining everyone who passed. With Brax and Ardent in the back, Valoria and Nathaniel looked like a young couple bringing goods from the north.

Valoria kept her gaze down, trying to look submissive when she'd been taught her whole life to hold her head high and stare at each person with confidence. Brax could always flash his royal seal and declare himself the prince. They were clear of the raiders, but that still left the castle vulnerable without its rulers, and they'd have to make their way back through the raiders' lands, whether they were successful in securing the blue fire or not. The less people who knew about the quest, the less trouble they'd stir up.

She held her breath as the guards' gaze fell over them. Nathaniel spurred the horses forward and nodded to the guards as if they had nothing to hide.

The guards stopped the caravan before them, peering under the leather tarp. Valoria's heart quickened. What if they recognized the prince? What would they do with Ardent?

She remembered Brax's words; *I do not live my life building plans around ifs.* If only she had his cool, logical nature.

Nathaniel reached over and put his hand over hers. "It will be all right."

The guards nodded, and the caravan before them moved on, entering the city. An older guard with gray in his beard and a broken nose approached them.

Nathaniel's hand remained on hers as a steady presence.

The guard's gaze dropped to their hands together. He studied their faces as if determining their relationship. He nodded, allowing them to pass.

Valoria breathed with relief as they entered the city. "We convinced them."

Nathaniel took his hand back. "I must be a great actor." He avoided her gaze.

A great actor? Valoria scoffed. He couldn't even remember his alias. No, the guard must have seen the natural ease they had with each other. It had only grown stronger each day they spent together despite her efforts to subdue it. So strong she could feel him near her.

People carrying baskets full of laundry, apples, fish, and other goods walked on either side of the road in an endless tide. The air smelled of fish, cooking, perfumes, and horses, each change of the wind bringing with it something different.

"I do not remember this town being so big, so crowded." Sad confusion spread across his face.

Valoria gave him a sympathetic smile. "Perhaps that is a good thing." She couldn't imagine coming back to a blackened ruin, or even another town built just like the first. Too many ghosts. "I'm glad it's different. They have said farewell to the past, something I must remind myself to do at times."

Nathaniel's face softened and grew warmer as he studied her. "You are wise beyond your years."

They traveled across the city to the harbor. Valoria peered between the buildings at the crisp blue waves.

"Have you ever seen the sea?" Nathaniel smiled, but it was sad. A dark cloud had hung over him since they'd arrived, and Valoria wished she could blow it away. But, she knew better. She had the same cloud over her head whenever she walked into her mother's sitting room at the House of Song.

"No. Before I came to Ebonvale, I'd never left the bluewood forest." She'd been naive and selfish about so many things. All she'd wanted to do was return home and play her music. But, the world needed her, and she would not let it fall to pieces. She cared about the people of Ebonvale as much as they hated her, and now about Ardent and the raiders as well. Lyric knew how much she cared about Nathaniel, and she was even growing to care for Brax in an odd sort of way.

"What do you think?" Nathaniel turned the wagon, and they passed an open space where the horizon sprang up in a carpet of shimmering blue. Seagulls dove to the water, and boats rocked with the tide.

Valoria sniffed the sea air and soaked in the wide openness. "I never thought anything could be more beautiful than the midday sun as it filtered down through the glass dome of the House of Song. I was wrong."

"You were not wrong. I have seen the sun light the House of Song and heard the minstrels play. Indeed, it is just as beautiful as the sight before us now." His gaze grew distant as if remembering.

"Where was I?" She would have certainly remembered such a face.

Nathaniel smiled as if he had a secret he could tease her with. "You were not yet born."

Chapter 20

Blueberry

Returning to Shaletown was more painful than Nathaniel could have imagined. The only bright light in the never-ending ache was Valoria's presence. She was right; he had to bid farewell to the past if he was ever to carry on.

When Nathaniel came to Ebonvale and became the king and queen's ward, he'd thought he had left it all behind. But, he could no more erase his origins than change his heritage. Trading ran in his blood, like his father before him. He'd watch his father barter with the soldiers and lords that came by the smithy. They took so many different forms of payment, from baskets of apples to loaves of fresh baked bread. His father knew the currency of life. He was good with people, and could make something of any deal.

The sights and smells of Shaletown awakened that talent in Nathaniel's veins. This was why Brax had chosen him for this quest and why it was up to him to find a decent place to rest for the night, and then a decent captain and ship willing to go where no man had gone in a long, long time.

But so much of the city had changed. Nothing looked like it should. Stores had different names, and taverns stood where baker shops used to be. How was he supposed to use his skill when all of his knowledge was archaic?

A swinging sign of a golden rabbit caught his attention, sparking memories from his past. The Grainvilles had run an inn called the Gilded Hopper. It used to stand back on Baker's Ave, next to the smithy, but the sign was the same, painted in blue, white, and gold. They were a kind family, although they'd refused to take in the albino who'd stayed at his house one night. The Grainvilles didn't like strange journeymen, but they took care of their own.

Would they know him? And even more importantly, could he trust them?

He parked the wagon on the side of the road next to a trough of water for their horses. "Stay here. I will not venture far."

Valoria stood in determination. Even in her servant's garb, she looked regal. "I want to go with you."

He shook his head apologetically. "You must look after...Axel and Ardent. Neither one can stand guard."

She nodded as if she'd forgotten and sat back down. Some people down here might recognize their prince, and they could hardly trust the boy. "Be careful." Her silver eyes were full of concern and hope. Their quest rested on him finding a private refuge. He wished he could seal their parting with a touch, or a kiss, but he settled for a nod. "I always am."

Nathaniel walked to the door of the inn and pushed it open. A bell rang, announcing his entrance. He stepped into an antechamber with hooks on the walls and scuffed shoes laid out on shelves. A painting of the old Shaletown hung on the wall. His chest ached when he saw the grey roof of his father's smithy in the background. A woman with curly brown hair sat at a desk behind a partition.

She finished writing and glanced up. "Can I help you?"

"Perhaps." How would he go about this? Nathaniel took off his hat and scarf, and bowed his head. "I'm looking for a family who used to own this establishment."

Her eyes widened. She had a small chin and a pointy nose, reminding him of a fox. "My family has always owned this inn."

His heart sped. "Are you a Grainville?"

"The last one living." She stood in astonishment as if his questions were impertinent. "And who, by chance, are you?"

"Nathaniel Blueborough. My father used to run the smithy."

She laughed in shock and blinked, studying him as if he were a painting coming into focus. "Nip?"

He froze, trying to recollect something about her curly hair or pointy nose. "My apologies. I do not know you."

"Blanca." She came around the partition and threw her arms around him. "I thought you were dead."

He stood frozen for a moment before he started to hug her back. The memory of a chubby little girl who used to stand outside the baker's shop and pull his hair came back to him. "Blueberry Blanca?"

"That's right. Although I don't eat any of those blueberry tarts anymore. I'm taller now, and my freckles disappeared, thank Helena and Horred."

"You look very different."

"I'll take that as a compliment." She smiled in a flirtatious way he'd not seen in her before. Maybe all of that pulling hair had been her way of getting him to notice her? "How did you survive?"

Her gaze turned angry. "I wasn't in Shaletown when the wyverns came. My parents had sent me to a boarding school in Innisborough—a dreary, dismal place. Although, traveling there saved my life. I was one of the many who came back and rebuilt."

Guilt burrowed deep inside his gut. He'd given up on Shaletown because it was too painful to come back. This woman had been braver than he was. "I haven't been back since."

"So, you were here when they attacked?"

Nathaniel nodded solemnly.

"I can't imagine how hard it must have been to have witnessed such a disaster. No wonder you never came back."

Nathaniel breathed with relief. Finally, someone understood and acknowledged his pain. "You do not know how consoling it is for me to hear you say that."

She smiled warmly. "So, what can I do for you? How long are you staying?"

"I'm here with some friends. We need lodging for one night, and a reference for a captain and a ship."

Disappointment settled in her features. "One night, 'tis all?"

"I'm afraid so. If you could manage it."

"Of course I could for you." She walked behind the desk and flipped through her parchment book. "How many people?"

"Four, and it has to be two private rooms. I can pay whatever it costs."

She dipped her quill in ink and scribbled. "All right. And I'll give you a bargain because we're old friends."

"No need for that." He didn't want to give her the wrong idea. "My companions would like to remain anonymous. Will that be a problem?"

"Well, aren't you a man of mystery." Her face turned sour. "My parents never liked suspicious guests. They used to turn people away all the time."

His stomach sunk. "I remember."

"When I opened the inn again, I told myself I was never going to be like them. I'd welcome anyone who came through the door, sometimes even if they can't pay." Her solemn face broke into a smile.

"That's very kind of you. And we can pay you very well. I promise we won't be any trouble."

She wiggled her finger at him accusatorily. "You were always trouble. But, I forgive you."

If he remembered correctly, she'd been the troublemaker. But, as a guest in her establishment, he wouldn't argue. "One more thing. You cannot tell anyone I've come back."

"I won't say a word." She pressed her finger to her lips. "Although, there's not many who'd know you around here now anyway."

He breathed with relief. The gods smiled upon him in strange ways.

She leaned forward, placing both elbows on the countertop and exposing the curves of two very large breasts. "So what have you been up to all these years?"

Nathaniel coughed and covered his mouth. This conversation had spiraled out of control. He couldn't leave Valoria unattended any longer. And he couldn't tell Blanca of his affiliation with the rulers of Ebonvale. Maybe Blanca could keep his presence a secret, but to have the prince of the land staying in her inn may prove too juicy for her restraint.

Just as he set down a pouch of gold, he thought of a brilliant answer that would have no lie in it. "You could say I followed in my father's footsteps in a way, working with swords."

Without another word, she handed him the room keys, and he sprinted away.

* * * *

"And who is this woman you've entrusted with our secrets?" Valoria whispered as Nathaniel brought the wagon down an alley and around the back of the blue painted inn. Jealousy rose up like wyvern's breath, and she had to mask it with anger instead.

"She's a childhood acquaintance. And I did not entrust her with all of our secrets. I told her who I was so we could get private rooms and a reference for a captain and a ship."

"You do not think she'll tell everyone who's staying at her inn?" Truly, Valoria had no right to be jealous at all. Sometimes she was so illogical, she could slap herself.

Nathaniel's face turned solemn. "Sadly, not many would know me. There aren't many original villagers living in New Shaletown. Most of them died in the blaze."

"My apologies." Guilt heated her face. How could she overlook such a blatant fact? "I just want us to be careful, that's all."

"What is this about being careful?" Brax emerged from the wagon with Ardent by his side. He'd put up his hood to mask his face so only his large jaw was visible to passersby.

"Nothing." Nathaniel untied the boy's restraints.

"I wouldn't do that." Brax warned.

"What do you suppose we do, march him through the inn as our prisoner? Won't that draw some unwanted attention?" Nathaniel threw the rope in the wagon.

Brax scowled and moved away. "Have it your way."

"I'm not going to run away." The boy rubbed his wrists. "I've eaten better with you than any other day in my life."

"He has a point." Valoria gave Brax an encouraging smile. Maybe she could wear him down over time and show him these raiders were people as much as he was.

"Very well." Brax gave the boy a hard, skeptical glance as if daring him to disobey, then turned to Nathaniel. "Show us these private rooms."

They entered the inn from the back door and climbed a rickety stairway up to the third floor. Nathaniel brought out two room keys and opened the door at the top of the stairs to the right. "This is your room, Val."

"Thank you." Valoria had to bite her tongue when she heard him say her nickname. Her childhood nickname coming from his lips warmed her heart. A little too much.

Her room was bright with a northern exposure and two large triangular windows. A simple four-poster bed with a pink quilt looked cozy after so many nights sleeping in the wagon or on the hard ground. Then, she saw the ivory washbasin, scented pink soaps, and bathtub and she knew she was in heaven.

"We'll be across the hall." Nathaniel called in, and Valoria realized she'd forgotten about them.

"Good. Thank you." She closed her door and peeled off all of her traveling layers.

Three buckets of warm water sat beside the washbasin. She poured them in, wishing Cadence was there. They'd always talk about their days while she took her bath, and she missed her handmaiden's responses. There was so much she'd like to tell her and giggle over. How Brax claimed he had no fantasies, how Ardent didn't like fancy cheese because it smelled foul, how Nathaniel liked to dip his biscuits in his tea. But she couldn't talk to Cadence about Nathaniel, could she?

Her handmaiden wouldn't hear of it.

Truly, there were things that Valoria had no right speaking to Cadence about. Perhaps it was fortunate Cadence wasn't there.

She dipped into the bath, immersing herself in the water. The soap smelled like the roses in her father's gardens. Valoria breathed deeply, rubbing the soap up and down her arms and legs. She would not think of Cadence's chastising glares now. Not even the hard truth would ruin her bath.

A knock came at her door.

Valoria stood and reached for a clean towel. "Who is it?"

"Just bringing in your midday, miss." A woman called from the other side.

"Very well, bring it in." Valoria covered herself as the door opened.

A curly haired woman entered bringing a tray with soup, a heel of bread and a bowl of fruit. Her eyes widened. "My, my, my. Nip didn't tell me his companion was so beautiful, and so young."

Jealousy surged. That must be Blanca, the woman who knew Nathaniel from his past. Valoria didn't like her calling Nathaniel by his old nickname. He'd been an adult for many years and deserved more respect. If only this inn maid knew how high up the command he'd risen.

Blanca studied her. "You don't look related."

"I'm his sister." Or she would be very soon.

She placed her hands on her hips. "He doesn't have a sister."

"When you knew him, he didn't. But, that was a very long time ago, was it not?" Honestly, wasn't she supposed to be the guest? As a princess, she'd never been treated in such an impertinent way.

"Hmmph. His sister, eh?" Blanca snorted and turned to the door. "Enjoy your meal."

"I will." Valoria waited for the door to close before she splashed back into the tub.

Thank Lyric and his golden lyre they'd only be staying a single night. After second thoughts, she preferred the wagon bench.

Chapter 21

Mercy

Nathaniel offered Ardent a glass of water and a bowl of soup. Thank Helena he'd been able to rush Blanca from their room with the excuse of his exhaustion from the journey. The more she asked, the closer she got to his secrets.

Hopefully, Blanca didn't bother Valoria. She'd always had a fiery tongue, and might rile Valoria up when she beheld the princess's glowing beauty. Valoria was a rose among wild flowers. Often, he wondered what the princess was thinking when she turned away from him with a melancholy look in her silver eyes, showing her delicate profile and high sculpted cheekbone.

"She likes you." Ardent slurped his soup without the spoon.

Nathaniel almost dropped his bowl. The princess? Fond of him? How would Ardent have any idea?

"You knew her when you were young?" Ardent chewed a heel of bread.

"Oh, the inn maid?" Nathaniel breathed with relief, and a little disappointment. "She has a strange way of showing it."

Ardent shrugged. "Strange or not, that's more than what I've got."

Compassion for the boy overcame any lingering longing over Valoria. How could he be preoccupied with a dead end when a lad needed his support to set him on the right path? "You're young. You have your whole life ahead of you."

Ardent shrugged and wiped soup off his chin. "No one will take a shining to a thief."

"You shan't be a thief forever, isn't that right?" Nathaniel handed him a cloth. Ardent could work on table manners after he sorted out his life, but a little nudge in the right direction wouldn't hurt.

"Once I'm in prison, I shall have a black stain on my reputation for life."

Nathaniel thought of all the stains on his: orphan, blacksmith's son, lesser brother. "One black stain is something that can be overcome."

A knock sounded at the door, and Nathaniel's heart jumped to his throat. He asked Helena, Horred, and their godly son for it not to be Blanca.

"May I come in?" It was Valoria's light voice.

"Of course." Nathaniel stood eagerly and opened the door.

The scent of sweet roses wafted up, making the blood flow through his veins. Valoria wore a simple white dress. She'd let down her braids, so her auburn hair fell in wavy curls around her shoulders. Her porcelain skin was pale and perfect like a lily's bloom.

He moved from the doorway and she slipped by him. "Where's Axel?"

"He had business in town." Nathaniel offered her a seat by the window.

"Business?" She glanced nervously to Ardent.

Nathaniel gave her an apologetic frown. "I could not stop him."

"Oh." She sat down and gazed out the window. "I'm not sure I want him to find what he's looking for."

That statement could have so many subliminal meanings, none of them good. Unease spread over Nathaniel as he sat down in the chair opposite her. "Perhaps he's purchasing supplies."

"Supplies…" She didn't take her eyes away from the window. "We'll need them where we're going."

The door opened, and Brax strode in with bags of apples, blankets, and dried meat. His eyes scanned the room and fell on Valoria. Did interest flash in his gaze? "I did not know you were here."

"I just stopped by." Valoria stood abruptly, as if she'd done wrong.

Guilt plagued Nathaniel's heart whenever Brax caught them together. At least they weren't alone.

"Wait." Brax placed the bags on the bed. "You should stay to hear the news."

"News?" Nathaniel stood. It was a better stance to come between anyone should they argue. All his life, he was used to keeping peace.

Brax straightened and adopted the commanding tone he used when giving a speech or ordering the army. "I have found a place for our raider."

Ardent stopped chewing and his mouth was still full of half-eaten bread. His eyes widened as if a judge delivered him his death sentence. Nathaniel stepped over to the boy and placed a hand on his shoulder.

Brax pulled an apple from the bag and took a bite. "I have spoken with a local fisherman who is in need of an oarsman. He is willing to take

Ardent on knowing full well of his prior indiscretions." Brax turned to the boy. "The work will be strenuous, but you will be paid adequately. You'll have to sleep on the boat for now, but with a couple months labor, if you save correctly, you will have enough for a small room in town."

Ardent dropped his bread. "You mean I'm not going to prison?"

"No." Brax shifted uneasily as if he wasn't completely comfortable with the idea. "You are not."

Valoria cheered and rushed across the room to Brax. She took both his hands in her own and kissed his knuckles. "Thank you."

Brax blinked in shock. Then, he regained some composure and nodded in deference. "You should thank yourself." Brax's voice softened. "Your arguments led me to this conclusion."

Jealousy ripped through Nathaniel. He smothered it immediately. There was nothing wrong with Valoria thanking Brax with kisses. So, why did it feel so wrong in his heart?

"I do not deserve this kindness." The tension in Ardent's voice stilled everyone in the room. The boy dropped both hands at his sides.

"You mean you will not accept it?" Valoria stared at him in shock.

Ardent sighed and pulled at the frayed edges of his pants. "I've been shooting arrows at passing caravans all my life."

Valoria stepped toward him and crouched beside him on the floor. "You've done it because Gibson ordered you too, because you had to survive."

Ardent shook his head. "I chose to, just like I told you back in the wagon. I wanted to keep on living, and I didn't want to become weak like the prey. But, I knew it was wrong." He wiped at his eyes. "I tried to honor the gods by delivering superficial wounds. But, about a year ago, I grazed this man's arm. I thought he'd survive. I intended for him to."

Valoria reached out and placed her hand on his arm. Sorrow touched her beautiful face.

Nathaniel could only squeeze the boy's shoulder. He wished he could have found Ardent many years ago, like the king and queen had found him in the ashes of Shaletown. He'd been lucky to have such loving saviors. This boy did not have half his luck.

"It's all right." Valoria patted his arm. "It's not your fault."

"But, it is." Ardent spat back in anger. "He died. Lost too much blood on the way to the city." The boy's hands shook. He pulled away from Valoria's touch. "I learned the man's name from a letter he'd had in his pocket. I had some people ask questions about the man's family. He had a son. My father died when I was young, and I took another boy's father away, continuing the cycle. I've turned my back on the way of Helena and Horred. I'm cursed."

Brax stepped forward and Nathaniel's chest tightened. Would he judge the boy harshly? Would he rescind his earlier bargain?

"Warriors kill many men in battle." Brax crouched next to Valoria on the floor. "They are taught to mourn their loss, but not to carry their deaths on their hearts." He offered his hand to Ardent. "'Tis time to right your wrongs, my son."

Ardent chewed his lower lip. This moment of indecision reminded Nathaniel of Bronford Thoridian asking him to join the Royal Guard. His life had balanced on a thin branch, and he could have fallen either way. He was glad he'd chosen the path he had. Now Brax was following in his father's footsteps, offering a second chance to a lad down on luck. Bronford would be proud of his son.

Ardent took Brax's hand. The warrior stood, pulling the boy up. "Come, pack your things. A new destiny awaits." His voice had turned lighthearted, or as least as lighthearted as Brax could be.

Valoria stood and studied Brax with a mixture of interest and awe. Nathaniel had never seen such admiration in her eyes when she'd looked upon him. She touched the warrior's arm. "I'm going to pack a few things of my own for Ardent. I'll be in my room if you need me."

Brax nodded awkwardly as if he didn't expect her to tell him anything of her whereabouts. "Very well."

Valoria glanced at Nathaniel and nodded, then left. The sunshine in the room went with her, along with Nathaniel's heart. Someday he'd have to come to terms with the fact she'd never be his. But, one tragedy at a time. Save the boy, save the kingdom, then save his own heart.

While Ardent packed, Nathaniel approached Brax by the door.

Brax had resumed eating his apple, but his gaze glazed over, as if his thoughts had gone with Valoria as well.

"Why?" Nathaniel whispered.

Brax raised his brow in question and bit off another piece of apple. He didn't answer.

"Why did you change your mind?"

"Something you'd said." Brax swallowed the bite of apple and a ponderous expression came across his face. "You said to acquaint myself with the treasures of her heart. Well, I listened."

Nathaniel nodded, surprised his advice had gone so far. He didn't think Brax would listen to him, never mind to Valoria. "That, you did."

* * * *

Valoria wrapped a fig cake in a cloth along with a piece of gold. Ardent's sad history had touched her soul. She could not imagine being forced into raiding to stay alive. But, deep down in her gut, she knew she'd have done the same. She didn't have her mother's wholehearted kindness, the kind that forgives so easily and places everyone's happiness above her own.

Valoria was a survivor. She'd rather endure pain than give in. She was her father's daughter, and she would make him proud, even if it meant marrying Brax.

That thought didn't have its usual harsh sting. Brax had surprised her. He'd shown kindness instead of judgment, thinking beyond the walls of right and wrong he'd so carefully constructed.

He'd said he did so because of her. Perhaps, she'd been the one to judge too harshly.

She opened her door. Brax, Nathaniel, and Ardent stood at the top of the stairs. Nathaniel had his hand on Ardent's shoulder. "Listen to the fisherman. Do as he says and be respectful."

Brax glanced in her direction and nodded. "Ready to see him off?"

"I am." Valoria approached Ardent and handed him the cloth. "Something for the road." Ardent consumed anything in front of him, so she didn't think her fig cake would go uneaten. As for the gold, maybe he could buy that room in town sooner than he thought. "Remember, you shape your own destiny."

Valoria smiled, but it felt forced. How much of that was true in her case? Could she shape her own destiny? Hadn't she been fated to unite the House of Song with Ebonvale since birth? Her statement was true for him but not for herself.

Ardent nodded gruffly and stuffed the cloth in the bag strapped across his back.

Brax cleared his throat. "Time to depart."

The warrior took the stairs two at a time, and Ardent followed him. A few steps down, he turned his head to Valoria and Nathaniel. "I won't forget this."

With the rhythmic sound of footsteps, they were gone. Valoria wished him a silent prayer and ran her fingers along the wood railing of the stairs.

Nathaniel turned to her. "Do you think he'll stay on the right path?"

Melancholy mixed with confusion made Valoria shift on her feet. What was *the right path*? The path we choose for ourselves, or the one laid out by our parents or, in Ardent's case, by his circumstances? "He has as much of a chance of any of us."

The raw truth of her answer surprised her.

Nathaniel gave her a questioning glance, and Valoria ignored it. To be alone with him after what Brax had done for the boy made her feel guilty in a sticky, tortured way.

Without another word, she disappeared into her room.

Chapter 22

Last Kiss

The morning cast a dull, grey light. The sea, the clouds, and the air had a misty, bleak quality that did not bode well for their journey. Nathaniel tightened his cape around his neck, eager to leave New Shaletown behind him no matter what the future brought.

"Where is this captain that your…lady friend recommended?" Brax spoke from the inside of his hood. Out of the three of them, he was the one who was most likely to be recognized, so he kept his face hidden at all costs.

"She's not my lady friend." Brax made her sound like a mistress. "I knew her as a child, that's all."

"But, you knew her well enough to trust her now?" Valoria sounded suspicious, as if he were withholding some secret relationship, which would not be wrong considering she was betrothed to Brax and not to him.

"Without her recommendation, we'd be choosing blindly. We do not have any other choice." He counted the ships at the dock. Blanca had said it was the fifth one in, double-masted with a flag of red and gold.

"There." Nathaniel pointed to an older, but sturdy looking ship. "That's the one."

They walked down the dock, their boots echoing on the wood. The sea lapped at their feet as if eager to swallow them whole. A seagull picked at an oyster on the top of a mooring, watching them with an orange eye. He cawed, and it almost seemed as though he warned of their coming.

An old, white haired man wearing a dark overcoat threw netting off the side of the ship. It fell in the sea with a splash and sunk to the dark depths below. The man gazed up as they approached. He had a timeworn, withered look, his long hair blowing every way of the wind, and a tattoo of a shark's fin on his neck. But his eyes were a bright blue, and when he smiled, his face was kind.

"What brings you to Amok's dock?"

Nathaniel gave Valoria and Brax a look that told them to let him handle negotiations. "A friend recommended we speak to you. We're looking for passage through the Sea Of Urchins."

"The Sea of Urchins, eh? That's not a place one crosses without a purpose, indeed." Amok smacked his lips together, then his eyes filled with mischief. "Depends on who this friend is, lad."

Doubt made Nathaniel hesitate. How much did he really trust Blanca? Somehow he doubted she was in it for the money, at least with him. "Blanca Grainville from the Gilded Hopper."

"Good ol' Blanca." Amok smiled fondly. "Poor girl. I knew her parents. They were kind folk, even if they were a lil' leery of eccentric strangers."

"Perhaps you knew my father then?" Nathaniel stepped forward. Saying his father's name took courage because it brought back his loss in full force. "Alhearn Blueborough."

Amok's eyes lit up. "Now that's a name I haven't heard in a long time." He jumped from the boat onto the dock.

Brax moved his hand to the hilt of his sword hidden underneath his cloak, but Nathaniel raised his hand to stop him.

Amok studied Nathaniel's face. Close up, the old man had more wrinkles than an old sheet wadded in the closet. "Ah yes...there he is." Amok pulled back and smiled. "You have his eyes and his nose. He'd be proud of the man you've become."

A wave of melancholy threatened to knock Nathaniel to his knees. He breathed deeply, stifling the sorrow. "Will you help us?"

"For the son of Alhearn, I'll do anything." Amok gestured toward his ship. "Climb aboard. The Manta's Tail is all your own."

Nathaniel turned to Brax and Valoria. Brax raised his brow in doubt, but he followed the old man and climbed aboard. Valoria smiled as she passed him. "Thank Lyric's lyre you came along."

"Lyric's lyre?" Amok noticed Valoria's harp strapped to her back. "Do we have a minstrel in our mist?"

"We do, and my harp is at your command." Valoria bowed to him. Brax offered his hand and she climbed aboard.

Nathaniel moved to climb on himself, but Amok held up a gnarled hand. "Hold on right there, lad." He gestured down the dock toward the town. "Looks like you forgot to give a proper farewell."

His stomach dropped. Blanca came running down the dock with veils trailing behind her, waving her arm wildly. The urge to jump on the ship overwhelmed him, and he glanced back to the bow, where Brax and Valoria stood staring.

Blanca had put them up for the night with no questions asked, offered to watch over their carriage and horses while they were gone, and gave him a great recommendation for a captain. Only a rogue would run away from her now.

He walked as fast as he could to meet her to get as far away from the ship as possible. He did not want anyone overhearing her flirtatious attempts.

"How could you leave without saying farewell?" She reached him, grabbing both his arms in her hands.

Guilt trickled over him. He'd been relieved when he saw an older woman sitting at her post. "You weren't at the desk, and we had to leave immediately."

"I forgive you." Her hands roamed up his back to his neck. "And I want to give you something for the journey."

Before he could ask what it was, she pulled his head down to hers and mashed her lips to his. Her hair blew in the wind, surrounding him in a curtain with no escape.

Nathaniel pulled back, but she was stronger than she let on, and her grip did not falter. She smeared her lips all over his mouth and sucked on his lower lip before pulling her head back.

She could have hit him over the head with a hammer and he would have been just as bowled over. But, it wasn't from love. It was from shock and embarrassment.

He turned his head, praying to all the gods that Brax and Valoria had gone below deck. But, they stood where he last saw them. Brax's eyes widened in surprise, and Valoria shot daggers with her glance before turning away. Amok grinned as if impressed.

Mortification froze his soul. Valoria must be disgusted. Never would he think to kiss a woman he hardly knew so flagrantly in front of everyone. He wanted to turn around and leave without another word. But, the sincere expectation in Blanca's face stopped him.

"Blanca…" He searched for the right words. How could he tell her he didn't love her? That he loved…

She placed a finger on his lips. "Don't say anything now. Take your journey and think about me."

"I could never—"

She shook her head. "You are too noble for your own good. You always were. We do not know what will happen on your journey, but give the thought of us a chance."

"Why me?" Nathaniel shook his head. "I was just a blacksmith's son who you used to tease." They had no long, tragic history, no sweet memories.

"You knew me before, back when I was young and the world had so many possibilities. To everyone else, I was the poor orphan child."

"So was I." He'd underestimated the tragic link binding them together. They were survivors from a bygone time, a time of innocence.

"I pushed people away. I didn't want their pity." Blanca wound part of her veil around her finger. "I was so caught up in rebuilding, in keeping the inn going, that I turned my nose up at offers. Now, I'm an old maid."

"You are hardly old." If she was old, he would be considered old as well, and Nathaniel refused to believe he had his best years behind him.

She laughed. "That's what I always loved about you, and why I teased you so much. You have a kind soul. I didn't appreciate it then, but I do now."

"Remember me with this." Blanca slipped a handkerchief in his hand. With a smile, she turned and walked back down the dock.

Nathaniel slipped the handkerchief in his pocket like a stolen item he didn't want anyone to see. He dragged his feet back to the ship. What would he tell her if he returned and his feelings were the same as they were now?

"Now there's a farewell." Amok chuckled.

Nathaniel breathed quickly to reply and thought better of it. To tell the old man he did not want her affection would only make him look like more of a scoundrel. He ignored Amok's taunting leer and climbed on board.

His lips ached where Blanca had kissed him, and he was certain red scratch marks ran across the back of his neck. His cheeks burned so hot, he thought he'd set his hair on fire. One thing was for sure, no one would forget that kiss anytime soon.

How he would restore his integrity in his party's estimation, he had no idea.

* * * *

The constant rocking of the ship made Valoria long for the hard, unchanging cobblestone in front of the House of Song. How a body of water could be so beautiful yet so unmerciful and relentless perplexed her to no end. Now she knew why sailors called the sea their love and their bane.

"The manta ray is a magnificent creature." Amok sat beside her as she tried to focus on the rise and fall of the horizon. "Despite their monstrous size, they do not kill large prey. Instead, they open their mouth and forage for the smaller creatures in the sea. They are not violent, or all-consuming like the wyverns. Instead, they survive on the leftovers."

She nodded, trying to find significance in his words. "I see."

Amok spread his hand over the water. "They cast a wide net and forage for the bits, much like I do to make my way in this world. The trick is to not get too greedy or you'll overfish your welcome."

"I'd never thought of it that way before." Valoria studied the tattoo on Amok's neck. The ink had seeped around the edges, making the image of the fin blurry. It must have been done many years ago when he was a young man. Did he regret it? Who was Amok, truly? An eccentric madman, or a sage seaman wizened by his years? Did he speak true wisdom or nonsense?

Valoria considered his words. "The wyverns pushed too far and that proved to be the end of them."

"Aye." Amok nodded as his eyes gazed out to sea. "Same with the undead. They'll overstep their bounds, and you have to rein them in."

Valoria studied him, wondering if he had an inkling of why they were sailing to the Sea of Urchins. Had word of the undead attack spread so quickly? "Easier spoken on the wind than enforced with a sword."

"That is why they have you." He pointed to her. "For you conjure your magic speaking on the wind."

"At least I try." She shivered, thinking of the necromancer's soulless black eyes and how he'd sucked a part of her soul dry. "I fear it will be the death of me."

"The death of you, or your rebirth." Amok winked. "Depends on how you look at it."

Valoria blinked, taken aback. Did he mean for her to allow the darkness to overtake her?

Nathaniel emerged from below deck, stifling any further conversation of the undead. He nodded in their direction, then walked to the railing on the other side. Jealousy reared up like wyvern fire in her chest. She'd known there was something between him and that overly bold woman. Why he'd tried to hide it from her, she had no idea. It wasn't like they were betrothed. He was free to kiss whom he chose.

It shouldn't have mattered to her, yet it tightened her stomach until she couldn't think of it any longer.

"Now there's a lucky lad." Amok smiled, but it was sad. "One of the few survivors."

As much as their conversation unnerved her, at least it was keeping the sea sickness at bay. "You knew his father. What was he like?"

"Honorable and just. You knew he'd live up to his side of the bargain. He knew how to trade and make both parties come out on top. One summer he traded me a silver fish hook every week for a pound of tuna and a lobster. I thought I was getting the better end of the deal, but he said at the end of the summer that his family ate like kings and thanked me for it. Made me feel worthy, like I was doing good in the world. Now that's a talent if I ever say so myself."

Valoria pictured Nathaniel as a small boy eating fish at his father's table. When she'd arrived in Ebonvale, he'd made her feel at home the minute he met her. "Nathaniel is the same way."

"You think highly of the lad?" Amok studied her and his bright blue eyes seemed to see too much.

"He's a loyal companion." She stood, turning her back on the real answer. The dizzying sway made her stomach pitch. "I'm not feeling well, I must go below deck."

Amok winked and patted her arm. "You'll get your sea legs. Don't worry about that."

Valoria nodded and stumbled to the wooden stairway leading to the belly of the ship. Gaining her sea legs was the last thing she had to worry about.

The ship pitched up, and her hands slipped down the moist railing. She fell down the stairs. Large hands caught her and held her up until the boat steadied.

Embarrassment burned in her cheeks. "Brax."

"My lady." He set her down gently. But he did not move to climb the steps. It was as if he'd forgotten where he was going. But Brax wasn't a scatterbrained man. He must have changed his plans because of her. "Are you well?"

"'Tis the sea." She moved by him, embarrassed to show her vulnerability. He already thought her a useless, naïve girl. "I really must return to my room."

"Wait." His voice came out as a command.

Valoria whirled around ready to deliver some barb about ordering her around when the kindness in his eyes stopped her.

He reached in his cloak and brought out a silver flask. "This helps with the sickness."

Although the gesture was kind, offering booze to a seasick princess was not the way to a woman's heart. "I do not drink ale."

He extended the flask toward her. "'Tis an herbal mixture I picked up yesterday in town."

She took it, brushing his sausage-like fingers with her own. He was always so warm, like a fire burned under his skin.

She unscrewed the cap. The liquid smelled faintly of lavender and chamomile. "How did you know I would be sick?"

"I didn't. I succumb to the pitch of the sea." Brax paused as if deciding whether or not to speak further. "The sway of the sea can bewitch the best of men."

Valoria had to suck in her cheeks to resist the urge to smirk. Strong, proud Brax drank herbal tea to calm his stomach? The truth made him more endearing, more human. He'd gone on a limb giving her the tea. It exposed his vulnerability, which was the last thing warriors wished on display. He'd done it for her.

She touched his arm, feeling warmth beneath his shirt. "You needn't say more. Thank you."

He bowed his head. "Glad to be of service."

Awkward silence filled the air between them. Should she stay? He was finally opening up. Her stomach churned and her knees wobbled. She needed to drink the tea, lie down, and dream of solid ground. Valoria turned and walked to her room.

Surely, there'd be more opportunities to spend time with him without the deck pitching beneath her feet.

She collapsed on her bed and popped the cap on the flask, running her fingers along the place where he'd put his lips, where she'd put hers if she drank the tea. She was procrastinating, and the truth made guilt settle in her gut. She wasn't as opposed to him as she used to be. A small spark of interest stirred inside her. If she encouraged it, the spark could develop into a flame. But would it burn as brightly as the one already blazing inside her for Nathaniel?

She hadn't run from Brax; she'd run from her own conflicted emotions.

Chapter 23

Soul Touch

Long sticks poked from the water as if giant pincushions lay underneath the surface. A scraping sound made Nathaniel cringe, reminding him of when Blanca used to draw her nails across the chalkboard in school.

He jogged up the stairs to the wheel where Amok stood, gazing into the horizon. Did he not hear it? Had the old sailor gone mad?

"Shouldn't we turn around?" Nathaniel couldn't imagine the wood of the hull lasting much longer.

Amok laughed. "Why turn around when you're in the right place?"

"The right place?" The man *had* gone mad. He moved to push him aside and take the wheel.

"The Sea of Urchins, my lad." Amok's voice stilled him. The old man waved his hand over the clusters of brown twigs rising on either side of them. Some of them were almost as tall as the masts. He leaned to the right, bringing the wheel with him, and the ship rounded a particularly large clump.

"Urchins?" Nathaniel had seen one wash ashore once. He'd probed it with the toe of his boot until his father had told him to let it be. But, that one had been the size of a coin. "What about the ship?"

Amok patted the wheel. "The Manta's Tail is sleek and quick. We'll be clear of them soon."

"And what about the ones tearing us to shreds along the way?"

"Silver fish hooks ain't the only thing your father sold me over the years." Amok punched his shoulder. "The bottom of the hull is plated in the strongest and lightest metal ever forged. They won't even leave a scratch."

An old memory flashed through his head. His father stood over the hearth, banging out slim sheets of a silver alloy. Nathaniel had asked him what it was for and he'd said he couldn't give up his customer's secrets, not even to his son. Nathaniel had been angry at him, he could still feel the irrational frustration underneath his skin. He'd thought he was ready for the tricks of the trade. Now, they'd gone with his father to the grave.

"Many a sailor has come unprepared." Amok pointed, and his face turned solemn. The remnants of a ship impaled by one of the urchin's quills stood adrift above the sea. The sails had been torn to shreds, and the threads blew like ghosts in the wind. A hole in the hull revealed a table on its side and a chair with a ripped, velvet cushion. "And don't go for a swim anytime soon. The spines will slice your leg open, not to mention the poison which fills a man's veins and turns him blue as the sea."

"What is the meaning of this senseless place?" Brax's voice pulled Nathaniel from his haze. The warrior climbed the steps two at a time. "I sleep for an hour and the world turns upside down."

"We are crossing the Sea of Urchins." Wonder lined Nathaniel's voice. "Amok says not to be deterred. How is...Val?"

"She has not emerged from her room." Brax glanced to the horizon. His gaze turned foggy and unreadable.

Nathaniel hadn't spoken with her alone since the Blanca incident. She'd mostly kept to herself or talked with Brax. "Have you spoken with her?"

"Only in passing yesterday afternoon."

"We should check on her." Nathaniel glanced to the stairs to the lower decks.

"The girl needs her rest." Amok gave Nathaniel a disapproving glance, as if he wooed every maiden he laid eyes on. "It takes time to get over the sway of the sea."

"You say not to worry, but what is that giant over there?" Brax pointed to a large mass of brown and white spotted shell moving in between two giant clusters of urchins.

"Dear Helena!" Amok's hands tightened on the wheel, making dread stir in Nathaniel's gut. "I thought I'd never see one in my lifetime."

"What is the foul thing?" Brax drew his sword.

"An urchin herder. The beast picks the spines clean." Amok turned the ship, but Nathaniel feared it wasn't soon enough. The shell turned, curvy ridges spiraling up as long, spidery legs climbed over the spines toward their direction. Amok's face turned white. "Best wake up the girl. We'll need her harp."

Fierce determination shone in Brax's dark gaze. He raised a hand, stopping Nathaniel. "Leave her be. She's safer in the cabin."

He was right. Did Nathaniel want to sacrifice her for her music? A little voice told him she could take care of herself. But, he wasn't going to take the risk he was wrong. She was too valuable, too precious. He drew his own sword, adrenaline coursing through his limbs. "Then let us battle it together."

The spidery legs picked through the spines with elegance, as if they'd danced around them for eons. The shell turned, revealing the opening where four large, red claws sprouted. Antennae unfurled, sweeping the air around them. Atop the red carapace sat two black orbs.

"Reminds me of the lobster I had for dinner." Brax spat on the ground. "This will be an easy kill."

Nathaniel wasn't so sure. Those claws could cut through steel. He'd cracked enough lobster carapaces in his life to know how hard that shell was.

The beast clicked its claws with a snapping sound and climbed toward them. Amok steered away, hand over hand on the wheel. The ship tilted, and Nathaniel grabbed the railing to stay upright. They turned around a giant urchin as a wave boosted them upright.

"Ha, ha, ha!" Amok laughed as if crazed. "The Manta's Tail can outsteer the best of 'um."

Urchin spines pricked the air above their heads as Amok steered through a narrow path. The spines scraped the sides, and Nathaniel jumped back as their pricks rose above the railing. If Amok wasn't careful, one of them would slice a mast.

The creature followed, scurrying over the spines faster than Amok could avoid them. Brax paced back and forth along the prow, ready to fight.

"Helena's grave!" Amok cursed as the ship caught on a cluster of spines. He turned the rudder, but it was no use. They were stuck. He glanced at Nathaniel apologetically. "Only the gods can save us now."

"The gods, or my sword." Brax lunged forward as the creature's leg stuck a hole in the deck, crashing through the lower levels. Thank Helena Valoria's quarters were on the other side.

Brax swung, and his sword clanged on the beast's leg without a nick. Another leg came down on him, and he deflected it with a single blow. "Find the weak spot!"

Nathaniel glanced up at the mass of legs, claws, and carapace. Everything was hard shell. Another leg splintered the deck beside him. He swung at it, and his sword banged right off the casing. He had no idea how to defeat this foe.

Brax swung at each leg as it tried to step forward. "Keep it back!"

The boat tilted backward as the weight of the beast pulled them down into the sea. Nathaniel slid forward. He could not meet Helena and Horred. Not this day. Nor could Brax. Without its prince, Ebonvale would surely fall.

* * * *

Valoria woke slowly. Clumps of lavender dangled from the ceiling above her face. They tilted in a strange way, as if the boat had pitched skyward to the heavens. Voices rose on the wind. The sound of splitting wood echoed through the ship's belly.

She shot up, and reached over the bed for her harp. Nothing.

Had someone stolen it? She was on a ship with only three other people. That was nonsense. She scanned the room. All of her things had piled on the far wall. The instrument lay with a heap of clothes. It must have slid across the room. Her bed scraped the floor, slowly skidding forward as well.

Lyric's lyre! Was no one steering the boat?

She jumped out of bed in her nightdress, picked up her harp and burst through her door. The floor pitched up, and she had to climb forward on her hands and knees toward the stairs leading above deck.

She emerged from the belly of the ship. A gust of fresh hair blew her hair back. A field of spiny pricks surrounded the boat. Nathaniel and Brax shouted from behind her. She turned to the stern and fell back with shock.

A crab the size of a mountain towered over the ship, swiping its claws at Brax and Nathaniel. They danced with their swords, struggling to keep their ground. Amok cursed as he climbed the masts with a large knife between his teeth. Meanwhile, the weight of the beast's legs pulled them into the sea.

Her fingers shook as she plucked a sour chord on her harp. She had no song for utter chaos such as this. Perhaps a minstrel army could hum deep enough to soothe the beast or scare it away, but a single woman? She could barely stand up right, never mind sing loud enough to get its attention.

A leg swiped at Brax, and he ducked, rolling away on his back. The appendage came toward Nathaniel, and he fell back as a sharp claw clacked inches from his face. He was positioning himself in front of Brax, and knowing him, he'd sacrifice himself to save the heir to the throne. If she didn't do something, she'd lose them both.

Valoria breathed deeply. Echo would have to forgive her. She'd have to break the minstrel's code yet again and expose herself to the necromancer's influence by using her ability. She needed the power of the sea.

Pushing her fear aside, she closed her eyes and delved into the deep, dark place within her, that place where the necromancer had left a black spot on her soul. Fear, isolation, and death waited for her there, yet she drew herself in toward it, on the brink of evil.

The necromancer's presence jolted through her. He probed her mind and traveled in her veins through her body.

"Where are you, Princess?"

She fought him, blanking her thoughts so she didn't give him any hint of their plan. Dark judgments lurked in the abyss. Her mother's death was her fault. If only she'd stayed behind that day instead of choosing her father, she could have saved her. Remorse suffocated her.

The darkness delved deeper, finding every one of her sins. She lusted after a man who was not her betrothed. With her recklessness, she could bring down both kingdoms. How could she be so selfish?

"Because everyone is selfish. Embrace your natural tendencies." The necromancer whispered to her. It was as if he spoke right behind her into her ear.

"No." Valoria shivered and fought against the darkness. She had a good soul. She would save the kingdoms, not destroy them. She drew the black power emanating from the abyss. It filled her with exaltation and determination.

She opened her eyes and summoned the sea.

The waves rose up behind the creature, pulling the water away from the boat. The creature scrambled against the tide, its legs digging into the sandy bottom. She pulled harder, churning up the sea until debris from the rocky bottom sifted to the surface.

"Yes, let the power overtake you." Pleasure filled his voice.

Valoria coughed and dropped her harp. It clanged on the slick deck and started sliding toward the sea. The power rode through her, and she cowered against its force. All she could think about was the darkness, the evil, and how it obliterated the pain.

She fell to her knees. Her harp had slid toward the edge of the boat. The golden strings caught the glint of the sun, and she remembered Echo teaching her the first note on a sunny day in the courtyard under the apple tree.

A minstrel values their music above everything else. He brought her finger to the harp. *This instrument will define you, challenge you, and make you more than you can ever dream to be.*

She was a minstrel, a harpist, and her music made her whole, not this dark evil. Valoria crawled to her harp. Her fingers dangled just out of reach of the crown. She had to overcome the necromancer's hold on her if she was to save it.

"It is you who should answer to me." Valoria spat. "You abandoned your people. Remember what you had before the darkness. What instrument did you play?"

The necromancer's thoughts poured into her mind. Long, strong fingers strummed a beautiful lute with painted leaves. A cottage by the House of Song sat along the familiar cobblestone road. Flower boxes held daises and herbs. An older woman sang as she washed the dishes in the window. An older man chopped wood in rhythm by the garden.

Regret, anger, and remorse cut through the beautiful images like a knife through a painting. Two figures approached on a winded horse. A young man jumped from the horse and helped a woman cloaked in veils. They approached the house, but the older couple shunned them. More minstrels came from their houses and shouted, tossing old vegetables and rocks.

They ran back to the horse, but the animal bucked and fell on its knees. The couple left it on the road and stumbled away on foot. A rock hit the younger woman in the head. She fell, her veils blowing away from her face in the wind.

Valoria gasped as everything made sense. She'd seen that face.

The young man did not save her. Guilt and shame overcame him until he could not bear to look at her face. He was not strong enough to endure their love. With one backward glance, he disappeared in the woods.

The power lost its hold on her and Valoria sucked in air in reprieve as if she'd held her breath for too long. She stumbled forward and grasped her harp before it fell into the sea. Stars blossomed as a dizzying spell came over her. She closed her eyes, holding her harp to her chest.

* * * *

Nathaniel clutched a gash in his right arm. If he lost too much blood, he'd be of no use to Brax. Two claws came toward him as he hacked his way across the stern. He could only fend off one. Nathaniel chose the larger one and lunged. He missed, and he braced himself for the second claw to snap him in half.

Both claws snapped over his head. Had the creature lost its aim? The creature fell back as if it had lost its footing in the sea.

Now was the time to act if they were to defeat it.

"The eye!" He shouted to Brax. "You go for the eye and I'll distract it."

Brax nodded and wiped blood from his brow. Nathaniel didn't know where the blood had come from, but he hoped it wasn't as bad as his own wound. He lunged forward, throwing himself onto the part of the deck that the creature's legs had splintered. The creature swiped its claw at Brax, forcing him to retreat. Brax jumped over the claw and landed farther back. The creature stepped forward once again, as if it had regained its footing.

If he didn't do something bold, they'd lose their chance.

Nathaniel ran at the creature and leaped, clutching its smaller claw. The shell was hard and pockmarked with sharp barnacles and irregular bumps. The rancid smell of fish and seaweed wafted up. Using his good arm, he swung his blade straight down. The tip cracked through the shell to the fleshy part.

The creature swung the claw to strike him, and Nathaniel's grip on the shell slipped. He held onto the hilt of his sword, straining his good arm as his legs dangled over a spiny clump just underneath the water.

Brax used the distraction to jump onto another claw. As the claw rose over the creature's head, he dropped with his sword in hand. As he fell, he brought up his claymore and stabbed the eye. The creature jerked back, and every leg curled into the shell.

Nathaniel's fingers slipped from the hilt. As he fell, he prayed to Helena and Horred his death would be quick and not painful. He hit the icy water and released his last breath.

Chapter 24

Lost Soul

Nathaniel awoke to sharp pain in his arm. Bright sunlight blinded him. He tried to move. Every limb was weighted down as if with stones. Was he dead?

"There's a good lad." Amok's weathered face hung over him, the old man's hair tickling Nathaniel's forehead. He stank of ale.

"Is he awake?" Brax's bass voice echoed from the back of the room.

"Awake as he'll ever be." Amok pulled away, and Brax's angular face hovered over him.

His usual stoic expression softened into relief. "Helena graced you with a second chance. Amok spotted you from the top of the mast."

"Pulled you out of the sea like a turtle." Amok chuckled and took a swig from a flask. He offered some to Nathaniel.

Nathaniel ignored the offer, staring at his hands. His skin didn't look blue. "The urchins?"

Amok patted his shoulder. "Didn't prick a hair on your head."

He breathed with relief. Then, panic shot up his spine. "Valoria?"

"*Val* is recovering." Brax gave him a hard look.

Nathaniel didn't care about nicknames at a time like this. "Recovering? Was she harmed?"

Worry, or was it disapproval, tinged the corners of Brax's mouth. "We found her lying unconscious on the deck, holding her harp."

"Holding her harp?" Nathaniel's chest tightened. She must have been using that black magic again to help them win the battle. But what had she given up in exchange? He pulled his head up. "I have to see her."

Amok gave him a stern glace. "You have to rest. Axel has been tending to her."

Axel. Right. Nathaniel dropped his head back on the pillow. Who was he to demand to see her? If he wasn't careful, he'd start to look suspicious.

"She is well." Brax lifted his sword from the seat. He'd cleaned it since the attack and the metal shone in the sunlight from the cabin's window. "I'll be on deck standing lookout if you need me."

Nathaniel nodded. Had Brax thought him too protective of Valoria? Or perhaps his obtuseness worked in Nathaniel's favor, at least this time. He'd have to be more careful. He'd promised King Thoridian to support Brax, not stand in his way, and he reminded himself of the promise each day.

"Did you see Axel harm that beast? Your friend's quite the warrior for an average street merchant." Amok's eyes twinkled as if he knew more than he should.

A street merchant? Is that what Brax had told the old man? Nathaniel tightened his mouth to keep from smiling. "He likes to practice with his sword."

"I'll say. For hours every day. I've caught him up before sunrise swinging that blade like it was a twig. Reckon it pays off when an urchin herder attacks your ship."

Nathaniel sighed. No one sees the person distracting the beast, only the one who slays it. But that was his place, to stand in Brax's shadow. He knew it well.

"I'd be careful if I were you." Amok took another swig from his flask.

"Why?" Nathaniel propped his pillow up so he could get a better look at the old man.

Amok wiggled a knobby, wrinkled finger at him. "Blanca's no fool. You so much as lay your eyes on another woman, and she'll hit you over the head with a shovel."

Helena's sword! Would he have to live with her kiss on his conscience forever? Nathaniel rubbed his eyes. "I'll try to remember that."

"You break that girl's heart and you'll have to answer to me." Amok narrowed his eyes. He stood, pushed his chair against the wall, and left the room.

Fantastic. Now he'd have to disappoint Amok as well. He might as well marry Blanca and make everyone happy.

But would Valoria be content with that? A little voice told him she would not.

* * * *

Valoria sipped the herbal mixture from Brax's flask. She'd almost opened up to him and told him about the necromancer's identity. But to speak of her connection to that evil would mean telling him the truth about everything—risking herself to save them, using black magic. Somehow, even though he'd demonstrated forgiveness with Ardent, she didn't think he'd understand her situation. He might not even believe her in the first place.

A knock sounded at her door. Now might be the chance she was waiting for. Valoria took a deep breath and prepared herself for judgment. "Come in."

The sight of Nathaniel brought a dose of relief mixed with reticence to speak with him. Since seeing him with Blanca, she did not want to interfere. She'd thought he might have felt something for her, but she'd been wrong. It was fortunate she hadn't explored her own feelings. She could have brought down both kingdoms for no reason.

"How are you feeling?" He stood by the door. His arm had been bandaged and an ugly red spot had blossomed under the white cloth.

"I'm well enough." She pulled the blankets up around her as if using them as a defense. "How's your arm?"

"It aches, but it will heal. Amok said I was lucky. The claw could have sliced the entire arm off."

She cringed, thinking of him with only one arm. "Who knew our captain was a healer as well?"

"He's a man of many talents." Nathaniel stepped forward. "May I sit down?"

She hesitated. What was the point of carrying on with their lengthy conversations? She would be with Brax soon, and he with Blanca. "I am very tired."

Nathaniel did not move. His face turned solemn, almost stern. "I know you used black magic again."

She glanced at the hallway behind him. Keeping secrecy was something he had to work on. Her tone turned annoyed and insistent. "Very well, close the door and sit down."

Nathaniel closed the door and took a seat beside her bed. There was no judgment in his face, only concern. He had such a pleasing face, it was hard not to want to caress it. "Did the necromancer find you?"

"He did." Valoria shivered. "But, I pushed him away."

Surprise lit his sharp features, making him all the more gorgeous. "How did you do it?"

Valoria tightened her fingers into a fist. She would have to limit their time together. He grew on her each minute until she couldn't get him off her mind. "I found out who he is…or was."

Aurbie Dionne

"Who is he?"

Valoria pursed her lips. Should she drudge up the past? What's done was done. What meaning could it have now? It would only explain the darkness in the man's soul. Not that she condoned it.

"You have to tell someone." Nathaniel pleaded with her. "Even if it's not me."

Tears threatened in the corners of her eyes. She wanted it to be him so badly. She wanted him to be the one she told everything, the one she spent all her time with, the one... "He is Sybil's lost minstrel love."

He gasped and covered his mouth with his hand. "How do you know?"

"I saw his memories. I watched as he returned to the House of Song with Sybil on his horse. The minstrels shunned him. They couldn't accept him stealing Sybil from the King of Ebonvale. I felt his anger, his remorse, and his shame."

Nathaniel reached out and took her hand. His touch was warm and insistent. "That must have been horrible."

"It was." She sniffed. She wasn't the minstrel. She hadn't made such an indiscretion. "I'd rather die than be unwelcome in the House of Song."

"You will always be welcome there, and in Ebonvale." His eyes were so kind, they almost made her forget all obstacles between them.

She had to remember her father's wishes and her promise to the queen. And Brax. "If I do what is expected of me, yes."

Nathaniel took his hand away and set it in his lap.

This was the impasse they'd come to all along. Why did he have to keep pushing the boundary and making her wish her life was different? Didn't he already have his own love?

Valoria glanced away at the waves lapping around the boat. At least they were free of the urchins. "I am tired. Leave me be."

Nathaniel's face turned solemn. "You must tell Sybil when we return to the castle."

That weak waif of a woman? She was already halfway to being a ghost. "It would kill her."

Nathaniel stood and pushed the chair back. "She would want to know. Besides, she might have a way to defeat him."

"Would she act against her one true love?"

"If he placed Ebonvale in danger, she would."

Chapter 25

Lady Love

Nathaniel leaned against the railing, staring into the horizon. It had been two days since the Sea of Urchins, and nothing had changed. The horizon lay bare, the waves lapped in an endless tide, Valoria avoided him, and Brax was as irritable as ever. Ebonvale would crumble and fall, and the dead would plague the ends of the continent before they even returned to shore.

"You trust this man to reach the Sapphire Isles?" the warrior grumbled beside him as he shaved his head with his dagger and some soap.

"He's brought us this far."

Brax used the tip of his dagger to point at a new scar above his left ear. "Right into the mouth of a giant beast."

"We brought him there. You forget, not many would sail us through the Sea of Urchins. Half his ship is torn to shreds." Amok had been drinking from that flask frequently these past few days, but Nathaniel couldn't blame him. The attack had frayed all their nerves.

Brax shrugged as if it were nothing. "I've already told him we'll pay the damages once he delivers us safely to the Isles and home."

His brother didn't understand sentimentality. A ship was an object that could be replaced, much like a town could be rebuilt. He didn't understand the melancholy feeling of losing something so close to you, you lost part of yourself with it.

"Do you miss your father?"

Brax stopped in mid shave and gazed out at the sea. It took him a moment to answer, yet his face remained plain. "He fought bravely and died with honor. I am proud to be his son."

"That is all true beyond a doubt. But do you miss him?"

Brax continued to shave. "That is the difference between us. You allow
your thoughts to wander where they make you weak. I might miss him
if I allowed myself to dwell on his absence. Instead, I think of the great
deeds he has accomplished and it motivates me to pick up my sword and
follow in his footsteps."

It was wise advice, but Nathaniel could not take it. To disregard his
own feelings would be to tell himself a lie. No, he relished sentiment. It
was what made him human. It gave him compassion for others. He took
those feelings head on. Brax might call him foolish, but in his own way,
he considered facing the darkest part of his emotions brave.

"Ahoy! Land ho!" Amok called from the bow.

Nathaniel turned, hope rising inside him. A speck of land so green it
could have been carved from emerald rose above the sea. He ran to the
bow, leaving Brax to finish shaving. Two more specks materialized on the
horizon, and the sea shone scintillating blue around them.

"The Sapphire Isles." Valoria spoke with awe beside him, making
Nathaniel step back in surprise. She hadn't left her room since the attack.

Her hair blew across her face in streaks of auburn as she approached
the railing. She still wore her nightgown, and it blew against her body,
showing her curves in the wind.

Nathaniel looked away, stifling the urge to hold her against him. "How
do you know it's the right place?"

"The water. 'Tis so blue it bests the sky on a clear summer day."

"'Tis beautiful." But, truly he didn't speak of the water.

"And dangerous." She placed both hands on the railing. Her knuckles
were white. "No algae grows in these parts. No fish swim, or seaweed
floats. The mermaids eat everything in sight. They wipe the sea clean."

Nathaniel imagined a sparkling, empty sea as a chill settled in his
shoulders. "You did not speak of this before when you told us of this
quest."

She turned to him, her silver eyes vulnerable and wide. "Would you
have still come?"

"Yes." He didn't take a second to think about it.

"Ahem." Amok approached them and glanced at Valoria's nightgown.
"Best dress in your battle gear, you might need it."

Valoria nodded. "How far will you take us in?"

Amok shivered and brought his hands around his shoulders. "Not far,
lass. The mermaids prey upon men who don't have a lady whom they
love. They find empty hearts the easiest to trick. I'd be a goner."

"You've never had someone?" Valoria's tone turned wistful.

"Me?" Amok wrinkled his bulbous nose. "I had a girl I liked a long time ago. Got this to impress her." He pointed to the tattoo on his neck. "You see, she liked this tough lad with ink all the way up both arms, pictures of creatures much like the one we met a few days ago. Anyway, turns out she didn't like my tattoo, and I was stuck with the ugly thing." He wiped at his neck. "Taught me you can't change yourself for love. If it's true love, you won't need a tattoo."

Nathaniel studied the old man, impressed by the wisdom of his words. He was off the mark with many things, but on this occasion, he spoke the truth.

Amok turned to Nathaniel. "Concerning those mermaids, you won't have anything to worry about, now will ya?" The old man elbowed him in the side.

Nathaniel stepped away, disgusted. Just because Blanca kissed him didn't mean he was in love. But, he nodded all the same, avoiding Valoria's gaze. "I'll be fine." He didn't mention the true reason.

Amok gestured toward Brax as the warrior ran his hand over his freshly shaved head. "What about your friend, does he have a love?"

Worry crawled into Nathaniel's heart. But, he couldn't speak of his doubts in front of the princess. To say Brax didn't love her would be underhanded. "I cannot speak for him, but he should."

Amok pointed his gnarled finger. "Make sure he does. If he goes out there with a free heart, then he's nothing but bait."

Brax caught them all looking at him and stood. He wiped the soap off his dagger and returned it to the sheath on his belt as he approached them. "What is this matter of which you speak?"

"True love." Valoria approached him with stoic determination. She set both hands on her hips. "If you do not have it, then the mermaids will capture your heart for themselves and eat it raw."

Brax didn't flinch. He crossed his arms with a bored look on his face, as if they told children's stories to scare each other at night. "They will not get the better of me."

"Very well." Amok moved to the side of the ship where a small boat lay underneath a tarp. "Get your things. You should move in while the day is new and the sun shines bright."

"Do they attack at night?" Nathaniel squinted into the water, but he couldn't see anything moving underneath the sparkling surface.

Amok handed him a paddle and rolled his eyes warily. "They attack every minute of every day."

* * * *

For her sake and his, and that of the quest, Valoria hoped Brax loved her. He certainly wasn't as annoyed by her as he'd been when he first met her. She'd like to think she'd earned a small degree of his respect. But love?

There was only one way for her to learn the truth.

Amok lowered them to the water in the small boat. Brax and Nathaniel held paddles, and she held her harp. She remembered the songs she'd learned as a child. "They are weak out of water, and they have no true power over humans. 'Tis all an illusion. In reality, they are mere fish in the sea." She said it to comfort herself as much as inform the two men.

A cool layer of mist hung above the water, making it difficult to see anything farther than a few feet away. Valoria pulled her cloak tighter around her. This was the place they'd traveled miles to reach, yet reaching it sent shivers across her arms and legs.

"Did you bring the pearls?" Brax's muscles bunched as he began to paddle.

Nathaniel tapped the upper pocket in his vest. "I've kept them safe."

"Let me see them." Valoria held out her hand. If anything, it would keep her mind off the fact they were paddling through mermaid territory.

Nathaniel dug into his pocket and pulled out a crimson velvet bag tied with gold cord. He upended the bag over her hand and five violet orbs shone in the sunlight. They were heavier and silkier than she thought.

"What makes you think these mermaids will trade their most precious commodity for a piece of jewelry?" Brax huffed as he paddled.

Valoria resisted the urge to glare at him. Sometimes, the brute was too logical for his own good. "The tales say these are precious stones of wisdom passed down through the generations. It is said King Pradarian, the great grandfather of King Artemus, tricked the mermaids with a deceptive peace treaty and stole them."

Brax snorted. "Ha! No King of Ebonvale would behave in such a manner."

"That is why the song is not sung in Ebonvale." She raised an eyebrow, challenging him.

Brax stopped paddling. "Are you accusing my bloodline of being thieves?"

Valoria straightened in her seat. "I am."

Nathaniel raised his hand. "Hold on. Stories can be twisted over time." He gave Valoria a knowing look. He believed her. She could feel it.

She wasn't going to surrender so easily, though. "We'll see when we meet them, won't we?"

"Shouldn't you be playing some music to keep them at bay?" Brax grumbled as he continued to paddle.

Valoria shook her head. He knew so little. "They are creatures of illusion and magic. Songs won't work on them."

"Then why did you bring your harp?" Brax curled the right corner of his mouth.

Valoria shifted uncomfortably. He'd pegged her with that one. "I feel safer with it."

Brax shook his head as if she'd disappointed him. "Two warriors around you, and a piece of wood with a few strings brings you peace of mind?"

Frustration built inside her. If he was any more insensitive, she'd climb off that boat and take her chances with the mermaids. Then, she noticed a small smile curve the corner of his lips. He was teasing her, almost flirting. Valoria raised an eyebrow. "Warrior skills will not help you in this place."

"No songs, no swords." Nathaniel rubbed his forehead. "We're doomed."

* * * *

The lush vegetation of the island hung over them as they approached. Vines hung from trees so tall they blocked the sun. Small black birds flew in a v shape overhead. Distant whoops of monkeys echoed from the hills. The waves that bore them closer crashed against steep ridges of rock. Their boat rocked in the turbulence.

"There is nowhere to cast anchor." Brax looked more annoyed than fearful.

"There won't be." Valoria stared in awe. "The island is only meant to lure ships close. No man has set foot in the jungle. 'Tis rumored there are underground channels that weave through the island where the mermaids take refuge during storms."

"Horred's grave!" Nathaniel jerked back from the edge of the boat.

"What is it?" Brax grumbled.

Unease crossed Nathaniel's face. "I thought I saw something."

Doubt clouded Valoria's mind, pulling her confidence apart. She gripped her harp to her chest and plucked a few strings to calm herself. They were here to save Ebonvale. They needed the blue fire and they had something decent to trade. But, she couldn't help but feel vulnerable and foolish, like a little girl who'd strayed too far from home.

"The mermaids can't touch you if you stay in the boat." She scanned the water. The crashing waves churned up pieces of shell and rock, and it was difficult to see what lay under the surface.

"There!" Brax pointed to the right by his side of the boat. "A tail like an eel."

"Over there!" Nathaniel pointed in the other direction. "A clump of kelp appeared and disappeared."

"Do not fall prey to their tricks." Valoria warned. She raised her voice. "Mermaids of the Sapphire Isles, we are here to trade."

The water bubbled around them. A pinkish fin slapped the surface. Webbed hands rose up, reaching up the sides of the boat.

"Valoria…" Nathaniel backed to the middle. "What do we do?"

She thought back to the songs. Was there a hierarchy among them? She shouted over the water. "We've come to see your leader."

When she turned back, Brax was leaning over the edge of the boat, staring at something in the water.

"Brax!" Valoria reached over and pulled on his arm. It was like trying to move a bull. "Nathaniel, help me."

"Helena's sword!" Nathaniel moved and grabbed Brax's other arm.

Brax's eyes glazed over, as if he saw beyond the water to a place he longed to go. She'd never seen him so melancholy, and it scared her more than the mermaids in the water. He muttered under his breath. "It cannot be."

Her fingernails dug into his skin. "Pull him back!"

"I'm trying." Nathaniel gritted his teeth and kicked against the side of the boat.

A face emerged from the depths below. Eyes black as ink with no pupils stared up at them as hair-like kelp lilted around cheeks frilled with gills. Blue lips opened to reveal uneven, pin shaped teeth.

"The creature is hideous." Nathaniel gasped with shock. "Brax, come to your senses."

"He doesn't see the mermaid. She's showing him what he wants to see." No matter how hard Valoria yanked, Brax leaned closer and closer to the surface.

The mermaid reached up with both webbed hands. Valoria's stomach lurched as Brax reached toward her. Their hands met, and in the blink of an eye, she pulled Brax under. Valoria fell forward with him, but Nathaniel caught her with both his arms around her waist. Brax's leather shirt slipped through Valoria's fingers. She fought wildly as Nathaniel pulled her back into the boat.

"No!" Shock and disbelief rattled her to the core. Another wave crashed, sending bubbles around their boat. When the water cleared, there was nothing there. "He's gone!"

She fought against Nathaniel, her whole body shaking. This was all her fault. She'd brought the rightful heir to the throne to his death. Desperation came over her as she reached over the boat. She'd have to go in after him.

"No, Valoria." Nathaniel pulled her back. With one arm he held her against him, and with the other, he ripped the velvet bag from his pocket. "Bring him back, or you'll never see your precious pearls of wisdom again."

"They don't want to trade." Tears stung Valoria's eyes as she crumpled into his chest. "I was wrong."

"I do not believe it." Nathaniel had such faith in his voice, it gave her a small thread of hope. He turned back to the waters around them. "Our companion for the pearls."

The water bubbled up again, and a mermaid crawled onto a rock a few feet away with quick and fluid movements reminding Valoria of an eel. She was smaller than the average person, her body thin and wiry like a starving child. Her skin shone a translucent white, her hair dark and slimy. She raised a webbed hand, and the water stilled around them. Even the waves eased.

"Your tricks do not work on me." Nathaniel shouted and drew his sword. "If you refuse, I'll slice a dozen mermaid heads off before they pull me under."

Valoria stared up at Nathaniel in awe. His strength at such a dire hour surprised her. She'd never seen him so fierce and determined.

"Why trade for that which is rightfully mine?" The mermaid spoke with a deep throaty voice, forming the words awkwardly in her toothy mouth. Her gills wheezed and dripped water down her chest. A starfish clung to her shoulder. Barnacles covered her body, opening their mouths to gulp the air.

Nathaniel pointed the end of his sword at her heart. "If he dies, your kingdom dies with him."

She clicked her tongue, and the water bubbled beneath her tattered fin. Three mermaids lifted Brax to the surface. His skin was pale, his chest unmoving. Small, red scratch marks drew across his forehead and right cheek.

Terror seized Valoria. She gripped the side of the boat, her hands trembling. Was Brax dead?

Nathaniel's face slackened, but he did not lose his ground. "Return him to us."

"Why so important?" The mermaid stroked Brax's jaw.

Valoria's chest tightened. Would Nathaniel dare to tell her the truth?

Nathaniel straightened and spoke as if she'd offended the gods themselves. "He is the future king of Ebonvale. He came to return what is rightfully yours in exchange for your aid."

A guttural sound came from her throat. "King of Ebonvale stole our pearls." Water dripped from her black lips. "Why help him?"

"Because if you do not, the sea will die. The undead will march on Ebonvale, and spread through the continent until nothing lives. Have you seen an undead?" He paused as the question sunk in. "They are relentless and they do not need to breath. They will march into your waters and turn your own people against you."

She swayed and her gills puffed. "This man can stop them?"

"With your blue fire, he can."

Her black eyes narrowed. "You offer us another treaty?"

"I offer you a chance to survive." Nathaniel's tone was even and calm as if he knew he had her beat.

Valoria tightened her grip on the boat, praying the mermaid believed him. She straightened and the mermaid's black eyes focused on her. "My people have made a treaty with Ebonvale for our protection as well. You hold my betrothed, the man who will unite Ebonvale with the minstrels of the House of Song. If you kill him, you have us to answer to as well. But if you allow him to live and give us what we need, you will make another ally."

The mermaid tilted her head up, scrutinizing her. She glanced at Valoria's harp, at the calluses on the tips of her fingers, and then her auburn hair. Did she look as hideous to the mermaid as the mermaid looked to her?

The mermaid raised a hand, and another mermaid leaned over Brax and covered his mouth with her own. When she lifted her head, Brax gasped in air. He coughed as water rose up from his lips.

Valoria breathed with relief. She could not dwell on the truth of the matter, that he'd fallen prey to the mermaids' advances, that he did not love her. She would deal with that knowledge later. For now, she had to settle for the fact he was alive.

Three mermaids carried Brax to the boat and dumped him over the side. Still coughing, he crawled to a sitting position as Valoria spread a blanket over his shoulders. His lips were blue. She touched him and gasped as her fingers turned to ice. It was as if his inner fire had burned out.

Nathaniel threw the velvet pouch into the water. It sunk into the depths. "And the blue fire?"

A webbed hand reached from the surface by the boat. The webbing unfurled to reveal a glass bottle stopped with a snail shell. Inside, a blue substance glimmered and swirled.

Valoria's heart quickened as Nathaniel leaned over the boat's edge and reached for the vial. She reminded herself he was not susceptible to the mermaids' spell. He had a love in his heart. Blanca. Now the truth was clear and it ate away at her insides like acid fire.

Nathaniel took the bottle and studied it in the light. "This is enough?"

"One drop will burn lake." The mermaid lowered herself waist deep in the water. Her tail undulated in the waves.

His eyes widened. "Why do you have something so powerful, it could be your demise?"

"We stole it from enemy." She'd slipped in up to her neck. Fins along her sides unfurled around her like wings.

"Thank you." Nathaniel bowed his head.

"Thank us by saving the world." She disappeared under the sea.

Chapter 26

Facing Truths

Valoria's arms burned as she paddled with Nathaniel back to Amok's ship. Brax huddled in the back under the blanket, his eyes staring at the horizon with a blank expression. He hadn't uttered a single word since they'd left the Sapphire Isles. Perhaps the mermaids had tricked them into bringing home a ghost.

"Will he recover?" Valoria whispered to Nathaniel, even though she doubted Brax would hear or care.

"He's had a tough blow." Concern crossed Nathaniel's warm eyes. "But he's stronger than anyone I've ever known." Nathaniel nodded to himself. "He'll come back. Give him time."

Give him time. The queen had asked her to promise as much. Valoria had given Brax time—days, weeks, almost a month. Hadn't she given him enough?

She knew the answer to that question. She had to give him as much time as he needed, whether it took days, months, or years. Or a lifetime. A rock fell in her stomach.

Valoria studied Nathaniel's perfect features. "You are fortunate to have such a love as to prevent the mermaids from reaching you." The words escaped her mouth before she'd had time to think upon them.

Nathaniel jerked as if startled. "Fortunate is not the word I would use."

Valoria snapped her head up in confusion. Who would curse love?

"Ahoy maties!" Amok shouted from the bow of The Manta's Tail. "Bring the boat about and I'll lift ye up."

They secured the boat to the moorings, and chains clinked as Amok turned the wheel and lifted them from the sea. Valoria wanted to pursue their conversation further, but Nathaniel turned away, watching the chains rise and fall around them.

Amok's wrinkled face peered over the railing. His eyes widened when he saw Brax. "Looks like someone had a fall."

Valoria cast him a glare that advised against further comments on the matter. Even though Brax had teased her and made her feel like the lowest form of princess in Ebonvale, she would not have someone treat him with disrespect.

Amok turned to Nathaniel. "Did you find what ye were looking for?"

Nathaniel nodded, providing no other explanation. "Help me take Axel to his room."

Amok positioned himself under one shoulder, while Nathaniel positioned himself under the other and they walked Brax across the deck and into the belly of the ship. Valoria followed them, wishing she could help more.

They dropped him onto his bed. Nathaniel retrieved a bowl of soup from the pantry as Amok went above deck to chart the course home.

Valoria pulled a chair next to his bed. "I'll stay with him."

Nathaniel nodded as if it was the more logical choice, handing her the bowl. "I'll be above deck making sure we don't run into any more mythological creatures."

She nodded and held a dampened cloth to Brax's forehead. If they did, they'd be in poor shape to fight with their boat falling apart and their best warrior down. Valoria wasn't even sure she had the energy to play her harp.

After Nathaniel left, she brought a spoonful of soup to Brax's lips. He ignored her, gazing out the window to the waves. She'd never seen this downcast side of him before, and she suspected he didn't show it often.

"You have to eat to regain your strength." She lifted the spoon again, but his lips wouldn't part.

"I thought it was real." His voice was soft and hoarse, as if he were waking from a long sleep.

"What?" She dropped the spoon. "You thought what was real?"

"In the water." His voice trailed off, his gaze still locked on the sea.

Here was a chance to glimpse his soul, to truly know him, yet he would not share himself. Valoria resisted the urge to push him. "It does not matter now. Have some soup."

He turned toward her, seeing her for the first time. "It does matter. I have failed you."

He had. She could not avoid the ugly truth. He did not love her. There was something in the water he wanted more, the key to his heart. She'd never have it. But, did he truly have the key to hers? He'd failed her as much as she'd failed him.

"Here." She dug in her cloak and brought out his flask. "You need this more than I."

Brax closed her fingers over the flask. "'Twas a gift. You must keep it."

"It does not belong to me." Nor did his heart.

"It will someday."

But would it, truly? She did not have the courage to ask. Instead, she set the flask on the bed beside him. "But not today." She pushed the soup closer to him. "Eat. You'll need your energy for the battle to come."

"I cannot eat until I have your forgiveness."

Had the mermaids shown him *her* heart, she'd be the one asking for forgiveness, not him. She gave him the spoon. "There is nothing to forgive."

* * * *

Nathaniel joined Amok at the wheel. Twilight spread across the horizon, and the first stars of the night peaked through the dull canopy. "How long until we reach shore?"

"The wind is in our favor." Amok winked. "With this northwesterly gale, I can skirt the Sea of Urchins and have you back in Shaletown in three days."

Three days. Nathaniel hadn't thought he'd be eager to return, but the quest had taken longer than anticipated, so he welcomed any way to speed their course.

Amok clucked his tongue. "You'll be seeing your sweetheart soon."

Nathaniel massaged his forehead. He still didn't know what he'd say to Blanca. Earlier in the boat, he'd said too much to Valoria when she'd spoken out about true love. How could he tell her *she* was the reason why the mermaids hadn't attacked him? It was impossible. But, how could he refuse Blanca after revealing there was a deep love in his heart?

It wasn't that Blanca was so unbearably dreadful or unsightly. She was a pleasant woman. But, he'd spent his whole life trying to forget about his past, and Blanca tied him right down to it. And he couldn't marry a girl who'd picked on him as a boy and pulled his hair. To her he'd always be that little rascal waiting outside the pastry shop for handouts.

What he wouldn't admit to himself was the real truth that ranked high above all others; Blanca wasn't Valoria. If he accepted that, he wouldn't be able to find anyone who would compare, and that thought made his chest ache.

"Know why I wasn't killed when the wyverns came to Shaletown?" Amok leaned over, narrowing his eyes against the horizon.

Nathaniel shrugged. It wasn't a subject he cared to talk about.

"I was in the sea, collecting conch shells for a local merchant who sold them at the market up north." Amok pursed his lips. "Saw them coming, I did. Like ribbons in the sky. First a few, and then a horde, flying right over my boat."

Nathaniel shifted uncomfortably. "What happened when you came to shore?"

"Everything was blackened ash. Not a soul in sight."

Nathaniel's stomach hollowed. The queen had found him in that pile of ash. "Did you have family in Shaletown?"

Amok shook his head. "I haven't had family in many years. But that didn't take away any of the heartache. I knew everyone in that village, watched the wee ones grow up and take on their own shops, like Blanca. The village was my family."

"And is it now?"

Amok shrugged. "I make do. They are all affable people. But, I miss the ones who came first, the ones who I had history with." He sighed. "'Tis not the same."

Nathaniel would have to make do with someone who was not Valoria. But, Amok was right, it would not be the same.

Chapter 27

Sharpened Blade

New Shaletown filled the morning light with tidy brick buildings and slate roofs. Valoria soaked in the familiar sight, eager to walk on land.

As Amok steered to their mooring, a young woman with a basket of chickens on her back sauntered across the dock. An older man smoked a pipe, and a young boy threw bread crumbs to the pigeons. It was hard to imagine such a horrible scene of tragedy had occurred so many years ago.

A woman in veils standing at the end of the dock caught her attention. Blanca. Had she been standing there every day waiting for Nathaniel's return? Valoria's stomach sickened, and this time it wasn't from the rock of the sea.

"There you are. Twice what we promised to cover the damage to your ship." Nathaniel handed Amok two bags of gold.

Amok shook his head in wonder. "I don't know how such a young man as you came about all this fortune, but I thank you all the same."

"We thank you for your silence on the matter." Nathaniel gave Amok a hard stare.

"Of course. Won't utter a word to a seagull." Amok pocketed the gold. "Glad to be of service."

Valoria approached the two men. When she caught Nathaniel's attention, she gestured toward the dock. "Someone's glad to see you."

He stiffened and his lips thinned into a firm line. "Wait for me a moment. There's something I need to attend to." With determination, he pushed by Amok and jumped onto the dock.

Amok clucked his tongue. "I'd look after my heart if I was her."

"Why do you say that?" Valoria's stomach was tied in knots. She tried not to watch, but she couldn't take her eyes off Nathaniel as he approached the innkeeper. She lowered her veil and reached out with her arms. Nathaniel stood apart, refusing to embrace her.

"There's something off about him. Something he's hiding."

Valoria turned back to the old man, studying his sharp blue eyes. Could he sense Nathaniel was hiding their true identities? Nathaniel hadn't been good at keeping secrets.

Blanca took a step back, covering her heart with her hand. She looked down, teetering as if she'd fall. Nathaniel did nothing to help her. He stood rigid as a dock mooring.

Valoria stepped forward and used her hand to shield her eyes from the sun. "What is he telling her?"

"What I suspected all this journey." Amok spit into the sea. "The lad's not taking her."

"Well, I'll be Lyric's teacher." A guilty wash of relief came over Valoria. She didn't like Blanca, but that shouldn't mean she shouldn't want her to be happy. And she did want her to be happy, just not with Nathaniel. Because he deserved someone who admired him for who he truly was, not because of his past. But who would that someone be? It couldn't possibly be her, even if she wanted it to.

Blanca dropped her arms by her sides and walked away, leaving Nathaniel standing alone. He waited a few heartbeats, then turned back to the boat. A calm, solemn expression stretched across his face.

But, he had a true love. The mermaids had sensed it. Valoria blinked in shock as he returned to the ship. Who had his heart?

"Better tend to your friend." Amok muttered under his breath.

At first Valoria thought he meant Nathaniel, but Brax had risen from below deck dressed in his traveling cloak and leather pants. Although he'd prepared for travel, his face was still pale and he moved with a slow hesitation, as if he didn't trust the deck to hold his feet.

Even though Valoria had a thousand questions to ask Nathaniel, she turned to Brax and met him at the railing. "Are you feeling better?"

"Well enough to travel," he grumbled, glancing at her with a cursory nod.

She moved to touch his arm and he swatted her back. "I can manage."

"I had no doubt of it." She pulled away as embarrassment and hurt burned in her neck and cheeks.

Nathaniel reached them as they walked the plank Amok had placed connecting the ship to the deck. "Blanca says a stable boy will bring our wagon. We can start our journey back."

"You do not want to say farewell?" Brax must have missed their recent exchange.

"I already have." Nathaniel's tone was curt and final.

Brax raised both eyebrows, but did not pursue the matter further.

"That you did." Amok wiped his dusty hands on his trousers.

Nathaniel clapped the man on the shoulder. "I did all I could, and I thank you for everything you've done for us. Watch over Blanca for me, watch over the town."

Amok nodded. "No need to ask."

By the time they reached the end of the dock, a small boy had pulled their wagon up with the horses well rested and fed. Nathaniel handed him a piece of silver and they climbed aboard, Brax in the back, and Nathaniel in the front. Valoria once again had to choose between them.

She climbed in the back where Brax had already begun sharpening his dagger, his favorite task. He glanced up and grumbled, "I wish to be alone."

Valoria ignored him and sat on the bench across from him. "Do you think Ardent's still here, working for that fisherman you set him up with?" Perhaps if she talked of what he'd done and not what he failed to do, he'd come around.

Brax shrugged. "Hard to tell."

"I bet Lyric's lyre he is." Valoria smiled and glanced around the wagon, imagining Ardent working on a fishing boat. "I bet he'll own his own boat someday, just like Amok."

"If you've come to talk of fantasies, then I'm not in the mood." Brax returned to sharpening his dagger.

She reached over and put her hand on his, stopping him. "Isn't it sharp enough?"

He gave her a warning look. Valoria did not take her hand back. What would he do? Stab her with the dagger? She knew him well enough to know he wouldn't hurt her, even if he didn't love her.

Brax pulled away, letting her hand fall, then returned to sharpening with a vengeance. "It will never be sharp enough for what's to come."

* * * *

Nathaniel whipped the reins, guiding the horses through streets that should have been familiar, but were not. His conversation with Blanca still weighed heavy on his shoulders, but it was something that had to be done. He couldn't marry her if he didn't love her. He owed her the truth, and the truth was what he'd given her.

Almost all of it.

He breathed deeply, taking in the briny sea scent and listened to the gulls cawing above him. He'd told Blanca he couldn't live in New Shaletown. She was brave where he was not. He had responsibilities elsewhere, and a life he'd made for himself that he could not turn his back on. All of it was true. But, what he didn't tell her was his heart belonged to someone else. The mermaids had only confirmed what he'd known ever since he saw Valoria's silver eyes.

If he could not have her for his own, then he'd lend his aid to her kingdom, fulfilling his promise to the late king. The path was so clear, yet to walk it took more strength and conviction then he'd ever known.

The leather parted behind him, and Valoria climbed out. She joined him on the bench. She'd braided her hair in a complex pattern down her back in tiny, amber rivulets. She'd tied a gold cord around the waist of her simple servant tunic, showing her tiny figure.

Nathaniel kept his eyes on the road, mostly. "How is Brax?"

"Grumpy as always." She crossed her arms over her chest and sulked. "I tried to cheer his spirits, but it's clear I have no effect on him."

Nathaniel shifted in his seat. She had an effect on *him*, that was certain. "He is a stranger to failure."

"Not one of us is perfect." Valoria plucked an idle note on her harp and the sound resonated like a bell. "The sooner he understands that, the better."

"He will always strive for perfection." Nathaniel turned the corner and the city gates loomed above them. The guards only inspected the people coming in, and the line of departing travelers only stretched to the first shop. They'd be in the countryside soon.

"Well, if I cannot bring him out of his gloom, maybe the raiders will." Valoria's hands tightened around her harp.

Nathaniel nodded, whipping the reins as the line moved through the gates. "He does thrive on battle."

Valoria suddenly looked small and vulnerable in the shadow of the gate. "Do you think they will attack us again?"

Nathaniel pursed his lips. The mermaids had bent to their cause once they were shown the alternative. He'd already seen how one raider could change. All they needed was a push in the right direction, and he had a few tricks up his sleeve. "I'm planning on it."

Chapter 28

Risky Venture

It didn't take long for the countryside to turn from green meadows to ash. The sun had disappeared behind the horizon, and twilight gave way to darkness. Nathaniel goaded the horses to increase their pace, searching for a decent place in the barren landscape to make camp.

Beside him, Valoria hummed and plucked her harp in a soothing rhythm. Her delicate fingers danced nimbly, deftly choosing strings to fulfill the tinkling melody. He never grew tired of hearing her play.

The leather moved behind them, and Brax poked his head through. "Why haven't we made camp?"

Valoria glared, but kept humming.

A current of anger rose inside Nathaniel. Brax was never one for polite conversation. "There hasn't been a decent place to rest."

Brax's eyes searched the gray twilight around them. "In this darkness, we could be riding into a trap and we wouldn't know it until it was too late."

"I'm well aware of that." Nathaniel gave Brax a stern glance. If the warrior hadn't sulked all day, perhaps he could have spotted something Nathaniel had missed. But, he wasn't about to start an argument in front of Valoria.

"There." Valoria pointed to a copse of bare trees with scraggly limbs reaching to the sky.

Brax stepped forward and leaned over Nathaniel's shoulder. "It will not cover the wagon completely."

Valoria's fingers swiped over the strings and the tune changed from calm to mysterious. "I'll sing the song of concealment and weave shadows through the branches."

Brax eyed her as if he didn't trust minstrel's music.

"'Tis our best choice." Nathaniel pulled the right side of the reins and the horses turned to the east.

Barren limbs scratched the sides of the wagon as they entered the dead grove. The horses balked, and Nathaniel spoke in soothing tones to calm them.

"Bluewood." Valoria studied the trunks. "Like in the Forest of Song."

"They're deadwood now." Brax reached up and snapped a branch with his fingers. He brought the end down and dug his nail into the dead bark.

Valoria gave him a tired, exasperated look. "Bluewood are more resilient than you think." She reached out her hand. "Give me the branch."

Brax hesitated. Nathaniel gave him a look of warning, and Brax handed her the branch.

Valoria dug her fingernail deep into the bark.

"It's dead. Nothing could survive the wyverns' fire," Brax grumbled.

Valoria frowned, picking at the bark. "Lyric's lyre!" She broke a fingernail and shook her hand, then stuck the finger in her mouth.

"We have to give the land more time to heal." Nathaniel didn't like seeing her disappointed. "Then, you'll see new growth."

"Stop!" Valoria stood, and she had to brace herself against Nathaniel to keep steady as he pulled on the reins and the wagon slowed.

She reached up and pulled on a branch over her head. The limb bent, but did not break. At the end, a tiny, white flower sprouted from the dead bark. It was so small it could have been a snowflake.

"Well, I'll be Horred's mother." Nathaniel marveled at the blossom, then he locked eyes with Valoria and smiled, joy radiating in the air between them. "They're coming back."

Brax also stood, but he didn't look at the blossom. He raised his hand and shushed them. "Someone is watching us."

Nathaniel jerked to attention. The dead branches reached all around him, pressing in. His hand moved to the hilt of his sword. "Which direction?"

"Northeast." Brax whispered. He sniffed the air. "There!" Brax leaped from the wagon to the ground.

Movement blurred between the trunks. Brax launched after it.

"Wait!" Nathaniel called out as he scrambled down from the bench. "I want him alive."

The sound of metal pulled from a sheath echoed through the woods as Brax disappeared in the shadows. Nathaniel bolted forward, branches scraping his skin. He pulled out his sword and hacked at the dead wood.

"Brax?"

Twigs snapped from the left. Nathaniel moved toward the sound. He didn't know what he feared more, Brax being captured or Brax killing the one person that could help them.

A figure barreled into him, sending them both rolling in the ash. Nathaniel struggled to keep his hand on the hilt of his sword as his elbow hit the ground. A small, wiry frame fought against him, pushing his face into the ground. He barely weighed anything, and his arm was thin as a chicken bone. Nathaniel kicked the figure off him. The wiry man scrambled away into the darkness.

Nathaniel jumped to his feet, running after him. This was no trained warrior. He was a boy like Ardent, struggling to survive.

Several feet away, a body hit the ground with a thud. Someone grunted, then Brax's bass voice echoed over the darkness. "'Tis over."

Nathaniel emerged into a clearing lit by the silver light of the half moon. Brax stood, pointing his sword at a young man's throat. Nathaniel blinked in disbelief. He'd seen that curly, red head of hair before. "Wait! Do not kill him."

Brax's sword lowered closer to the young man's neck. "This boy was part of a raider attack killing two of my men. We cannot keep him as a prisoner. He'll just slow us down and time grows thin."

"We need him." Nathaniel crouched next to the young man. He was one tough little guy to survive the sword wound and the swamp. Surprisingly, Nathaniel was relieved to see he was safe. "Do you work for Gibson?"

He spat in Nathaniel's face. "I've seen you before. Spoiled castle folk."

Nathaniel wiped his cheek on his sleeve. "If you will not help us, I cannot save you from his sword."

The young man's eyes shifted back and forth, as if he was trying to figure out a way of escape.

"There's no escape this time." Nathaniel leaned closer, risking another attack of spit. "What were you doing in this forest?"

Brax pushed the tip of the blade into the young man's neck and a spot of red blossomed. Nathaniel breathed deeply, restraining himself from pushing Brax's hand away. He had to trust him not to go too far.

"Spying." The young man strained his head back, away from the tip of the sword.

"For Gibson?" Nathaniel persisted. Brax pressed the tip of the sword in further. A ribbon of blood trickled down the young man's neck.

He nodded.

"Now we should kill him." Brax growled.

"No!" Nathaniel shouted. Brax had a few things to learn about negotiations. He turned back to the young man. "Take me to this Gibson."

"Have you gone mad?" Brax's voice held disbelief.

Had he? He'd grown tired of years of fighting, of dead men on both sides. Brax had stopped the raiders from reaching the castle, but did his tactics truly work? Or were they adding to the problem? Nathaniel turned back to Brax. "We need more allies on our side if we're going to win this battle against the undead."

Brax shook his sword. "And you think these vermin will help us? They refuse our aid."

"They will if we explain the situation. If we offer them pardons, like we did with Ardent."

"Pardon them?" Brax sounded as if Nathaniel proposed they hand them a seat on the throne. "And shall we free all of the thieves and murderers in the dungeon as well?"

Nathaniel shrugged. "We may have to give anyone with two hands a sword."

His urge to negotiate with the raiders came from more than the need for soldiers. This young man reminded him of his real brother, Pill, and every other country boy that had lived in these lands. These were his people. If the queen hadn't found Nathaniel in the ash that day, he would have become a raider himself. Watching Valoria argue on Ardent's behalf had stirred a sense of compassion inside him, and the sight of that white flower sparked hope. If the bluewoods came back, then so would the crops. Suddenly, everything became clear. "We must give them a reason to come back to Ebonvale, to farm this land."

Brax frowned, staring at the young man with such disgust, Nathaniel thought his cause was lost. "They are not to be trusted."

Nathaniel stood and placed a hand on Brax's shoulder. "You take Valoria back to the castle and use the blue fire on the swamps. I'm going back with this young man to meet Gibson."

Brax shook his head. Concern lit in his dark eyes. He did care for Nathaniel, even if they didn't see sword to sword. "This is foolishness. They'll kill you or offer you for ransom."

Nathaniel sighed. "Either I'm dead now, or when the necromancer knocks on our door. I'll take the chance they'll listen to what I have to say."

Brax's face softened, making Nathaniel realize how much he meant to the warrior. "I'm not giving you up to the enemy."

"You have no choice." Nathaniel faced him with a steady look. "I've followed you in every way since you became Commander of the Royal Guard. But, this time I will not back down."

Nathaniel turned back to the young man. "Will you take me to Gibson?"

The young man nodded and grinned. "Gibson will reward me for bringing such a prize."

Brax raised his sword off the young man's neck and turned to Nathaniel. "If I cannot convince you otherwise, then I will go with you."

Nathaniel raised a hand to stop him. "You are too valuable. They need you at the castle."

Brax shook his head. "They will only believe a pardon if it's from the prince's own mouth."

* * * *

Anxiety crawled up Valoria's spine as she marched with Brax and Nathaniel to the raider's main camp. As much as she wished to help them, this plan was far beyond anything she would have imagined. Time was already short, and they held the one thing that would save Ebonvale in their hands. If anything happened to them, the kingdom would surely fall.

Determination set in Nathaniel's jaw and conviction shone in his eyes. She had to believe in him. More allies meant a greater army, and who knew how many undead were swarming in the mountains of Sill?

Brax's shoulders were tense and his jaw taut. He didn't seem as taken with the plan, yet he strode with strong-willed steps. When he committed himself to a cause, he did it wholeheartedly. That much she admired in him.

Valoria gripped her harp with white knuckles, hoping she didn't have to use it. More and more her music entwined with the black magic, and she had a hard time separating the two. Her dreams had turned dark, and those black eyes followed her wherever she went.

The red-haired young man leading them moved sinuously in the darkness, as if he'd been hiding in shadows all his life. They climbed a nearby hill, then descended into a valley of dirty rainwater and muck. The half-moon shone in the distance like a beacon growing dim as they climbed down an incline to an old mine shaft.

"You do not mean to take us in there." Brax spoke with disbelief as he stopped at the opening to the mine. Chills crept over Valoria's spine as she stood at the mouth of darkness. Only death waited in there.

The young man smirked as he picked up a small torch in the corner and lit it by sparking two pieces of flint. "If you wish to meet Gibson, then you have to follow me."

Nathaniel nodded without hesitation, gesturing for them to follow. "Take us in."

A damp chill surrounded them as they entered. The torch cast flickering light on walls of rock and caked mud. Old rail tracks led into the depths. The young man brought them down a winding tunnel that grew narrower the farther they traveled.

Brax and Nathaniel had to lean over to fit through. Valoria touched the ceiling with her fingers, fearful it might cave in on her head. They passed another tunnel, then entered an open area where crumbled old mine carts heaped in a pile. Small pieces of coal littered the ground. A metallic scent hung in the air.

"You'll have to leave your weapons here." The red-haired young man commanded them as if he were king.

"I'd rather die on my own sword." Brax growled and lunged at the young man.

"Enough." Nathaniel raised his arm to hold Brax back. "Do as he says."

Valoria clutched her harp to her chest. "This is no weapon." She couldn't imagine leaving it in the dirt.

"We will leave our swords if you allow our companion to keep her harp." Nathaniel glanced at Valoria and winked.

The young man eyed Valoria and nodded. "Very well."

Valoria scoffed silently. Apparently, she didn't look threatening. How little these people knew of minstrels.

They approached a doorway guarded by two older men with ash smeared over their faces. The red-haired guide approached them and whispered in one of their ears. Valoria could hear every word. "Tell Gibson I got something good coming his way."

One of the men nodded and ran ahead. The other one sneered as they passed. The corridor was wider with lit torches on either side. They emerged in a cavern with a lake. Small huts made from clay nestled around the shore. Children scurried inside at the sight of them, and women with pale, dirty faces coughed and clutched babies to their chest.

Guilt panged in Valoria's gut. She'd expected a gang of thieves, and instead she saw families scrounging to survive. They must have escaped into the mines when the wyverns attacked and never come back out. To grow up in such darkness and suffering horrified her. Why hadn't Ebonvale reached out to its people?

Nathaniel and Brax gaped at the clay structures as they passed. Valoria followed them, wondering if they had the same thoughts. Would this change the way Brax ran the kingdom? Maybe so, *if* they escaped with their lives.

The young man brought them to a ridge of stone where two men stood guard. The mouth of another cave flickered with firelight. The skulls of cows, oxen, and sheep hung on the walls around the opening.

Drums sounded from within, and a stone-faced man with a swath of black hair streaked with gray and a short beard emerged from under a piece of bear's fur covering the opening. The guards around him bowed and retreated.

He glanced down at Valoria, Brax, and Nathaniel with suspicion and disgust in his cold, tired eyes. Guards filled the cavern around them, making Valoria's unease spike. Archers were stationed in ridges over their heads, and men with spears stood at every exit. If negotiations turned sour, there would be no easy escape.

Nathaniel stepped forward. "You are Gibson?"

He nodded curtly. "What's it to you?"

Nathaniel bowed his head. "I am Nathaniel Blueborough, adopted son of the queen and the late king. This is Braxten Thoridian, Prince and heir to the throne. Beside me stands Valoria of the House of Song, Princess and future Queen of Ebonvale. We have come to ask for your aid in return for a full pardon."

The middle-aged man laughed. He had two gold teeth and quite a few missing. "The prince of Ebonvale? Asking for our aid?"

Brax growled deep in his throat. Valoria tightened her fingers on her harp, waiting for the right time to strike a chord.

Nathaniel held his hand up, silencing Brax. "That's right." He held his ground. "We need your aid in making Ebonvale the glorious kingdom it was before the wyverns came."

Gibson leaned over, towering above them on his protected ridge. He smirked. "Why should we help you?"

Nathaniel's gaze held so much conviction, not even a thief could distrust him. "If you do not help us with the northern front, undead will break through the ramparts and spread into these lands."

Gibson waved his concerns off. "We'll stay underground. We survived the wyverns, and we can live through this."

"And who will you rob?" Valoria spoke up as anger got the better of her. "The undead have no gold. They do not eat nor drink. The land they cross is plagued with swamp and blight. Lest you board up that entrance and never come out again, they'll find their way down, and then there's no stopping them."

Unease crossed Gibson's face. He shifted from foot to foot as if deciding what to do. Then, he signaled the archers, and all around them, bows pulled taunt. "We'll ransom you all to the queen and have enough supplies to outlast the horde."

"Chickens!" Brax shouted. "You'll run out of food and die in this hole."

"But not this one." Gibson pointed to Nathaniel. "He'll suffer the same death as you paid my brother. Speared through the chest—you remember that, my prince? You dragged his body to the front line and chopped off his head."

The image of the head bouncing from the upturned bag flashed through Valoria's mind. She wished she'd closed her eyes, but she'd stared instead, watching those soulless eyes gaze right at her. Brax had said it was the leader of the rebels. Had Gibson taken his brother's place?

Brax growled. "He betrayed our people. He killed members of the Royal Guard."

Gibson pointed a finger at the prince. "Your father betrayed us, running off while the rest of the army holed up in that castle as the wyverns burnt every last meadow."

Brax shook his fist. "My father was fighting with the brunt of our army in Scalehaven, battling the wyverns at the source."

Shock registered in the faces of the guards and the onlookers surrounding them. Perhaps they hadn't been told the whole truth.

Gibson's eyes turned sinister and remote. There was no reasoning with him. "Just as you killed my brother, yours too will die."

As he brought down his hand to signal the archers, Valoria whipped out her harp and strummed the chord of power. Everyone fell to their knees, covering their ears. But the effect would only last a few seconds. She needed more than her minstrel music to save Nathaniel, and for him she'd call on the necromancer himself.

Valoria closed her eyes and reached to the brink of darkness residing within her. The evil welled up faster than before, as if it traveled through known channels. The necromancer's black holes for eyes stared back at her, and his voice resounded through her mind.

You cannot fight the power. You will always return for more.

The power flooded her veins, bringing an ever-burning fury along with it. She opened her eyes and cast the anger at Gibson. He fell to his knees, blood trickling from his nose and ears. Around them, every arrow fell in mid-flight, raining upon the lake and the crowd. People covered their heads, but the shafts broke in the air, littering the ground with harmless splinters.

"Valoria, no!" Nathaniel beseeched her. He turned to her with horror in his eyes.

Valoria couldn't stop the surging power. It consumed her, eating away at the person she once was. The darkness poured in, along with debilitating anger so strong, it boiled the blood in her veins.

Strong hands held her, but all she could see was soulless undead, their empty minds numbing her pain. Through them the fury was bearable, and the more bodies she could collect, the thinner the anger spread.

Call them. The necromancer beseeched. *Begin the spread of the horde.*

"Come back to me." The words came from another place, another world. Valoria felt strong arms holding her and smelled a familiar pine scent. A hand cupped the back of her head, holding her face against warm skin.

Nathaniel.

She opened her eyes, and the power faded as fast as it had come. Nathaniel held her against him, rocking her back and forth.

She wrapped her shaking arms around him. "You saved me."

"No, you saved me." Nathaniel laughed in relief, running a hand along her face. "I thought I'd lost you."

"You did." She shivered, remembering how cold and hopeless that dead world was. Every time she tapped into the power, the evil consumed more of her soul. If she employed it again, she'd lose herself forever.

She pulled away from Nathaniel and glanced around her. The crowd gaped, some of them making the sign of the sword across their chests.

Brax had climbed the ridge and was holding his sword to Gibson's neck. He shouted above the clamor. "This man has told you lies. My father, the late king of Ebonvale, traveled with two armies—the minstrel army from the House of Song and Ebonvale's Royal Guard—and defeated the wyvern brood where they hatched."

Brax paused, scanning the crowd to see who was listening. They'd all stayed to hear what he had to say, and they stood in silence at his command.

Brax sheathed his sword, leaving Gibson to cower beside him. "Another threat lurks on our northern border. A necromancer has raised an army of undead and will attack in less than a fortnight. If we do not have an army large enough to hold them off, the undead will break through and plague this entire land. You may be able to hide for a while, but you will have nothing on the surface to come home to if they succeed."

He paused again, surveying the crowd. Inner confidence shone through him, and Valoria saw the king rise inside him. Brax was becoming the person he was born to be. "Help me protect the border before the plague of the dead spreads beyond control. Help me make this kingdom what it should be. I will not force you, I only ask you to abandon this hole and follow me to the light. Stay here and hide if you will, or follow me into a brighter future."

Some people retreated to their clay huts. But a few members of the crowd nodded their heads. Others grunted with approval. Most of them stayed, even if it was to see who would follow him.

Brax raised his hand as if taking an oath. "As the prince of Ebonvale, and the future king, I will pardon every one of you who returns to the castle with me and helps me fight for our right to survive. Those of you on our side, come with me this day. Let the future begin now."

He jumped from the ridge and landed by Nathaniel and Valoria.

"Come with me." Brax moved forward, and the crowd parted before him.

"Can you walk?" Nathaniel helped Valoria rise to her feet.

Valoria nodded, and they fell in step behind Brax. Valoria glanced over her shoulder as they made their way through the ramshackle dwellings. One at a time, men and women filed in behind them. They held spears made with broken glass and small knives. Some of them looked like they were barely old enough to hold a weapon and others were too old to do any good. But they followed all the same, and in this battle every soul counted.

Chapter 29

Homecoming

Valoria watched the sun shine on the distant fields of grain surrounding Ebonvale as she sat next to Brax on the wagon bench. Behind them, their makeshift army marched. This kingdom was capable of such ugliness, and such beauty. She'd feared it at one time, but now she'd come to call it home.

Word spread quickly once they reached Ebonvale's farmlands. At first, farmers were concerned to see an army of raiders marching on Ebonvale, but when Brax revealed himself as the prince, they cheered and sent riders to alert the queen at the castle.

They treated them as heroes returning from battle. But, the real battle loomed.

"I want you to send word to the minstrels once we get back." Brax turned to Valoria. Nathaniel rested in the back of the wagon, so she'd decided to try once again to develop a rapport with the prince.

She raised an eyebrow. "I was hoping you'd ask."

Brax glanced at the horizon with a weary expression stretching across his broad forehead. "I was a fool to discard them so easily."

He had been. But, the eve of battle was not the time to point fingers. "No one had any idea of the challenge Ebonvale has to face."

"I thought I could succeed by myself." Brax sighed, whipping the reins as the horses slowed to chew long grass on the side of the road. "I was wrong."

She touched his arm. "It does not matter now."

He moved away from her touch. "It was not I who won the fight with the raiders. It was you. I could not have won this army without your aid."

A deep gratification came over her. She'd been waiting for him to acknowledge her fully. After she'd dropped the arrows and felled Gibson,

Brax had walked past her, leaving Nathaniel to haul her from the ground. Granted, he was busy reclaiming his people, but even one look of concern would have showed his gratitude.

"Ebonvale and the House of Song need each other."

Brax smiled sadly. "'Tis the universal truth neither house can reconcile."

"Until now." She reached toward him, and he pulled away again. Rejection stung in her cheeks as Valoria placed her hand in her lap. Perhaps he still hadn't come to terms with their union. Would he ever?

* * * *

Onlookers threw roses on the cobblestone at the horses' feet as their wagon rode the thoroughfare toward the castle. Nathaniel had woken and joined Valoria and Brax on the bench.

Despite the rising triumph inside his chest, a wave of melancholy came over him. Their journey was at an end. The three of them had accomplished so much together, and they might never be together again. Certainly, he'd have to distance himself from Valoria when they reached the castle, and that thought hurt the deepest of all.

The queen stood on the temple steps waiting to receive them. Brax jumped from the wagon and strode in confident steps to his mother. Nathaniel helped Valoria from the wagon and they followed Brax in step.

The queen opened her arms. "Helena and Horred smile down on us. You have come back to us unharmed."

"My queen." Brax bowed and presented the vial of blue fire. "We bring you the answer to our troubles."

The queen took the vial in her hands carefully and held it to the light. The shimmery liquid moved with purpose in the sunlight as if eager to escape the confines of the glass.

"And we bring you an army as well." Brax stood and gestured toward the ranks standing behind the wagon. "Our people have returned to us."

In response, the raiders cheered, and the onlookers took up the applause.

"You have accomplished the impossible, my son." She placed a hand on his shoulder.

"I did not do it alone. Nathaniel and the princess are just as deserving, if not more." Brax turned toward them.

Surprise hit Nathaniel like cold water. His brother had never acknowledged him in such a way before. He'd always taken a second seat to the acclaim and now Brax brought him before himself.

Brax clapped Nathaniel on the shoulder. "Come, let us feed and equip these new soldiers and assign them quarters in the barracks."

Eager to get started, Nathaniel nodded. He turned to Valoria to bid farewell, but she'd noticed her old music teacher in the crowd and ran to embrace him. Her servant joined them, and the three of them smiled and walked up the temple steps.

His time with her was over.

* * * *

Valoria glanced back in longing as she walked arm in arm with Echo. She'd forgotten to say farewell to Nathaniel. He marched with Brax, directing their new army to the training grounds. It was better this way, for him to travel his path and for her to travel hers. Yet, a bond had formed between them, and even though they parted, she felt the connection strong as ever, binding their souls in an unspoken truth.

"I will send word to the minstrels immediately." Echo climbed the steps beside her. "You have made me proud."

Valoria glanced away with guilt. He would not be proud of what she'd done to achieve success, But, such conversations had to wait until they were free of prying ears.

"I'll finally be rid of these impractical dresses." Cadence huffed as she picked up her skirts in her arms, climbing the steps. Now that the prince had returned, they needn't keep her secret any longer.

"I thought you were eager to have them?" Valoria raised an eyebrow.

Cadence rolled her eyes. "I was. But, after having a boy throw a rock at me, thinking I was you, and another servant girl with a hatred of minstrels spit in my food, I'd like to have my comfortable clothes back, thank you very much. I won't even go into detail about the country nobleman who wanted to steal me away for my alleged ties to the House of Song."

"Sounds as though you've had quite a time of playing princess." Valoria glanced down at her riding tunic and leggings. She'd miss the ease of walking and riding. And of talking to Nathaniel like they were friends. Somehow the large dresses separated her even more from him, like a barrier they couldn't cross.

"I'm happy you're back." Cadence smiled. "By the way, Brax seemed proud of you." She gave Valoria a sidelong wink.

Valoria nodded. "We have developed a sort of mutual respect." But that was all. If she looked for anything deeper, she'd be fooling herself.

"Mutual respect is a good start." Cadence reached the top of the steps and released her skirts in a flurry around her legs.

"I bid you farewell." Echo bowed to both of them. "I'm off to send a message to the House of Song. Is there anything in particular you'd like to say to your father?"

Valoria paused. Would he be proud of what she'd accomplished? She might have saved the kingdom, but she did not win Brax's heart. "Only that I continue to follow his wishes."

Echo nodded as if committing the words to memory. He patted her on the arm. "Get some rest."

"I will." Having Echo back at her side grounded her. He'd always been there for her, giving her pieces of advice in their music lessons. She'd make him her chief advisor when she became queen.

Cadence turned in the direction of their quarters, but Valoria didn't follow.

"You're not coming back with me?" Cadence frowned as if hurt. All this time they'd been apart, and she'd have to wait again.

Valoria gave her a sympathetic smile. She was a different person than the young lady who'd traveled in the carriage with her handmaid always at her side. "I have important business to attend to."

"In your servant's clothes?"

"This cannot wait."

"Very well." Cadence waved her hand. "Off with you. I'll be pressing your evening gown for the feast." She began walking down the corridor, then stopped and whirled around, narrowing her eyes. "I hope it's not with that lieutenant."

"No." Although Valoria wished it was. She kept a straight face. Cadence could never know her true feelings. "It's with the queen's mother."

"That madwoman?" Cadence lowered her voice. "I hear her from my window at night. She sings strange songs with spine-chilling cadences in a language I've never heard of. People say she speaks of the past as if it's the present, and the future as if it's the past. What could you possibly want with her?"

"'Tis a private matter." Valoria could say nothing more.

Cadence nodded, biting her lip and walked away.

Valoria watched Cadence leave, melancholy swelling inside her. Would they ever be as close as they once were? There was a time when she had no secrets, but now everything was so complicated, and her life full of responsibilities and allegiances. Playing princess meant walking a fine line.

Valoria climbed the steps to the tallest tower. Rumors said Sybil had chosen the remote location to stay away from the jeers and whispers. Although her daughter, the queen, had forgiven her for riding off with a minstrel lover and leaving her and the king of Ebonvale, the people of Ebonvale were not as merciful.

As Valoria learned from the vison, neither was the House of Song. Shame and guilt had pushed Sybil's minstrel lover to the dead lands. If both kingdoms had been more forgiving, would the undead army still be at their doorstep?

The steps wound around and around. Windows showed the castle growing smaller underneath them, and the people in the courtyard scurrying around like ants. She reached a small, triangular oak door at the top and knocked gently using a rusted silver ring.

"Come in." The old woman sounded sane enough.

Valoria pushed the door open. A room no bigger than a storage closet stretched in front of her. A small bed lay perched against a single window with a view of the western mountains. Old, tattered dresses hung from hooks on the wall, and a cracked mirror stood against a chest. Two sparrows bathed in her washbasin, shaking water onto the floor.

When Valoria entered, the sparrows fluttered out the open window. The old woman rose from a chair in the corner. She wore a simple white shift with bare legs and feet. Her thin, white hair hung long and unbraided around her shoulders. Hands with bones like a bird's placed a book with no cover on the floor.

Valoria wondered what thoughts were written on those pages.

Her one good eye shone bright green with surprise while the other one stared blindly under a milky white sheen. "My, the princess, come to visit me? Don't worry, they'll be back. Come in, come in. What can I help you with, my dear?"

Who would come back? Did she mean the birds? Valoria stood awkwardly in the doorway, not knowing where to sit or what to say. "I've come bringing news."

"You should tell the queen, my dear. She would benefit from any news." The old woman shuffled her bare feet across the floor. At first, Valoria thought she walked with no purpose. But, the old woman was more alert than others would think. She reached beside the bed and unfolded a chair. "Sit, please."

Valoria sat in the unfolded chair while Sybil sat across from her. "This news doesn't concern her directly."

Her bright eye blinked. Age spots covered every inch of her face, but Valoria could see she'd been quite beautiful with delicate, foxlike features and fine-boned cheeks. "It cannot possibly concern me."

"It does."

The old woman started as if Valoria was the madwoman. "Nothing has concerned me for fifty years."

"This news is more than fifty years in the making, my lady."

"Call me Sybil. That's what my father calls me. He's coming to see me soon." She folded her hands in her lap like a schoolgirl.

Her father? It could not possibly be true. He'd be long in the grave by now. Doubt clouded Valoria's determination. Why cause this old woman more pain?

Nathaniel's insistence came back to her. *She has a right to know.*

"Sybil, do you remember visiting the House of Song?"

"The House of Song." Her hand touched the side of her face where a crescent scar decorated her cheek. It was the same place the rock had hit her. "That's where you're from, my dear? Is it not?"

"Yes, but did you ever go there?"

Her lips trembled. "I didn't stay long. Not long enough to hear the music. The minstrels were unhappy. Told us we had no right to come. That we'd start a war. I wanted to hear the music, but I didn't stay long." Her face broke into a sorrowful, fearful expression.

Valoria reached over and held her hand. Should she bring up more pain? The sudden urge to change the subject overwhelmed her. There were so many other subjects to talk about. Why not ask about her birds?

The kingdom might need the answers hiding in her memory. Valoria breathed deeply. "Do you remember who you were with?"

She nodded and wiped her good eye. "He didn't save me."

"I know." Valoria squeezed her hand. "He left you in the forest while the minstrels threw rocks."

"I thought he loved me."

As unpleasant as they were, Valoria thought back to the necromancer's memories. "He did. But he wasn't strong enough to bear the humiliation. He's regretted leaving you all this time."

Sybil eyed her with a look of suspicion. "How would you know of this? Have you found him?"

Valoria paused, not knowing how to tell her the man she'd loved had become a monster. "In a way, yes, I know where he is."

Sybil's face filled with hope. "For many years I did not want anything to do with him, but now that I'm old and time has healed my resentment, all I have left are my memories." She grabbed Valoria's hand. "Will he see me?"

Valoria swallowed hard. "Seeing you might be the only way to save him. That's if you're willing to try."

"Why? Has he followed a dark path?"

"Darker than the blackest, starless night."

Sybil covered her mouth with her hand. "What has he done?"

"He's raised an army against us."

Sybil gasped as if it were her last breath, and her face contorted in pain. "The necromancer. No, tell me 'tis not him."

Valoria's heart broke apart. Regret, guilt, and shame piled on top of her. Whether it was because she'd inhabited the necromancer's mind, or because she felt a connection to the old woman, Sybil's pain was her own.

A single tear formed in the corner of her eye and ran down her face. It was enough to show Sybil she spoke the truth.

Chapter 30

Horizon's Secret

Nathaniel surveyed a young man as he swung a gleaming sword in an arc above his head. "Remember, it's heavier than the weapon you are used to. It will take more time to reach its target, but the blow will be devastating."

"This armor feels like rocks are in my boots." He wiped sweat from his brow.

"But it will protect you from the undeads' teeth." Nathaniel tapped on the arm plate. "One bite and you're a goner."

"They're saying we're all goners." He swung again, this time hitting the scarecrow in the chest. Hay cracked and fell on the ground.

"That's it!" Nathaniel clapped his shoulder. "With an arm like that, the undead are the goners." Despite his encouragement, unease crossed his mind. These people were trained as thieves, not warriors. They didn't even know how to properly wear armor. Some of them had never held a real sword in their hands.

"They're goners to begin with." The boy laughed and hacked again.

At least they had spirit. Nathaniel smiled and walked to the next trainee. Out of the corner of his eye, he saw a head of hair. He changed direction.

The same young man who'd brought them to Gibson stood with a bow and arrow, aiming at a target board. Nathaniel approached him as he let an arrow loose and it hit the bull's-eye. Perhaps they weren't all inexperienced.

Nathaniel clapped, and the young man turned around.

"What are you looking at?"

Nathaniel crossed his arms over his chest. "I did not expect to see you here."

"I didn't expect to be here." He scowled and leaned on his bow.

Some of the raiders who'd followed them had turned around, and others stayed for the hot meal and then fled. Still others had taken their swords and disappeared. But he'd remained. "You mean to fight?"

"I mean to make a place for myself."

"What's your name?"

"Flip."

Nathaniel laughed.

"It's a decent name." He glared defensively. "Given to me by my late mother, Helena bless her grave."

"That's not what I find amusing." Nathaniel stepped closer to him. "My name is Nathaniel Blueborough, but as a boy people called me Nip."

The young man studied him with suspicion, but Nathaniel knew the truth would sound sincere. "My late mother named me after the blizzard she had me in."

"So why did you give it up?" Flip scratched his head, looking younger than he usually let on.

Nathaniel shrugged. No one had asked him that before. "I suppose I wanted to be taken seriously by the castle folk. After I was adopted by the queen and late king, everyone asked what I was doing here at the castle. I felt out of place, and I missed my home. So I tried to leave the past behind and move forward. In my old life I was known as Nip, but in this one, I was to be Nathaniel."

"Does that mean I'll have to change my name?"

Nathaniel smiled. "Not if you do not wish to."

"I want to keep it." Flip picked up his bow. "I want to remember where I came from." He aimed another arrow at the target.

"Then keep it, and do not let anyone convince you otherwise." Nathaniel watched as the arrow hit the bull's-eye once again.

A horn blew, and Brax jogged across the field to meet him.

"What is it?" Panic rose inside him.

"A warning." Brax gestured for him to follow him to the battlements. "The queen is about to employ the blue fire."

Nathaniel followed him, anxiety creeping into his gut. "Do you think it wise to draw their attention before the minstrels reach our front line?"

Brax tapped his hand on the hilt of his sword. "She wants to see what's under the swamps. We cannot defend ourselves from an enemy we cannot see. What if they are already at our doorstep?"

It was a gamble, but they'd waited long enough. Nathaniel increased his pace, taking the stone steps two at a time. He reached the battlements along with the other soldiers, forming a line across the turrets. The queen stood at the highest point where the wall rose on top of a hill. Dressed in her armor, she held the vial above the swamps. Valoria stood beside her like an apprentice in training.

Brax clapped Nathaniel on the shoulder. "Now we will see if the princess is right."

"She's always right." Nathaniel had full faith in her. Valoria had powers he could never understand, but there was also a goodness inside her that prevailed against all odds, as if the gods themselves kissed her steps.

The queen upended the vial, and the shimmery blue liquid spread in a line, sparkling in the sun as it fell.

Nathaniel held his breath. The liquid splashed into the muck, forming blue puddles. It disappeared as it dissolved.

"Damnable mermaid nonsense!" Brax pounded his fist on the stone. "And they said my ancestor was the trickster."

"Wait." Nathaniel refused to believe the minstrels' songs were based on a lie. Everyone in Ebonvale thought them sly swindlers, but he knew Valoria's integrity firsthand. He'd known her father as well, and Valorian had always been kind to him. There was more to the minstrels than magic and deception.

A few soldiers turned away, cursing. Nathaniel stayed, watching intently. "Look! Over there!" The horizon shimmered, like the sun baking the cobblestone on a hot summer's day. The shimmering spread until the entire swamp glittered like a thousand diamonds.

The soldiers beside Nathaniel collectively gasped as the shimmering diamonds burst into specks of stardust, disappearing in a chain reaction. When the stardust cleared, dead trees, old carriages, bones, and muck stood uncovered.

Everyone began to cheer. Joy spread through Nathaniel, and he jumped and hollered. Brax clapped both his shoulders. It was one of the only times he'd seen his brother smile from pure triumph. They'd done this together.

Cries of shock and outrage cut through the celebration. Nathaniel turned back to the horizon, where soldiers with faces full of fear pointed to the swamps. Dread chilled his stomach as the horizon moved in an endless tide of bodies.

The undead were on their way.

* * * *

Valoria stepped back in horror as innumerable bodies writhed on the horizon. There were so many they could trample the entire continent, killing all life in their path. Victory seemed impossible.

Aurbie Dionne

The queen unsheathed her sword. "All elderly and children are to be brought to the inner keep. Everyone that can fight will suit up." Ferocity burned in her eyes. The undead had taken her father and her husband. Valoria couldn't imagine the vengeance burning through her veins. She pointed her sword into the swamp. "Let them come."

Her courage brought Valoria to her senses. They had a few hours at most. The minstrels wouldn't arrive for another two days. She needed her harp, but most of all, she needed to find Sybil.

Valoria threw herself down the steps as chaos broke out. The fastest way to Sybil's tower lay across the courtyard. She turned left and shot through the main corridor, bumping into a servant holding all of her belongings in her arms.

Was she abandoning them?

Valoria didn't have time to judge. Three men passed her by, running toward the battlements dressed in thick leather and metal armor. A noblewoman clutched her baby to her chest, jogging toward the inner keep.

Valoria leapt down the main steps toward the courtyard. Daisies bloomed unaware of the coming horde around the fountain where airborne dolphins and mermaids dove and twirled. Would this stand as a relic of a long-lost people while undead shuffled across the cobblestone forever?

"Valoria, wait!"

She whirled around expecting the necromancer to entrance her with his dark eyes, or for Nathaniel to give her a sweet, parting farewell. But, it was neither. 'Twas the last person in the world she would have thought would seek her out.

Brax ran toward her. His armor gleamed in the sun, polished to perfection. She must have misheard him. Why would he bother with her at a time like this?

Brax took his helmet off, revealing his blunt forehead, thick nose, and shaved head slick with sweat. He panted as though he'd been running hard. "I was looking for you everywhere."

Valoria stared at him with disbelief. "Should you not be with your army?"

Brax shook his head. "I must speak with you first."

Valoria hesitated, speechless, waiting on his words. What could possibly be more important to Brax than preparing for battle?

Brax gestured toward the fountain. Valoria sat on the edge underneath a mermaid holding a stone fish. Brax sat beside her, closer than he'd ever ventured before. "I should have told you back on Amok's boat, or even back at the first dinner feast, and I'm sorry I waited so long."

Valoria's heart beat quickly as he took her hand. Disbelief mixed with confusion perplexed her. She'd attempted closeness like this so many times and failed, and now that he was in her grasp, she had no idea what to do with him. She did not feel lust, or attraction, or excitement, but she wasn't repulsed, either. He'd grown in her estimation from a brute to an honorable man. What would he say?

"I lied to you."

Her stomach dropped. Had he loved her all this time? The thought was preposterous.

Brax wiped sweat from his forehead. Words did not come easily for him. "When you asked me if I ever had fantasies of my own, I told you no. But, I do have fantasies, dreams I keep secret from everyone in the world. I saw those dreams in the waters with the mermaids, and that is why you will never own my heart."

Valoria's stomach hollowed out. Was he turning her away?

Brax touched her cheek. "I have come to admire and respect you, so much so, it would be dishonorable to marry you."

Shock stole her breath away. Hadn't she wanted this ever since she saw him drop that head on the floor of Ebonvale's great hall? The undead were knocking on their doorstep, and he decided to reveal the truth. It didn't make sense. "Why are you telling me now?"

"I want to free you from obligation. If anything happens to me on that battlefield, I want you to live your life and choose your husband. Do not live alone to honor me. It would be a false life."

She opened her mouth to respond, and he pressed his finger to her lips. To any onlookers it might have looked as though he was consoling his love before battle. How wrong they would have been.

"There is a scroll on my desk in my study freeing you from any obligation. You may present it to the queen in the case of my death. And if I live, I will proclaim it as my burden only, so you will not disappoint your father. Let Ebonvale take the blame."

Tears sprung to her eyes, even though his words were the most sensible notions she'd ever heard. "I have failed. We both have."

"No, we haven't. We've united Ebonvale and the House of Song in a just cause. If we triumph, let that be enough."

Brax stood and placed his helmet back on his head. With a final wave, he jogged back toward the battlements, leaving Valoria in shock.

She did not have to marry Brax. He'd called off the wedding. So many consequences spouted from those two truths, but she didn't have time to explore all of the options. If the undead broke through, there'd be no options for anyone.

Valoria pulled herself up and continued toward Sybil's tower. The future was shaping up into something she could live with, now she had to claim it for herself.

Chapter 31

Sybil's Redemption

"Fire!" Nathaniel shouted and brought his hand down. Two soldiers cut the ropes holding down a rock the size of a boulder, and the catapult squeaked as it hurled the projectile over the wall.

"Another one!" Nathaniel ordered. "Keep them coming."

Brax, along with three other soldiers, rolled the next boulder from the stockpile. Nathaniel sprinted up the steps to see where the boulder landed. They'd missed three times before they started hitting the front line of undead, and they only had so many boulders left to throw. The undead moved quicker than he'd estimated, and the boulder had hit a clump in the middle of the army. More bodies eddied around the stone, taking the place of the ones lost in an endless tide.

"Again!" Nathaniel refused to be deterred. This time they had solid rock blocking the gateway, so they could spread all the fire they wanted.

"Archers!" He gestured for everyone with a bow to climb the battlements and waited. Too soon, and the arrows would fall short of the front line. As the archers pulled back their bows, Nathaniel lit the end of each arrow. "On the count of three."

He took his own bow from his back and lit his arrow with the flame before it flickered out. "One…two…three!"

They fired, and streaks of red flame cut through the air in an arc. The first few shots landed in the muck and sizzled out. But the undead moved forward without fear or logic. They stumbled right under the brunt of the force, and the front line burst into flames.

Cheers erupted as the soldiers hooted and pumped their fists in the air. It was a small victory, because another wave crawled over the first, and slowly the flames burned out.

Archers began to hit them as they came within reach of the wall. "Not too close!" Nathaniel shouted. "Do not let the bodies pile up."

He turned back to the swamplands, and a distant black figure too tall and skinny to be a man caught his eye. The figure sucked light like a shadow, blinking in and out of existence in unpredictable places. On his head, he wore a crown of teeth. The necromancer.

Dread chilled Nathaniel's bones and he prayed to Helena and Horred that Valoria would not use her magic. That horrid monstrosity of a man would not have her.

The figure raised its hands over its head, and a ball of lightning sparked between them. The necromancer hurled the lightning toward the walls. The rock shook underneath Nathaniel as a crack sprung between his feet.

Horred's gambit. They had less time than he thought.

The bodies of undead were piling on top of each other despite the archers refraining from hitting any too close to the wall.

Nathaniel turned back to the courtyard. The time for hand-to-hand battle was upon them. He'd held them off as long as he could, a pitiful try. At this rate, Ebonvale would be taken by nightfall. "Swordsmen come forward."

The army, along with the raiders marched in single lines and formed a barricade along the wall. They would not hold them back for long.

* * * *

Valoria emerged from the tallest tower facing the battlefield. Undead swarmed the battlements, toppling over the edge with the force of a tidal wave. They fell over the rock wall, then stumbled forward on broken feet and cracked limbs, uncaring of their own incapacities. Soldiers met them on the ground, but too many were dying too fast.

She strummed her harp, calming her racing thoughts. Ironically, when her future seemed limitless for the first time in her life, she wouldn't live to see its fruition. Not if she wanted to keep those she loved alive. She spotted the necromancer holding lightning above his head. His face was gaunt, his cheeks sunken in. He hurled a lightning bolt at the wall, and an ominous cracking sound, like a mountain splitting in half, rumbled through her gut.

He'd have a hard time working his magic if someone else stole it away.

"Valoria, don't!" Echo distracted her. He stood below her tower waving his arms. "It will be your undoing."

"So be it!" She'd locked the door behind her. Even using his most potent song, Echo would need time to break through.

"You'll turn, just like the undead." Echo shouted in despair. "Please. We do not need two necromancers."

Amok's words came back to her. *The death of you, or your rebirth.* He might have been a madman, but he held some wisdom as well.

Below her, Sybil stood atop a white horse, approaching the wall in only her white nightgown and bare feet. She gazed at Valoria and held up a hand in salute. Her face was solemn and determined.

The time of reckoning had come.

The necromancer shot another bolt of lightning at the wall, and a hole burst from the lower battlements, spewing chunks of rock at the soldiers in the front line. Undead trickled in as soldiers raced to meet them.

Valoria closed her eyes and called up the dark magic. It swelled within her, lighting her limbs on fire. Sheer power seduced her, bringing her to another level of consciousness where she stood over the physical world as a god.

The necromancer sounded pleased. "Welcome, Valoria. My army is at your command."

The urge to spread the plague overwhelmed her. So much anger, pain, resentment festered in the living. If only they knew the numbness of the plague, the world would squirm and be still. They would bow to her command.

Remember who you are. Valoria fought against the tide. *You do not wish for power. You don't even want to be queen of Ebonvale.* What did she want, truly?

The answer came from deep inside her. Nathaniel. She wanted Nathaniel. She always had since the first day she met him. If she allowed the undead to spread, she'd lose him to the horde.

No.

Valoria opened her eyes and spread her hands. The undead fell back in a line leading to the necromancer. Sybil kicked her horse, and galloped through the hole in the wall. Valoria fought to hold the undead from Sybil's path even as the evil festered inside her, claiming her soul.

* * * *

Nathaniel tried not to look at the faces of the undead he slayed or think of how they were once people, fathers, sons, daughters, husbands, friends. He'd lost his army in the endless tide, and he felt like the lone survivor of the end of the world. His arms ached from slashing through the bodies, yet they came with fresh vengeance. They did not tire nor falter, not even when he cut off a limb.

A body of a woman in a red dress hurtled toward him. She blinked out of existence, then back in again five feet closer and snapped at his face. He fell back, raising his sword as she leapt on top of him. The blade cut through her stomach. She kept snapping as she slid down his blade toward him.

She would have been beautiful once, without the clumps of mold growing on her cheeks or the dark circles around her eyes.

An arrow hit her head with a thump and she dropped unmoving on top of him. Nathaniel glanced up to see Flip standing on a carriage above him. He offered his hand. "Get to higher ground."

Undead swarmed the city, pounding and scraping on doors and breaking through windows. The army had retreated to the buildings around them, staunching the flow as it eddied around them. If he took the boy's hand, they'd be stranded, but at least he'd be alive.

Nathaniel grabbed Flip's hand, and he hauled him up to the top of the carriage. Undead climbed from all sides, and they scrambled to kick their hands off. The carriage rocked underneath them with the flow of the horde all around it.

Flip wiped sweat from his brow. "I only have three arrows left."

"Save them." Nathaniel didn't have the heart to add *for ourselves*. Instead, he glanced at Flip and smiled with irony. "Are you still glad you chose to come?"

Flip shrugged and laughed. "At least I had a good meal."

"Was it that delicious?" Nathaniel kicked at a man's thick white fingers as he clung to the carriage top. He prayed Valoria had reached safety. If only he could have saved her. If only he could have saved them all.

Flip used the end of his bow to whack an undead from the back of the carriage. "'Til the last bite."

* * * *

Valoria knelt on the side of a bed. Her mother lay before her unmoving. She cried, holding her mother's hand against her cheek. The skin was warm and soft, smelling like freshly baked bread and lavender. Her mother's eyes opened suddenly. They were violet, unlike her own silver eyes, or those of her father. She stared accusingly. "You left me here to die. You're just like your father. You love him more."

A whimper caught in Valoria's throat. She'd always favored her father, and the guilt thickened on top of her like a blanket, suffocating her until she fought for tiny breaths.

Her mother smiled, but it was cruel. "You have failed him."

One of the undead reached out to Sybil's horse, and the beast tumbled to the ground. Sybil crawled from underneath the weight, her leg bent at a crippling angle. Undead closed in, snapping their teeth.

No. Valoria fought against the vision. Her mother had always scared her. She'd be kind, and then change in a heartbeat, throwing words like daggers. She'd resented Valoria because her father loved his daughter but not his wife. Valoria had buried that truth deep within her. But now she faced the spitefulness of it for what it was, and it did not have power over her anymore.

An undead man with an arm hanging by a few tendons snapped at Sybil, tearing flesh from her wrinkled hand and sealing her fate.

Valoria pushed the vision of her mother away and clapped her hands, sending the undead sprawling around Sybil as she crawled toward the necromancer.

Valoria turned all of her will on the necromancer. "Now you shall see."

The necromancer dropped his hands at his sides as Sybil approached. The figure, black as night, bowed to the vison of pale white. All at once, he lost his hold on Valoria, and the evil trickled from her body, leaving her shattered and weak.

The old woman reached to her lost love with the hand bitten by the undead. Black spread through her fingers down her arm. They had seconds together, if that.

The necromancer reached down and took her hand, and all of the undead stilled as if they were puppets with no strings. Black met white, and Sybil and the necromancer melted into each other. With a flash of light, they blinked out of existence and were gone.

The horde crumpled to the ground, lifeless.

It was done.

Valoria collapsed to her knees and closed her eyes, praying to Lyric that Sybil and her love were finally together and free.

Chapter 32

Aftermath

Pounding came from the door behind her. Valoria crawled to the door. It took all of her strength to stand and lift the lock from its hinges.

Echo burst in. "Lyric's last breath!" Echo ran toward her and cupped her face in his hands. "You're alive."

"Mostly." Exhaustion threatened to knock her to her knees, so she leaned against the old man and held him close. "The others?"

"Cadence sealed herself in the inner keep." Echo smoothed over her hair. "I thought I'd lost you to the necromancer's magic."

"You almost did." She pulled herself back to look in his eyes. "What about Brax and the queen?"

"Both are accounted for." Echo hefted her toward the door. "Now we should get you to your bed for some rest."

"And Nathaniel?" Her heart stopped.

"They are still looking."

Panic surged inside her until she couldn't breathe. "What do you mean?"

"He'd been separated from his squadron."

She pulled away from him and straightened with new determination. "Where?"

"They last saw him at the back gate."

"The back gate?" The last she'd seen, it had been swarming with undead.

Valoria pushed by her old music teacher. Her knees wobbled, and she ignored them, hurling herself at the door.

"Where are you headed?" Echo shouted after her.

She didn't stay to answer.

Valoria had to climb over undead to reach the thoroughfare leading to the back gate. So many had died. How could she begin to hope the one man she cared for had been spared?

"Nathaniel!" She shouted, scanning the piles of bodies. She imagined his familiar head of brown hair among the debris. Horror knocked her over, and she had to pick herself back up again to continue. If he was here, she'd rather know. She'd rather find him and lay eyes on his face one last time.

She climbed her way to the back gate, where a single carriage stood amidst the bodies as if the horses had abandoned it mid-trip. Two pairs of boots lay on top.

Valoria climbed on top and fell to her knees when she saw him. Nathaniel lay with the red-haired young man from the raiders. Hope and fear intertwined, Valoria crawled beside him. She examined his arms and legs for bites, but could find nothing piercing the armor. She placed both of her hands on his face. "Nathaniel, Nathaniel wake up."

His eyes fluttered open. "Valoria? What are you doing here?"

"The undead are defeated." Valoria propped his head up with her palm. "Ebonvale is safe."

"Or what's left of it." The young man sat up beside them and shook his head. "And I was about to stick an arrow through my own heart."

Valoria stared at him in shock.

He ran his hands through his curly red hair. "I fought for Ebonvale and all that. So now, where can I find a decent dinner?"

Valoria pointed to the castle. "There'll be medics there as well."

"I don't need a medic. I need a roasted chicken." He jumped off the carriage and picked his way through the undead.

Valoria turned back to Nathaniel. He studied her face as if it was the most gorgeous sight he'd ever seen. "Brax and the queen?"

"They are safe." She offered her hand. "Come, let me get you to the castle."

"You should be with them, not with me." Nathaniel plopped his head back down on the carriage.

Valoria paused. Should she tell him what Brax said? He had a love, as the mermaids had proven, but was it Blanca?

She'd confronted her inmost fear, beat the necromancer, and climbed over a sea of undead. She had enough courage to tell him the truth.

"Brax does not want my company."

Nathaniel waved her off. "Give him time."

"That's just it." Valoria tried to think of a polite way to say Brax had denied her. "He does not want time."

Nathaniel perked up, raising both eyebrows. "So what does he want?"

"For me to be free. He called off the wedding." She thought she would have been embarrassed, but to speak it brought her relief.

Nathaniel's eyes widened in shock. "Free?"

She nodded.

"You mean you are not to be married?" He sat up and blinked, wiping dust from his eyes as if he wasn't seeing the world correctly.

"Not to a prince of Ebonvale." She smiled. "Unless, there's someone else who'd want me—"

Before she could finish her sentence, Nathaniel rose and pressed his lips to hers. He kissed her so fiercely, she fell back and he fell on top of her. They laughed, and he kissed her again, running his hands through her hair, then along her neck and down to her waist.

Valoria ignited under his touch. He tasted of sweet passion, and she opened her mouth, kissing him deeper, wanting more. She ran her hands through his hair, just like she'd dreamed of doing so many times and pulled him down against her, thinking she'd never release him again.

Epilogue

Valoria took her father's hand. Sparrows chirped from above as they walked through the sparkling chains of dust motes hanging from the bluewood pines. A crowd sat in white chairs in a meadow beside the domed House of Song. Cadence sat in the back row, followed by Echo, and the other music teachers in the village. On the other side, the queen of Ebonvale sat with Brax and members of the Royal Guard. Finally, the houses would be united.

Nathaniel stood at the end of the aisle dressed in the blue robes of the House of Song. His brown hair had been pulled back, showing his sharp features. He caught her gaze and smiled, intensity burning in his eyes.

"Shall we?" Valorian glanced down at her and squeezed her arm. Gray streaked his long hair, but his silver eyes shone strong as ever. This was the first time he'd have to face Danika Rubystone, and he'd accepted the challenge with courage.

"Are you proud of me, Father?" Valoria hesitated. This was not what he'd wanted. The houses would be united, but not by blood.

"More proud than any father in the land. We do our best, and the Thoridians have always been stubborn in their ways. Thank Lyric for Nathaniel."

"Yes, he is wonderful, isn't he?" Valoria smiled, catching Nathaniel's gaze once again.

They stepped forward, and ten harpists fanned out around the party brought their fingers to the strings in glorious glissandos. For once, Valoria was content not to play with them. She had better things to do.

They approached Nathaniel, and Valorian placed a kiss on her cheek. He turned to Nathaniel and held out an emerald pendant framed in gold. The pendant dangled, catching the rays of sunshine. On the back was the royal crest of the House of Song, a lyrebird. "I gave you this once, a long time ago, when you were a boy."

"I remember." Nathaniel nodded with deep respect. "You handed it to me to distract me so I'd hide in the carriage while the kobolds attacked. You told me it is held by the prince and rightful heir to the House of Song."

"I did." Valorian smiled. "I was sorry to have to take it back. I'd wanted you to keep it then, and I am more than proud to give it to you now."

Nathaniel took the pendant and hung it from his neck. "I shall treasure it, and Valoria, always."

Meet the Author

Aubrie Dionne is an author and flutist in New England. Her books have received the highest ratings from Romance Times Magazine and BTS Magazine, as well as Night Owl Reviews and Readers' Favorite Reviews. She has guest blogged on the USA Today Happy Ever After Blog and the Dear Teen Me blog and signed books at the Boston Book Festival, Barnes and Noble, and the Romance Writers of America conference. Her books are published by HarperImpulse, Entangled Publishing, Astraea Press, Spencer Hill Press, Inkspell Publishing, and Lyrical Press. When she's not writing, Aubrie teaches flute and plays in orchestras.

In case you missed it, keep reading for a sample of Danika and Bron's story:

MINSTREL'S SERENADE

The Chronicles of Ebonvale, Book One

He's sworn to protect her, but can he save her from himself?

Danika Rubystone has hated the minstrels ever since her mother ran away with one. As Princess, she's duty bound to marry Valorian, a minstrel from the House of Song. But problems in the kingdom are mounting. With her father dead, she's the sole heir to an imperiled throne, and wyverns attack Ebonvale's southern shores. But after Danika finds a lone survivor of a wyvern's attack who holds the key to protecting the kingdom and she finally meets the enchantingly sly Valorian, everything changes.

As Ebonvale's Royal Guard sails with the minstrels to smite the uprising of wyverns, Danika dances a line between sticking by duty like her father, or following her wild heart like her mother.

A Lyrical e-book available now.

Learn more about Aubrie at
http://www.kensingtonbooks.com/author.aspx/30585

Chapter 1

Fire's Mark

"No lady should see what evil lies beyond the ridge." Bron blocked the exit of the carriage with a great wall of muscle, sweat and dark skin. Plumes of smoke rose like great fingers brushing the sky behind his broad shoulders.

Danika focused on the strength in his dark eyes. "Nonsense. Every ruler must bear witness to the devastation afflicting her people so she can make the right decisions to protect her kingdom."

Bron's stance didn't change.

She narrowed her eyes; bodyguard or not, he had to follow her orders. She could force him to let her pass, but, maybe this one time she'd play his game. "So she can enact the most deserving form of revenge."

"That's more like it." Bron smiled, thick lips curving. "Spoken like a true warrior."

"Flattery will get you nowhere. Let me through."

He sighed with a gentle rise and fall of his broad chest, ran his hand over his shaved head, and stepped aside. "If you insist, Princess."

She placed her fingers in his war-hardened hand and allowed him to guide her to the blackened earth. The air stank of soot and ash, searing her eyes and the smooth skin on her cheeks. She blinked through the wave of heat and summoned her courage. "Show me the site of the greatest devastation."

"As you wish, Princess. The smoke spooks the horses, so we'll have to trek up the cliff on foot."

"Walking doesn't frighten me." She'd worn her thigh-high riding boots underneath her damask underskirt for such an occasion. She ripped the top layer of silks off, revealing the same leather leggings warriors wore under their tunics.

Bron averted his eyes. When his gaze returned to her, he seemed to appraise her with newfound interest.

She stashed the frills in the carriage, hiding the burning flush in her cheeks. Surely the heat had raised her temperature. She refused to blame Bron's attention. "Lead me to Shaletown."

"Or what's left of it."

Bron picked his way through charred trunks, presenting his hand whenever the footing grew treacherous. Although the ground steamed and the soles of her feet burned, she made her way on her own, refusing his offers. As the new ruler of Ebonvale, she had to show strength in a time when fear spread like the plague of the dead.

They crested the ridge and she covered her mouth with her sleeve. The blackened village lay before them as dead man's land. People had walked the cobblestones that morning going about their everyday business, unaware of the impending devastation. Anger boiled inside her, followed by a black void of loss sucking her dry.

Danika cleared her parched throat. "Has anyone searched for survivors?"

She knew the answer before Bron opened his mouth.

"No, my lady. The clouds from the blaze obscure the sky and the wyverns may still hover, waiting for stragglers. Besides, the chance of any surviving such devastation…"

She scanned the remains from her raven perch, balancing her boot on the stump of a sizzled tree. The brick foundation of a tavern stood without its thatched roof or bluewood walls. Black stains streaked across the town square where the fire's breath licked its way through. Skeletons littered the ash, their black-splotched finger bones grasping through the soot to seek salvation. This kingdom belonged to her now, and she couldn't let the provinces fall to ruin because of a swarm of vermin from the south.

Her heart raced as ire shot up through her chest, splitting her apart. "How could they destroy innocent people?"

"They're beasts, Your Highness. There's no logical reasoning to their onslaught."

"But we've stayed clear of Scalehaven. Unless something lured them to our lands?"

Bron shrugged as if the wyverns' attack were inevitable. "The beasts' population brims with hatchlings. Scouts have reported the yearlings as far north as Brimmore's Bay." His voice danced, careful and light, as if he wanted to protect her from the truth.

She ran her mother's satin scarf across her blistering forehead. Sweat stained the pink fabric red. "My father would know what to do."

Bron's gaze dropped to the ash as if her words defeated him.

Danika cursed her weak tongue. She knew better than to speak of the late king in front of him.

He met her gaze once again. "I have full faith in your rule."

Helplessness trickled through her, threatening to weaken her knees. Danika pulled away, straightening her back against the rising channels of smoke blotting the sky. She wanted to lean into him and borrow his strength, but such a gesture led toward a doomed future. To choose such a lowly man, albeit the Chief of Arms, when so many more lucrative prospects remained, would place her kingdom in further jeopardy. Especially in times as dark as these.

A blur of earthy brown scrambled between an overturned carriage and the remnants of the smithy. Danika's concerns flew from her mind as she focused on the form huddled behind the coal pit.

"There." She thrust her finger into the smoke. "A small child."

Bron grabbed for her arm but the silky fabric of her sleeve slipped through his fingers. She threw herself forward, stumbling down the cliff's side.

"Princess, no!"

Her arms flailed as she scrambled between slabs of malachite, the sharp edges exposed by the wyverns' breath. Halfway down, a keen wail rode the wind, slicing her ears. Black ribbons flickered on the horizon.

"Danika, stop! They're coming back!"

She jumped the final five feet and landed on her hands and knees beside the smithy. So many had died. If she could save just one…

The boy cowered with his arms covering his head.

"Boy! Come here." She waved to him but his eyes were shut as tight as a noblewoman's purse.

"Horred's grave." She'd have to sprint to make it. She skirted a pile of flaming wood and jumped over the wall, the broken glass tearing her bell-shaped sleeves like wyvern's teeth. She stumbled forward on her hand and knees, ripping the fabric to free herself.

A bronze plate three sizes too big hung on the boy's sagging shoulders. Had the armor shielded him? Surely not. The fire would heat the metal to near melting, sizzling a layer of skin.

As she ran toward him, he turned in the direction of her footsteps and peeked through narrow eyelids. He must have recognized her, because his eyes widened as big as two chicken eggs in a face covered in thick, black ash. Surprisingly, he had no burns.

"Follow me." She hoisted him up, and they scuttled through a hole blazed into the foundation.

The boy tugged on her arm to hide underneath the anvil. "It's too late. They're here."

Danika fought him as she glanced at the sky. The ribbons grew thicker, spiraling through the air like glittering pennants on Festival Day. The pattern of swirls mesmerized her as the horde unfurled.

She blinked, tearing her gaze away. "We can still make it."

The boy had stopped battling her, hypnotized by the sky. "It's too late."

"No." She yanked him around and screamed her throat raw. "Run!"

As they neared the cliff, Bron stood above them like a chiseled statue of a war god, unsheathing his golden claymore. A pang of worry pierced her stomach like a dagger. He'd stayed behind to distract the wyverns' attention to cover their escape.

Why had she been so foolish?

The first wyvern landed with a gush of wings on the outskirts of the village behind them, while a second flew straight toward Bron. Danika climbed, knowing full well she might have sent the two-time war veteran to his death. She lifted the boy and pushed him up the hill.

"Burrow's Bucket! I can climb by myself." He swiped her away and paused, throwing off the breastplate before scrambling up the crag. Danika grabbed at weeds, pulling them out as she struggled for a handhold. Although she should have focused all her energy on climbing, she gazed up at Bron.

The wyvern dove and lunged, smacking jaws longer than Bron's claymore. Bron ducked and swung, sinuous muscles bunching and stretching. He missed its shimmering hide by inches. The warrior excelled in hand-to-hand combat, but if the wyvern ignited its belly of fire, he'd have no defense.

"Over here." The boy had found a path up the incline. He reached down over a ridge and grabbed her hand, trying to pull her up. His scrawny arms shook as Danika slid through his sooty fingers. Her heels skidded backward until they hit a rock. "Don't wait for me. Go!"

The boy dangled his arm, waving her to him. "Come on."

She could make it. She took a step back and ran, leaping toward the ridge and catching a bramble. The boy grasped her arm. Thank the gods for all the secret training Bron had given her. Danika hefted herself over the edge. She grabbed the boy's hand and they scrambled toward the carriage.

She glanced at the place where Bron had stood. Nothing remained except a darkening sky with wyverns writhing through the air. "B-Bron." Panic rose inside her, along with a feeling of sheer loneliness. What if he'd died for her impulsiveness?

"I'm here, Princess," he thundered from behind the carriage. He'd rigged the horses and collected the reins in his hand.

The boy jumped in without a word. Danika shot Bron a look that would have killed an ordinary man.

"I thought you'd died."

"Princess, you know better than to traipse off while wyverns rule the sky."

Danika gestured to the boy kicking his heels against the carriage seat. "I couldn't leave him."

"So be it." He threw a tarp over a lump of steaming scales, shining oily green black in the twilight. "You have a new trophy for your mead hall."

"Honestly, I prefer the wall bare." Disgusted by death, she jumped in the carriage.

Frenzied screeches filled the sky behind them like mad raven calls.

"Hi-ya!" Bron whipped the reins and the horses galloped forward. Danika pressed her cheek to the glass. The wyverns became threads in the darkening sky. Her castle had a bastion of archers, but there were many more beasts than in her nightmares. Her stomach sank to her knees. In time, the writhing masses would overcome Ebonvale's ramparts as well.